Hannah 1980

A Time Travel Novel

By

Paul Gilbert

The story, all names, characters, and incidents portrayed in this production are fictitious. No identification with actual persons (living or deceased), places, buildings, and products is intended or should be inferred.

2023 FIRST EDITION

Copyright © 2023 by Paul Gilbert

All rights reserved. No part of this publication may be reproduced, distributed, or transmitted in any form or by any means, including photocopying, recording, or other electronic or mechanical methods, without the prior written permission of the author, except in the case of brief quotations embodied in critical reviews and certain other non-commercial uses permitted by copyright law.

HANNAH 1980

By Paul Gilbert

9:30pm
Friday
27th June
1980

THE BEGINNING

Laura surveys the Corner Pin public house from the safety of her taxi and tries to make a decision.

She reads the letter again to the check she's got the right place.

Hi Laura,
I'll be at the
Corner Pin Pub,
Rye Piece Ringway
Bedworth
Warwickshire
CV12 8CC
Any time after 8
Can't wait to meet you again
Tina x

The taxi had pulled up outside the side door and Laura stared at the 'Rye Piece' road sign. This was definitely the place. She looked at her watch. Snoopy's arms were pointing to nine-thirty. She was late.

Even the summer twilight couldn't show the place in a good light.

Maybe coming here was a mistake.

With a twinge of snobbery and shame, her heart sank a little. Her cousin, Tina, had spoken fondly of her former place of work, but, from the outside at least, Laura wasn't impressed.

Admittedly, Laura was a country-girl, escaping from a backwater sleepy town for the bright city lights, but there were no bright lights here, just dirt and grime.

"I'll help you with your bags," the taxi driver tells her. He sounds like he's doing her a favour in one way, but he clearly doesn't want to be here a minute longer necessary.

Before Laura could offer an alternative suggestion, he was out of the car and making her decision for her.

She took a breath and told herself she was being silly and this place can't be as bad as she's imagining it or Tina wouldn't have invited her here.

"Once you find Tina," she told herself, "it'll be fine."

She put her hand on the door handle and looked at the pebble-dashed walls of the pub, now all dash and no pebble.

"It'll be fun," she insisted. "You'll see."

She opened the door and stepped out of the car.

It was a hot night. Laura was still wearing her 'travelling clothes'; a t-shirt and jeans. She had been worried she might be under-dressed. That was no longer a concern.

Then, in a dent to her attempted optimism, she heard voices from inside the pub. Angry voices. An argument of some sort.

Laura asked herself, *Am I really going to walk into this place, an eighteen-year-old girl carrying a suitcase, and say I'm looking for 'my cousin Tina', who I haven't seen since we were nine or ten?*

The driver had the boot of the taxi-cab open and was about to haul out her case.

"Could you hold on for one second, please?" she said.

He looked up and pulled a face. "Are you staying or not?" he said, demanding an answer.

The shouting in the pub was intensifying. Laura could hear tables and chairs scraping on the floor, men yelling inaudible instructions and, she was sure, a dog barking. A big dog by the sound of it.

"Do you know where Park Road is?" she asks the driver.

He shook his head. "I'm a Coventry cabbie," he says, "I don't like coming out to these backwater towns." He added a mumble to himself, "They're all bloody backward out here!"

Then, from the pub, she heard clearly. "Get back! Leave me alone!"

The man's scared pleas were met with angry voices roaring back.

It sounded like one person being picked on by a mob, which didn't feel right to Laura no matter what the circumstances.

"Miss?" the cabbie asked.

Laura turned to see him gesturing to the suitcase.

The pub doors flew open and a young man burst out, staggering backwards, almost losing his footing.

Blood ran from a cut above the corner of his eye.

Laura could only stare as three men, all twice the size of their apparent victim, step out the door and fan out.

"Get back," the boy shouted.

He looked no older than her, but wore the clothes of someone from a different era; army boots, baggy woollen trousers, a tatty white shirt and a well-worn tweed jacket.

"Jimmy," the tallest of the three men says. He looks old, in his fifties, but he's well-built. He is at the centre of the pincer movement that is circling their prey. The other two guys are younger, and even bigger.

"Why did you try to rob me, Jimmy?" the tall man says.

"I didn't rob anybody," the kid shouted at him, "How do you know me? Who are you?"

"You know who I am. Get back inside."

"No!"

"Where you gonna go?" the man asks.

Jimmy risks a glance over both shoulders as he continues to back away, but he doesn't even seem to notice Laura or the taxi.

The tall man spearheads the approach as the half-circle closes in.

There's a loud bang to her side. Laura jumps and shoots a glance to see that the taxi-driver has slammed the boot of the car. He's leaving. Her suitcase is on the ground.

She turns back to the confrontation. The boy back-pedals too fast to stay on his feet and is now scrambling on all fours.

Laura grabs her suitcase, gets to the car and wrestles open the back door.

She throws the case in and stands with one foot in the car and one on the ground.

The driver stares at her in outrage, but seems unable to form words.

He revs the engine and puts the car in gear.

"Don't you dare!" Laura commands him.

She turns back to the boy.

He is back on his feet and about to make a run for it when she orders him, "Get in!"

He sees the opportunity and takes it, diving into the taxi, the two of them fall onto the back-seat and, without needing any encouragement, the driver speeds away.

"What's happening?" Jimmy asks.

It's not a question directed at Laura specifically, it's a more general enquiry as to the state of the universe.

"Who are you?" Laura says to him. Then asks, "How did those men know you?"

"They don't know me," he says. "Well, one of them did once."

He speaks then a thick accent that makes Laura think she's misheard him.

He pronounces them as 'um' and did as 'dit'.

His confusion seems to be seeping into her own thoughts.

With a clean handkerchief from her pocket, Laura had cleaned the blood from the boy's eyebrow. She stopped the bleeding, but the surrounding yellow skin promised bruising.

They were stood on wasteland behind a row of terraced houses.

She watches the taxi-driver literally throw her suitcase from the car boot.

"Could you be careful with that please?" she shouts.

The driver slams the boot and runs to the car door.

"Why are we here?" she asks Jimmy.

The taxi does a U-turn and speeds away.

Jimmy had directed them to this spot where two rows of terraced-houses gave way to sprawling fields.

From where she stood, Laura could see three more pubs on this road alone, The Royal Oak, The Cricketers Arms and The Woolpack. She could also see the small spires of the town centre. It had taken less than a minute for the taxi to get here from The Corner Pin. Bedworth is much smaller than she had imagined. If anyone tried to look for them, they wouldn't have to look for long.

"I live here," Jimmy explained, "but-"

He is staring at the low-walled remains of a cottage in a nearby field.

"Clearly, you don't live there now," Laura tells him. "Do you mean you *used* to live here?"

Jimmy looks at her. He doesn't know the answer.

"Listen," Laura says, "I don't know anyone here. I'm new here. I have nowhere to go."
Jimmy nods.

"Will those men come looking for you?"

"I don't know," he says. "Maybe."

"Where can we go?"

"I don't know," he says again.

Laura feels a panic rise in her stomach. How has her life changed so drastically in just five minutes?

She can't go back to the Corner Pin now, they'll recognise her.

She could go to Tina's flat, she had the address. She'd have to wait outside until she finished her shift in the very same Corner Pin and then what about 'Jimmy'?

She couldn't abandon him. She wasn't capable of turning her back on a victim of bullying. Many times she'd got into trouble before for sticking up for people against bullies, but she wasn't going to change now.

She was going to help him, but he needs to help himself too.

She retrieved her battered suitcase from the side of the road and stood in front of him. When he raised his eyes, she said, "I'm Laura."

She extended her hand for a formal handshake and he took it.

"I'm Jimmy," he said.

She pumped his hand firmly twice.

"Good," she said, "we need somewhere to hide, so what's the plan?"

"The lime kilns," had been Jimmy's answer.

He had proven quite resourceful once he had grasped the situation. Within minutes of Laura asking him what the plan is, the two of them were free-wheeling on a bicycle down a country lane, her suitcase on her lap and she on his, with some help from the crossbar. Of course, she had to wrap both of her arms around him for balance, and he hadn't complained. He hadn't spoken either, but that was OK.

Her plans had collapsed the moment she had arrived in Bedworth. She was scared and uncertain, but at the same time, she felt safe with this man.

As the downward slope petered out after a quarter of a mile or so, they coasted along to a gravel side road. Jimmy applied the brakes and they trundled to stop.

Reluctantly, Laura released Jimmy from her arms and dismounted.

Jimmy looked around, again seemingly confused by what he saw.

"Nobodies been here," he said aloud.

All three of the huge round brick-built open-air structures were as dilapidated as the cottage where he had first taken them, but they were quiet and out of the way. They had followed a short, overgrown footpath from the gravel driveway. In the moonlight, they could've been in an exotic movie scene. Here they could get shelter, but, again, he seemed surprised that the brick-built furnaces were no longer in use. The weeds that flourished around them were two feet high, and every inch of the ground was thick with weeds.

She hadn't asked where the bicycle had come from.

Jimmy had propped it against the wall, and the two of them sat themselves in the open furnace.

"So, Jimmy," she said, "What was that about?"

She said it with a smile, almost teasing. Jimmy still looked fragile, but not threatening.

"I-" Jimmy started, but struggled to expand on it.

"Let's start with something less complicated," she said. "Why don't I introduce myself?"

"Yes," he said, "that's a good idea."

She turns to sit facing him and crosses her legs.

"I'm Laura Wallace, and I have arrived in Bedworth this evening after an eight-hour journey by train, bus and taxi, from Lowestoft, Norfolk, to meet up with my distant cousin who works in a public house called The Corner Pin."

This seems to register with Jimmy as he offers a concentrated nod once she is finished.

"I think you know the rest," she says.

"I see," Jimmy says.

Laura waits a moment, then prompts him, "Now it's your turn."

Jimmy nods, much like before, then says, "I-"

Laura pulls a face, tired of the overuse of the single word 'I-' sentences.

"I found myself here," he says.

Laura frowns. "You found yourself here?"

"Yes," he says, "I don't know how."

"OK," Laura says. "Well, that's-"

"There was an air-raid," he says.

"There was a what did you say?" She was sure that he had said 'air raid', but maybe she'd misheard his accent again.

"And," he went on, "I shouldn't have been where I was, I'm ashamed to say."

He looks to be lost in his story, his blue eyes fixed on hers but his mind elsewhere. Laura doesn't interrupt.

"The house was empty. I knew they'd be in the shelters, and I was hungry," he says, "and, as I say, I shouldn't have gone inside, but they had food. So I went inside and it was a good job I did cos that was when the bomb hit and I was thrown across the room. There was dust everywhere, I couldn't see and I was scared. Petrified. I staggered about and outside was boom boom boom so I saw this WC and hid in there."

Laura nods slowly and says, "OK." But she hasn't understood a word of what he's said. Not really.

"Then I must've passed out," Jimmy surmised.

"So," she says, "you were in someone else's house-"

"Only for food," he insists. "I'm not a thief. Well, I was hungry."

Pained that she has upset him, Laura instinctively reaches for his hand. "I know, I know," she says, "you were hungry and you went inside and something happened."

"Yes," he says. He looks at her hand on his and gently wraps his fingers around hers.

Laura takes his other hand in hers and squeezes them both.

"You've been through a lot," she says. "I want to help you."

"I should go back to the house," he says. Thoughtful.

"Yes," Laura says. Disappointed. Realistic.

Jimmy seems to jump into life. "Will you come with me?" he asks.

"Yes," she says, "Will it be safe?"

"Should be all clear at one o'clock," he says.

Laura tilts her watch in the moonlight to illuminate Snoopy's arms. She tells herself that she's too old for a Snoopy watch, even though he is cute as ducks. What would other people think? What would Jimmy think?

Indeed, he seems curious about what she's got on her wrist, but Laura pulls her sleeve down and says, "It's nearly half-past eleven."

"We can go back in an hour," he says. "If that's alright for you?"

"Yeah, sure," she smiles. "I don't have anything else planned."

The two talked and talked and Jimmy gave her his jacket and put his arm around her to keep her warm. She leant up against him and didn't feel cold at all.

To Laura, it was like a game, a magic game no less, as Jimmy spoke about the shelling of Coventry and how the German planes had turned for home and unloaded their remaining bombs to lighten their load. These bombs fell over Bedworth.

Laura joined in with equal seriousness with, "collateral damage."

Jimmy didn't understand.

He also didn't understand her reference to the Coventry Blitz.

After a mildly awkward silence, she asked him about his family. Jimmy had a mother and a brother, who he lived with, 'in the cottage'. His father had died in a mining accident when Jimmy was young.

His earliest memory is of the neighbours gathering to slaughter a pig in their backyard. His mother had kept pigs in the yard and neighbours would bring scraps to feed it. She would then butcher the pig and apportion cuts of the meat to the neighbours, according to the amount of scraps they had provided. He remembered when his mother had finished there was nothing left but blood on the cobbles.

At half-past-midnight, they had walked back into town; her pushing the bike, him carrying her suitcase.

The house that Jimmy referred to is, in fact, a shop of some kind.

The two of them have walked into town, having left the bike once they left the country lane and it being a Friday night there were still people about although it was now past midnight.

Jimmy seemed to know his way around. They stayed away from main-roads, gave The Corner Pin a wide berth, and arrived at the back of the shop just before one o'clock.

By the time Laura got her bearings again, they were in an empty car park at the rear of the shop. The place was lined with a six-foot wall, one entrance and gateways for each of the surrounding properties. Laura leant the bike against the wall, hoping that it might somehow find its way back to its rightful owner, but needing to focus on her own situation right now.

"In here," Jimmy whispered as he opened a gate marked 'Do Not Enter'.

"Are you sure?" Laura asks him, but he has already led her by the hand into a delivery yard and across to a back door.

In his other hand, he held her suitcase.

"How do we get inside?" Laura whispers, unable to hide her nerves.

Jimmy doesn't answer, but turns the handle, and the door silently opens.

"I unlocked it when I came out," he whispers back to explain.

It's pitch black inside.

Jimmy enters.

Laura hesitates. "Do you know your way from here?"

Jimmy looks back at her and smiles. "Yes," he says, "this way." He points.

Laura looks back at the gate and takes a breath.

"I'm not sure about this," she says.

Jimmy steps up close to her and puts his arm around her waist.

And she feels safer.

They take a few steps into the darkness.

Laura can make out that the vague shapes in the room are some kind of goods on display, but no more than that.

"Nearly there," Jimmy tells her. "Look."

Laura peers into a storeroom ahead of them. There's a skylight which offers some illumination, but it doesn't make up for the fact that they're going further into the bowels of the property.

"I can't-" Laura says, but then there's another voice.

It comes from outside.

"Sarge!"

A policeman.

"What is it?" says another voice.

"Door's open."

With that, the ceiling is lit up by a torch beam that flickers around the open door and touches on them both.

"Hurry! Hurry!" Jimmy shouts.

"There's someone in there!" shouts the policeman.

Laura can't move. She feels literally rooted to the spot, but she can she Jimmy beneath the skylight, his hand reaching out for hers.

And she wants to take it.

"Come with me!" he says.

She wants to go with him.

But she can't.

She hears that back gate being shoved open and boots clatter across the yard. Jimmy's hand reaches inside his jacket and he throws something onto the floor just in front of her.

Laura breaks her paralysis. She takes two steps forward, reaches down and grabs the tiny bound booklet.

"Find me!" Jimmy shouts.

Laura looks at the bound booklet, is an identity card of some kind.

And even as her fingers wrap around the edges of the card, they too are caught in torchlight as the door bursts and a heavy hand lands on her shoulder.

Laura watches Jimmy. She can just make him out in the dark, praying that his eyes can see hers and they can somehow pass on meaning.

She's sorry.

She shouldn't have hesitated.

She will find him.

No matter what.

"Where is he?" the policeman demands.

Laura is pushed aside as the torch beams searches the storeroom.

"He's gone," Laura says.

And her tears bite into her cheeks with a pain she has never felt before.

Hannah

Earlier that same day...

Friday
27th June
1980

CHAPTER 1

I'm in Stubbs Toy Shop staring at a wall of Star Wars toys that rises from the floor to the ceiling.

The 'bricks' of this wall, the ends of the boxes, which have a black background and white lettering, contain the name of the toy and the 'Empire Strikes Back' logo. It's in cinemas right now, so Stubbs has gone *big* on Star Wars inventory and taken over a whole back wall of the shop. The Subbuteo display has been compressed to half its normal size, relegating Hornby Trains to a table in the centre of the room and Barbie to a stand-alone display near the back wall where she stares pleadingly into space. Even the Six Million Dollar Man has been pushed aside and all twenty of them don't look happy about it.

Only Airfix has successfully stood its ground, its soldiers, models and paints display defiantly holding firm. There is a stack of 1980 Airfix catalogues on the display, the cover showing an eclectic range of models from a Lancia Stratos Turbo GR5 Alitalia sports car, a Harrier Jump Jet and a Kingfisher.

But, today, I've come here for Star Wars only.

There are hundreds of boxes. When viewed as a single mass, it's overwhelming and confusing.

Especially when you're looking for a particular item.

Especially when you shouldn't be there.

There are four toys that have deemed to be big-ticket items and therefore exposed, full-frontal-style, for all to see, but, worryingly, there's no Falcon. There's an AT-AT, a Land Cruiser, Tauntaun (with open belly rescue feature), X-Wings, but after a while the boxes all look the same.

I know what I want. The biggest big-ticket there ever was. Han Solo's Millennium Falcon. My profit margin on that one item is huge.

It's not for me, by the way, just in case you thought that was my thing, you know. I'm a toy-trader. Its my chosen profession, you might say.

I look again at the hundreds of boxes that stand before me.

My head spins. Maybe there isn't a Falcon here.

My hair falls over my face just to compound my situation.

I joke with myself that maybe I should ask for assistance, but that cannot happen.

I shouldn't even be here. I shouldn't be doing what I'm doing here and I cannot, under any circumstances, draw any attention to myself.

The shop, formerly a town-house, is divided into two rooms of equal size and a former kitchen at the rear. The front room includes the main entrance, the counter and the little kids' toys; dolls, soft toys, plastic tea sets, sit in cars, little kids' toys. The shopkeeper, a smiling elderly gentleman who could be the result of a Google search for 'elderly toy shop owner'. He has the wire-rimmed glasses, the white hair and an amused smile. He is stood behind his counter serving a steady stream of customers.

I'm in the back room, the Star Wars wall stands between me and the shopkeeper, and I'm unseen except for a tiny reflection on a curved observation mirror placed at the intersection of the two rooms. There's no CCTV, there are no shop assistants to keep an eye on me, no other customers and certainly no store detectives to pounce if someone tries to steal something. In fact, there's nobody here but me.

And I shouldn't be here. I'm an interloper. An invader. If I get caught, I'll have some explaining to do, like who I am and how I got here.

So I'm careful, and I won't get caught.

I have meticulously ensured that I blend in; I have my black Doc Martin boots, my Shrink To Fit Levi's jeans, my Adidas t-shirt (in green and white piping and the three stripes on the shoulder to the bicep cuff, (I love it)), and my also beloved black Harrington jacket. It's all original 80s stuff, ironically from this very era, but where I'm from you have to hunt it out; four word eBay search notifications just won't cut it if you're looking for gear that doesn't show forty years of wear and tear.

The only thing I have with me that is 'new' is a perfect reproduction of a classic Gola sports bag. I would have loved to own an original, but sadly, none have been known to have survived intact. I normally stay away from reproductions, but I need the right bag for this operation.

So visually I absolutely blend in. I look like any other eighteen-year-old in this town. The problem is I'm the only eighteen-year-old in a toy shop. The shopkeeper, who has seen me here many times over the last few months, must be getting suspicious. I'm careful, but I have to come and go through the storeroom at the back of the shop. It's a long story, but we'll get there.

For now, I need to find my Falcon.

Let's start again, I tell myself: I will scan each of the boxes, starting from the top left, working my way down each column in turn. I focus. I will not get distracted. I will resist the urge to glance back at the shopkeeper. I will follow each column from left to right, top to bottom.

I begin.

Top left is the AT-ATs. Then another. Then the Speeders, then the Tie-Fighters mixed in with X-Wings.

I keep going, but it's like flicking through a deck of cards looking for the nine of diamonds. After a while, as card after card flashes before your eyes, they all look the same, and it doesn't register when you do see the card, and then it's too late.

Or maybe I'm over-thinking it.

Of course, after checking all four columns, I fear that maybe they don't have one, and then I see it. Up high. I have to squint to read it, but beside the text, the image of that round spaceship is the most recognisable vehicle on the planet. Han Solo's Millennium Falcon.

Hallelujah.

Even though I'm not short, I'm 5'5, and the box is way above my head.

In the corner of the room, to my left, I spy a set of wooden step ladders and I manoeuvre them into position. There's a small squeak as I open the A-frame, but I'm sure it's inaudible to anyone but me.

I climb up three rungs, but it's not enough. I go another two and my head is now close to the ceiling, but I need to get close enough to read the tiny print of the serial number before I go any further.

I retrieve a scrap of paper from my jeans pocket and hold it beside the box. My instructions are that the serial numbers must be an identical match.

I read first the numbers on the paper, then the number of the box.

Cat No. 33364

The numbers match.

Result.

This is where things get tricky.

As far as I can see, this is the only Millennium Falcon in the shop, which makes this a once-only opportunity.

They pack these things in so tight they are a major pain to extract. There's a huge risk that the box could sustain some kind of mark or microscopic dent which, even if only detectable by high-resolution thermal imaging hardware, means that it would grade at less than pristine. And that impacts my profit.

I have some lint free gloves, which may be a bit over the top, but you can't be too careful. I slip off my red LED digital watch (set to 1980-time) in case the metal case or the chrome clasp scratches the box. I love my watch, its proper retro 1970s and you have to press the button for the time to come up in red numbers.

(I bought it from this very shop just two months ago, in fact, I bought four at £9.99. I kept one and sold the other three for £150 each.)

I press side button.

11:06.

Just for fun, I press it again and it tells me the date. 27:06:80.

I love this watch.

It goes safely in my jeans pocket and I put on my lint-free gloves, admiring my professionalism if not my style-sense, but needs must.

The box has to be teased out with the utmost care and the gentlest fingertips, despite me tottering on this dodgy step-ladder. I can't even allow myself to consider the possibility of the shop-keeper berating me for scaling the rock-face of Star Wars toys.

It's at this point that my hair somehow swings across my face to cover my eyes. I have what I can best describe as 'circa-1980 Kate Bush bed-head'. It's long and dark brown and it can get pretty wild, but how it manages to blindfold me when it knows that my hands are tied up is beyond me. A few deep breaths and sharp blasts guided by my upper lip scatter it away, allowing me to concentrate on the job at hand.

The marks and dents I do inflict are to neighbouring boxes only and once I've edged a thumb's length of the box from the wall, I'm confident enough to go for a full extraction and it slides out with a satisfyingly sweet 'pop'.

With the box in both hands, I make some wobbly steps back to terra firma and breathe a much-deserved sigh of relief.

Some kid has wandered into the back room and is staring at me without talking.

If he thinks he's going to snag my Falcon, he's got a shock coming and my raised eyebrow and evil fake smile tell him as much.

He saunters off to inspect some Action Men as I place my Holy Grail of Star Wars toys on the Hornby Train-filled table in the centre of the room and put the step ladders back.

I allow myself a minute to fully check over the box for any previous damage, although, it's kind of irrelevant as I'm not letting it go now unless it has a complete tear or something equally catastrophic, which, I'm pleased to note, it doesn't.

I shove my gloves in my jeans pocket, slip off my Harrington jacket and place it on the table, then make my way to the front of the shop.

When I die, I want to be buried in my Harrington, or one of them. I have four all together. They are as much a part of my personality and identity as my own face. My preference, for practical but not personal reasons, are brand new, accurate reproductions of the originals, which actually means Baracuta G9 jacket as worn by James Dean (red - Rebel Without A Cause), Elvis Presley (slate blue - King Creole) and Steve McQueen (navy blue - Thomas Crown Affair). Of course, everyone in the 80s, not just movie stars, wore Harringtons (named after the Ryan O'Neil character in the US TV show 'Peyton Place'). Everyone here has a black Harrington, other colours were available.

Time for Stage Two of the operation.

With the Falcon box carefully secured under my arm, I stop at the rack of action figures. I'm desperate for an Imperial Commander to complete a set, but there's none here, so I grab Luke, Han and Leia. Easy money. They fetch a decent price as single items but when sold as a set, that price doubles.

I take my place at the counter behind a young man buying six tins of Airfix paint and a tube of glue.

I'm constantly impressed by the apparently endless stock of Stubbs toy shop. They seem to have every conceivable item that any child could ever want. It is indeed a little slice of heaven in Bedworth town centre.

The front room of the toy shop is for the little kids. Dolls, teddy bears, prams, kites and toy guns. There's shelving on every available inch of wall-space, and every inch of shelving holds stock. There are more tables for

Matchbox cars and farm animals and plastic tea sets and Lego. Mobiles, roller skates and small bikes hang from the ceiling, and every uninhabited space is populated with more dolls, some of which are Trolls, some are Tiny Tears.

It's so cute, it's like Santa's grotto without the fairy lights.

I wait patiently in the 'queue' and allow my glance to drift outside. The large shop window is covered by a clear green plastic film which, I assume, protects the window's display items from fading under the sun's rays. It gives the outside world a Wizard of Oz appearance, which I can appreciate, particularly as I've never been outside. And I'm tempted. Very tempted. I would love to wander among the hurried shoppers, mobs of kids, and older couples just to glimpse into their lives, but it's not wise and who knows how many butterflies and how many effects I will create without even knowing it.

Mum had drummed it into me ever since I can remember: We can go, and we come back, but we must never affect anything. I would nod. As long as I got my toy, I was OK with anything else. I knew I must never leave the shop, never go outside, but it was many years before I asked my mother how she went outside without affecting anything. And by that time I knew very well that she affected a lot of things, nearly all bad.

Still, I would love to walk amongst the people and take in the sights.

I watch as a woman in her fifties, my mother's age, mopes past the window. Although it's late-June, and according to my watch, it's 11 o'clock, she's dressed in assorted layers of grey clothes that seemed designed to hide every contour of her body and present a round shapeless mass from her chest down to her calves. I can't quite imagine my mother choosing any of those garments from her vast wardrobe, whatever the occasion. All the women in 1980 look twenty years older than their 2020 counterparts.

My mother has never been back, as far as I know.

When I started coming back, I didn't tell her. She didn't need to know. But I promise myself I would honour her advice and stay within the confines of the shop. My objective is to acquire items I could sell for profit, nothing more. And that objective is also confined to Stubbs. I could branch out into records, books, and comics especially are profitable and easy to transport, but I don't. And I don't need to. I get by on selling on items from Stubbs and Stubbs alone.

I can't deny I have aspirations of being a major dealer in 80s memorabilia, but although it's a grand daydream, I know that it's unsustainable. I often mentally work through the business model for my own amusement, plus it helps me not think too much about the ethics of what I'm doing.

My mother used to bring me here when I was three or four years old, pre-school age, although I was pretty much home-schooled until I was fourteen. Although, we moved around so much that I say I was road-schooled. I enjoyed learning, but by January each year, mum would say, "You've passed this year with Distinction! Congratulations!" and that was the end of the curriculum until September.

We'd go to the 'magic place', which was the third stall in the ladies' loo of the Bear and Ragged Staff pub, and she'd say 'Close your eyes sweetie' and I would and then she'd say 'Now open them' and we'd be there; in the toy shop. And then she'd leave me there, for an hour or sometimes longer, and I would look at the toys and pick one I wanted. Then mum would return and she'd buy me the toy, and we'd sneak back to the 'magic place' and I'd sit on her lap again.

"Hold on to your toy, Hanny!" she'd whisper, and I'd close my eyes and get that funny feeling in my tummy until she said, 'You can open them now, Hanny'.

And then we'd be back. In the pub.

I never asked any questions. Why would I? I was four, I got to spend hours in a toy shop and I got a toy.

If I had to guess how it works, I'd say it's a kind of quantum-physics where, when a atom moves somewhere, there is a time when it is in two places at the same time. This could be how my time-travel works, and the 'Magic Place' where this quantum-physics works. Or maybe it's where two ley-lines cross.

I don't know and I don't ask questions.

Who am I going to ask?

My mum has been trying to find out for decades and, as far as i know, she doesn't have any answers.

So now, when I go, I just go, get what I need, and come back. I've been doing this, initially being taken by mother, for years. I don't know how it happens, but I know that when it does, I come back approximately forty years, well, thirty-nine and a half. Or 39.64 years to be more precise. 14470 days. It's always the same, every time. Same time of day too.

There's no danger to myself. I've done it hundreds of times, and the only real danger is if I somehow change the course of history, even in a minor way. But I've been careful, and I will always *be* careful. And, for the record, I have no idea what happens if history is changed. Hopefully, I will never find out.

So as I see it, there's no harm in coming here, no one gets hurt, and I don't change anything (except for it having one less Millennium Falcon toy, Cat No. 33364, in 1980 until this deficit is corrected in 2020).

The next phase of this operation is just as fraught and dangerous as the first.

For maximum profit, the item has to leave the shop without even a micro-scratch.

This is where the interaction with the shopkeeper becomes mission critical. He could mark it with his watch face or, God forbid, drop the damn thing whilst he's flipping it around looking for the price tag. To be fair to him, he's very respectful of the product he sells, which is very much appreciated, but, all the same, I always make sure I present the box to him with the price tag on the end of the box is literally staring him in the face.

"It's a present for my little brother," I say, meaning please don't dent the box.

He smiles, "You should bring him in sometime."

"I will," I say, "although he'll be a little overwhelmed, this would be his favourite place on earth."

The shopkeeper laughs. "That is kind of the idea," he whispers to me with a smile.

I smile back as we share the in-joke.

With the Falcon safely back on my side of the counter, I lay out the three action figures. He handles these a little too carelessly for my liking, but the plastic packets are more robust than the huge cardboard of the 'treasured item', so I let it slide.

The Falcon is £16.33, the action figures are £1.59 each.

He manually rings up the total on his till. "That will be a total of twenty-one pounds and ten pence, please."

I hand over four five-pound notes and two ones and as he busies himself with my ninety pence change, I open my Gola bag.

Now, this isn't any normal Gola bag, circa 1980 or any other time. First, it is very large, the size of the Head bags that became popular in the 90s, the ones that could hold twelve tennis rackets or enough clothes for a week-long school trip to France.

Second, inside I have inserted an aluminium frame with slabs of polystyrene foam on the sides. This is how I protect my merchandise in transit.

With practised skill, I lift the toy from the counter and slide it very carefully into the Gola bag, where it lies snugly encased in polystyrene protected by the frame. I pull a towel over the top of it, lay the action-figures on top and zip up the bag.

Now I'm nearly home-free.

The shopkeeper gives me my change.

I thank him.

I remind myself I have done nothing wrong.

How I got here might be dubious, but that aside, I don't have to feel guilty about any of this.

Besides, it's something I've done for as long as I can remember. I don't break any laws, {except maybe some laws of physics}, I don't harm anyone, and I don't do anything wrong, certainly not wrong in a legal sense. I just buy some things, with legal tender, and then leave.

Most important, the single most critical thing, is that I don't change anything. I don't cause anything. I keep interaction to an absolute minimal. There's no cause and no effect.

I make sure of that. I'm careful.

All I do, literally, is buy toys and leave.

Well, I say 'leave', but that's not strictly true.

I never 'leave'.

I get to the door and open it. Then, fortunately for me, a stream of girls swarm into the shop, followed less enthusiastically by two frazzled mothers. I hold the door open. All the girls and their mothers offer me a 'Thank you' as they pass.

Immediately the shop is transformed from a library-quiet church of toys to a choir of excited six-year-olds, all of them shouting out names of the treasures they discover as they swarm throughout the room.

"Simon Says."

"Hungry Hippos."

"Strawberry Shortcake!"

"Where?"

"Where!"

I look back.

The girls are crowded around a single display, jostling for position, the feeding frenzy reaching fever pitch.

The shopkeeper. and provider of this joy, has a genuine smile.

He catches my eye and nods a farewell.

I nod back and go to leave, but freeze at the door. "Oh," I announce to myself, "I forgot my coat."

The nosy kid, who I'd forgot about, having seen the girls, has retreated into the back room. He gives me a funny look as I pass, but I don't rise to his bait. I don't need him to get curious right now.

I grab my Harrington from the train-table and head for the back of the room. There are two doors in the far corner, side by side; a door to the backyard and a door to the storeroom marked "Staff only". It's obscured by a stand-alone shelf of a hundred Barbies, and a few Kens, my co-conspirators. who look the other way. I step behind the shelf and am out of sight of everyone.

The door should be locked, but I'd unlocked it from the inside when I arrived a few minutes ago. I push it open and I slip into the storeroom. Once inside, I release the latch and the door is locked again.

It's dark inside. There is a light, but I never use it. A dirty skylight offers a degree of illumination that's enough for me to navigate to the staff toilet. It's a single stall. I assume it's used by both male and female members of staff, and, I also assume, that it happens to be in the same place as The Bear and Ragged Staff's toilet (in forty years' time), because of the position of the sewage system.

To protect my new purchases, I hold the Gola bag in front of me as I push the door labelled 'Toilet' in black marker pen.

I step inside, turn around and sit on the lid.

I leave the door unlocked.

Time to go home.

I relax.

I clear my mind and try to doze.

I find thinking of nothing helps. Blank white spaces with no sound create the perfect environment for the process to start.

It takes three minutes or so before things do start to happen.

This relaxation time is not essential. I can push things along, but it makes the experience of travelling so much more enjoyable. The best way for me to explain it is a vague rising sensation to a heightened euphoria with a gradual and very pleasant come down. And there are no after-effects.

The way it works couldn't be easier. All I have to do is relax in the white space, and to allow the thoughts of travelling back to arrive in my head unhindered. These thoughts are like timid animals at first, easily startled, but after a short time, they feel safe and are joined by more. As I don't panic, the process starts to happen. It's a gradual process. My senses of sight, touch and hearing arrive there before I do; I can see my new surroundings superimposed on the current. I can hear things, I can feel things, which means mostly I can feel the new loo seat beneath me and all I need to do is shift my butt to accommodate it and sit back down. The only sense that does not participate is that of smell, although, weirdly, after I have travelled, there is always a scent like sweet Blue Tac, strange, but it always happens and lingers for some time after.

And when I feel totally comfortable and perceive no threats, I arrive back in my own time.

11:23am
Friday
7th February
2020

CHAPTER 2

I step out of the ladies' loo and survey the bar of The Bear and Ragged Staff pub. There's always a few punters no matter what the time of day, and right now there are a dozen or so.

I head directly for the door. There's the usual crowd of regulars, most of them on their phones. The pub has a 'no TV and no Jukebox' policy, which means that individual conversations carry around the room with an indistinct drone making every word audible, but none of them decipherable. Not that I have any interest in anything that's being said.

Relative to Bedworth's other public houses, this place is way ahead of the competition and was once nothing short of palatial, but its high-quality fittings, carpets and wall-coverings are now showing the ravages of time. It's been twenty years or so since Whetherspoons moved into these premises. Some might say it's in need of a refit, but there are enough drinkers who believe that it's fine as it is, and, crucially, there's enough of them to sustain a profitable business.

Holding my Gola bag to my side, I take long strides to the door.

The only eyes that follow are that of an Alsatian sat beside a table of three men in tracksuits and baseball caps. When I stare at the dog, it looks away.

"Miss!" someone shouts.

I know the voice is calling me, but I ignore it and continue on my B-line for the door.

"Miss!" the same voice shouts louder, more assertive.

One of the guys hanging around the doorsteps in front of me and points at the bar.

He doesn't speak, but raises his eyebrows.

I get the idea. I don't want a scene or any more attention than is absolutely necessary. I turn around and raise my head inquisitively.

The barman is stood where I had been sitting twenty minutes ago.

He points at my glass and says, "You didn't finish your drink!"

When I arrive, I always buy a drink and sit at the bar for ten minutes before excusing myself and going to the loo. Sometimes, I sit for a while and scroll on my phone. I'll maybe have two drinks, as if I'm waiting for someone or killing time. It depends, but as long as I don't look like I'm only there to use the time-travel portal in the third stall of the ladies' loo, then I'm good.

Hey, you can't be too careful in this game.

The barman nods at the glass on the bar and when I don't respond he pushes it towards me about six inches, which considering I'm thirty feet away, is a pointless gesture, but he's giving me a 'check mate' look like it's game over.

I'm certain that all the clientèle have frozen in incredulity at the pronouncement that I have knowingly and willingly not finished my drink. Those at the back are craning their necks to see what kind of inhuman primate would consider leaving a glass that wasn't empty.

I look at the glass. It's a vodka and orange. I don't really like vodka and orange, but when I bought it I had no intention of drinking it.

And I still don't.

I just need to protect the contents of my bag from accidental contact, so I feign a panic.

I wave my hand in a frantic 'don't worry about it' gesture and offer the explanation, "My babies been sick!"

Nobody sees this excuse as justification for abandoning the half-full glass and I realise that 'My house is on fire' might have been better, but I can now only play the cards I've dealt myself.

The barman gives me a shrug that tells me I still have time to finish this drink and your baby will be fine. Trust me.

I hate this because I know he'll remember me now and I don't want to be remembered.

"You have it," I offer, the kindness of my heart bursting from my lips.

I don't stop to see if he takes me up on my offer as it seems to have bought me some time and I use that time to slip through the crowd at the door. Ignoring the bemused stares, I step out onto King Street.

The sun is shining, but it's a cold late-winter's day and, as such, it's freezing. I zip up my jacket to the collar and wrap my arms around myself.

Pedestrianisation and brick-paving has replaced the thoroughfare that it was, but apart from that, the scene is very similar to what it was. Lloyds Bank is now TSB, and the Fruit Shop is now a Vape shop, but there's very little difference. The stand-out shops are the Sunshine Travel Agents and the tattoo shop next door, both equally garish but with very different personalities, happy together in their non-competitive relationship. The launderette opposite, by contrast, looks dark, dinghy and dejected. It can't even be bothered to declare whether it's open or closed, and if ever a shop was screaming out for anti-depressants, then that was it. The charity shop that it leans against at least tries to put a brave face on things. 'Come on mate, cheer up. No one wants to be here, but what can we do?'

I count twelve people milling around the shops, and that is classified as 'heaving' by today's standards. The sun brings them out, my mother used to say as if their appearance was due to a Pavlov's Dog's response to sunshine, which it might be. Who am I to argue?

Besides, I have things to do.

There's always a delayed come-down on my return. A sad reminder that I'm back in my own time, where I belong, except I don't feel like I belong here. Not at all.

If there was any justice in the world, like even a feint smear of it, I would 'identify' as an 80s kid. Life, however, is nowhere near accepting 'era-re-alignment' as it is a multitude of others (you can make your own top ten if you can be arsed).

The phrase 'Go Back To The 80s' was, to me, not an invitation but an age-ist insult as if I was a fifty-year-old loser reminiscing about my youth, except I didn't get the actual experience, I only got the nostalgia. I didn't have the S, but I got the TD. I would contend, however, that my second-hand nostalgia was every bit as distinct and detailed as the veterans who were there, if not better. In short, I'd done my homework and knew my 80s shit.

It was always going to be an uphill battle trying to get along with my generation when I was the only one who could see the error of their ways. Every man jack of them was gleefully sleep-walking into oblivion by selling their soul to technology's promise of convenience and connectivity. I valued my soul more than a few Casebook likes or Re-tweets and don't get me started on Instagram.

I preferred to be alone with my thoughts rather than bombarded and measured by everyone else's. Naturally, this rendered me a bit of a weirdo. Obviously I was either socially inept, hiding something sinister, or simply born an emotional cripple, and beyond any hope of rehabilitation.

And maybe I was. Who knows? Who cares? I was self-sufficient. I could survive as an island. I could *thrive* as an island.

I had friends, or acquaintances, or classmates, depending on your definition of interpersonal relationships, but really these friendships were renewed on a daily basis, neither of us owed each other anything. Each day we chose whether to continue with the friendship or not. I didn't see anything wrong with that. In fact, it seemed healthy and pro-active.

As Finn once told me, my friendship was a 'zero hours contract'. Like that was a bad thing.

Maybe it's because I moved around a lot as a kid, or because I was home-schooled, or because my mum was both over-protective and undisciplined, or a million other reasons, but it isn't something I think about a great deal.

It was how I am.

And I liked it.

The only times I really felt fulfilled were during activities I performed alone.

I've studied enough On-line Psychology courses to know about human-conditioning and had therefore recognised that I, myself have been conditioned to know how to keep secrets. It was like a family trait, passed down at mother's knee.

'Remember honey, never ever tell a living soul about our secret,' my mother would smile.

'I promise, mommy,' I smiled back. And I didn't.

As I grew in years, however, I began to feel that itch of curiosity and to probe these 'rules of nature' with the simple question - 'Why?'

And mother provided the perfectly formed single-word answer - 'Trust'. 'We can't trust other people. We can only trust each other. You and me, Hanny'.

And I never really stayed anywhere long enough to learn to trust either.

Besides, I didn't really need anyone else except my mother, who had provided me with both secrets and trust.

My earliest memories are of going to the toy shop, but never being able to tell anyone. On the rare occasion I was asked where my huge toy collection came from, I would shrug and smile and say "I don't know." It usually did the trick. And anyway, we would move away somewhere before too many questions were asked.

And nobody ever found out, ever, right up to today, nobody ever knew our secret. Mother was right. If we trusted each other, we could keep their secret forever.

But I had been a smart-arsed teenager long enough to know that I wasn't going to stoop so low as to learn anything from a worn-out cliché, so that advice was ignored. I hate clichés in any form. The problem was, as I saw it, responsibility was boring and negative. It was like a sneaky trick disguised as a desire, it crept up on you, did rabbit ears behind your head, beat you to the punchline of a joke, lead you into temptation and trapped you with obligations. I was absolutely not a fan of the aspiration to be responsible, in fact, I was drawn more to its evil counterpart, that of being irresponsible.

However, I made a terrible rebel and apart from the aesthetic claims to the opposite (mainly t-shirts, music and posters) I lacked the commitment to be irresponsible towards the only meaningful authority figure in my life: mum.

But I did, however, question the moral pillars of my mother's ethical foundations. And that usually only ends one way.

When I asked these probing questions was the first time I saw my mother stressed and without answers or an explanation and a plan to make us safe yet prosperous.

"If we had to keep the toy shop secret," I'd ask, "why was it OK for us to use it? Wasn't it wrong?"

She'd shake her head. Frown. Go to speak and stop. This was very unusual for my mother, who would usually begin her answer before most of the question had been asked.

Then I would push a follow-on question onto her to compound her faffing - "And if it was wrong, and we kept it secret, should we trust each other?"

"Hannah!" she would shout. "That is ridiculous! We have built our trust together for years. It is our most precious possession and our greatest achievement."

I look her in the eye and say, "But is it right, mum? Is it right what we did?"

At the time, I thought it was so brave of me to shake the foundations of our Temple of Motherly Love, but in truth, I was cowardly and pathetic and I knew it. The real question that was burning in my mind was - 'On our last trip to the toy shop, why did you come back white as a

ghost and wailing with blood on your face? And where was Jimmy? You said he was coming to live with us.'
But, of course, I never asked that question.

CHAPTER 3

I give up trying to get warm and instead increase my pace in order to get to shelter as quickly as possible. I do, however, take my hand from my pocket so I can check my phone as I walk up King Street heading to the library.

I have two missed calls from Mia and a WhatsApp message from the buyer of the Falcon-

SkyW@1kerOn£ - any joy

Me - got it

I get to the door when he responds.

SkyW@1kerOn£ - 33364? original serial number? u sure?

I answer his question with the disdain that it deserves.

Me - collect today?

Before sending I give the question mark considerable thought. I decide it looks good, imposing, and demanding.

I go with it and press send.

The message comes back almost immediately.

SkyW@1kerOn£ - pix?

God dammit! Why are people like this? They're super-keen until it comes to the business end of the deal, then they come out with excuses.

The library does a sterling job considering the lack of funding and lack of general interest. If people lost interest in borrowing books then the library could rebrand itself The Bookshelf Museum as there's examples from the past sixty years on display. From the sturdy 1930s, 'built-to-last', oak monoliths that will outlive us all, through the 1970s sheet metal structures with the corners that could puncture a lung to the modern day, balsa-wood strength, cheap and disposable sort.

The place is almost empty, with two book browsers and one person in the CD section (I can't believe such a thing still exists), all three of them look like they've nowhere better to be but are not exactly thrilled by their library experience. I can't really blame them.

For me, the attraction was a quiet space, hiding place and public internet access.

I head for an isolated corner table, take a picture of the side of the box and WhatsApp it to SkyW@1kerOn£ with no message.

He's back in seconds.

SkyW@1kerOn£ - omg that looks mint like MINT

Me - it is

He sends a thumbs-up emoji.

I hate emojis.

I repeat my message from a minute ago - collect today? But change it to - collect now?

SkyW@1kerOn£ - how much

Me - 925

Then I add - as agreed

Thirty seconds go by, but I can wait.

SkyW@1kerOn£ - deal im on my way

Me - cool c u @12 ugly mug cafe CV12 8HA

Done.

Another deal agreed and another step closer to my next milestone: use my earnings to build an online memorabilia store, publicise it globally and maintain a strong presence. That's my end game.

And I'm getting closer.

But, before I can even allow myself a victory-fist-pump, two vague shadows appear on the table before me.

I look up and say, "Oh, it's you."

CHAPTER 4

Mia and Finn, the only real friends I have (or want) in the whole world, are standing before me.

Mia, in ripped jeans, an open puffer jacket and a crop top beneath. How does she not have hypothermia? She has her arms folded. I hate ripped jeans. They epitomise everything that is wrong with modern values and represent life as a fake aesthetic. They are a condition that represents time and erosion that can be bought over the counter.

Finn, in joggers and a Super Dry hoodie, has his hands in his pockets.

I'm sure that Finn thinks Super Dry is an exotic Japanese brand, crafted by retired Samurai warriors from the rarest silkworm cotton and exported from Tokyo by fire-breathing dragons, all because of their use of Japanese characters (which actually had little or no meaning). For some time now, I have been wanting to tell Finn that the Super Dry Company is from Cheltenham.

I have known these two since I started at Nicholas Chamberlaine Secondary School in Year 9. There was a music appreciation class after school and I went, mostly to avoid going home, and partly to meet new people, although that gave me so much stress that even when I got to the door, I nearly turned back. I looked inside and saw Mia and Finn and thought they looked OK. That piqued my curiosity enough to overcome my reticence. In the short few weeks that I'd been at the school, I'd watched these two blossom into minor school-celebrities: Finn for his athletic achievement and breakthrough into the football team and the good graces of the hot-girls, and Mia for her progressive style, what she did with her hair, and how she blinged her school uniform to stand-out whilst staying, almost justifiably, within the rules.

They're both what I call 'sixth-form attractive', meaning they developed late, but develop they did. They look like a couple, but they're not. None of us are. But we did become a kind of trio of amigos.

I was OK at sports (individual events but not team sports) and bonded with Finn as the only person willing to match his parkour stunts. And I also provided a retro-perspective to Mia's forward-thinking fashion projects. That gave me a foot in both of their camps and we were rarely apart for my two years at the school.

Mia expected me to follow her to Nuneaton Technical College, where she is studying both Business and Beauty, but that wasn't going to happen. I was going my own way, despite Mia's attempts at emotional blackmail. 'I thought we were a team?' It didn't work.

Finn earned himself an apprenticeship in plastering, which meant working as a labourer for four years and spending one day a week at Nuneaton Tech where he lunches with Mia and her friends.

I admire them both. They are committed to controlling their own futures. But we're on different paths.

"I've called you twice this morning," Mia tells me. "I needed to speak to you, Hannah. Why didn't you pick up? Didn't you get my voice-mail?"

"I was busy," I tell her.

"Are you turning off your phone as well as everything else?

"As well as what?", I ask, even though we both know 'what'.

"As well as closing your TicTok and Insta accounts?" Mia says. "Did you actually do it?"

"Mia," I say calmly, "we discussed this."

"You're insane! Why are you doing this?"

"I've explained why."

"You're waging war against social media," Mia says, "but what about us? What about your mates?"

I have to look up to talk to them. "We're still mates, aren't we? Or are we only friends on Facebook?"

"Of course, but I needed to speak to you, Hannah," she tells me. "Maybe if you hadn't cancelled your accounts, you might have got my message."

"Mia," I say, "I can't be part of social media any more. To me, it's doing as much damage to *us* as burning fossil fuels is doing to the planet."

Mia says, "I'm not buying that, Hannah, I know you. There's something you're not telling me. Don't you trust me?"

"Of course I do," I tell her. But in truth, I don't. At least, not entirely. "There's no big secret Mia," I soothe. There is a big secret, but it's so big, its weight would crush you.

As much as I genuinely love Mia and highly value her friendship, I am acutely aware that she doesn't have the ammunition, weaponry, or tactical warfare skills to match me in a debate. She is also unable to comprehend why I have grown to hate social media. Mia doesn't have the cruel cunning to manipulate me, but it's fun watching her try.

They both sit, already resigned to the fact that they won't change my opinion or reverse my actions. They've learnt that's impossible, and they're still here.

"How did you find me?" I ask.

"I tracked your phone," Finn says, but he goes all goofy-cute as he can't keep a straight-face. He's not techie, he likes his apps to be intuitive. He couldn't track a Royal Mail registered delivery package.

"We tracked your body odour," Mia says and *does* keep a straight-face. We've been best friends for a long time, at least in my world, and although we're growing apart, we're still inseparable. We're like conjoined twins trying to push each other away.

I am curious though as to how they knew I was here. I thought I had a secret hide-out but apparently not. I mean, who goes to libraries these days?

I wait for the third answer, and then Finn says, "Public internet. The preferred portal of all paranoid criminals."

"I'm not paranoid," I say.

"You're not a criminal either," Mia adds to protect my good name.

They finally take a seat.

"So you've gone all anti-socials? What's that about?" Finn says, pronouncing the word 'anti' as 'an tie'.

"It's the future," I tell him. "Remember where you heard it first."

"Going backwards is the future?"

"Yep, of course. I can't believe you had to ask."

Finn sighs, "I feel you Han, but we're worried about you."

"And I'm worried about you Finn," I tell him. "I'm worried that social media is dictating your choices to you, demanding perfection from you, judging and punishing you. All of us. We created this monster! Not Mark Zuckerberg or the geniuses at Google. We inflicted this self-flagellation on ourselves."

Finn smirks. "Does self-flagellation mean-"

"No!" I stop him before he does the hand-signal. "It means beating ourselves up, doing ourselves harm," I explain. "And future generations will say 'Why did you do it? When you could see the damage you were doing, why did you carry on?'"

"Yeah, I hear what you're saying, but," Finn implores me, "how are you gonna check out my hot Insta?"

I laugh. "Well, since you never send me nudes, I stopped checking you out months ago."

"Woah!"

"No wait," I say, "it was after you sent nudes that I stopped. My life is full of disappointments."

"In your dreams," Finn chuckles.

Mia is clearly not comfortable with the serious/stupid on/off switching of how me and Finn banter.

Over Mia's shoulder, I can see the librarian, a hefty woman in her fifties who visibly exudes her allegiance to library-law. She has identified the offenders and is making her way over.

Mia is also clearly not finished with the initial debate. "Hannah, we all accept there's good and bad-"

"Do you mind?" the librarian chimes from ten feet away.

Mia does a one-eighty head-spin and turns red instantly. Before confronting authority she needs to get worked up, but turns to jelly when blind-sided.

She freezes for a second, then squeaks, "Sorry."

We all get a dirty look of equal length, as she returns to her gun-tower.

"Mia, online bullying is a bloodsport for some people, it's fun for them. Is that good or bad? And the people who control social media encourage them to do it. Children are bombarded with self-harm and suicide propaganda, is that good or bad? "

"It's the way things are," Finn says, "as long as you protect yourself-"

"They demand that we either sell our souls or be outcast and isolated. I'm just choosing to cast myself out on my own terms."

"No one's buying your soul, Hannah," Mia sighs.

"Can't you see how much of yourself you have to give them?"

"I do see, and I'm OK with it," she says.

"Only because they conned you into thinking that you're OK," I tell her, "but I'm not OK with it. I'm not OK with parents shoving tablets in front of their babies so they don't have to teach it how to talk or smile or interact with another actual person." I am trying not to get preachy, but that ship has sailed.

"I don't see the problem," Mia says and looks away.

"All I'm saying, Mia," I say as reasonably as I can, "Why can't we, me and you, enjoy a meal, or a day out, or listen to music, without us having to share it with the entire world?"

"What are you afraid of people knowing?"

"Everything! Once it's there, it's there forever!"

"But it's forgotten in days."

"No, Mia, it's never forgotten. Every bit of data you share is filed next to your name and used against you. Why else did they train you to share that stuff? It's so they can tailor-make their bullshit to the flavour you will absolutely love. The bullshit flavour that they know you will find irresistible. That's why."

That was my big finish, but Mia, who may well be my best friend in the world, is hardly even listening.

She lets out a long breath and says, "Do you have to be so-"

Then she shrugs as if she can't even be bothered to think of the word that I am 'being so'. It's all too much effort and no reward for her.

And this is the big obstacle that has crash-landed on the landscape of our relationship, We've managed to build around it and cover it up, but it's always there. And it's that Mia thinks that by being my friend she is doing me a favour. Sometimes it's like she's doing her bit for society by donating her a percentage of her friendship to the less fortunate.

Me? I disagree. I can honestly say that should our friendship terminate, which I absolutely do not want to happen, but if it did, I would think of Mia far less than she would think of me.

I move on and I move on quick. It's an experience I've had thrust upon me more than most and a skill I've honed over many years.

How many times did she come home from school, wondering what's for tea, to see the suitcases and boxes in the hallway ready to go? The next day I'd wake up in a strange house and we'd live in a different country for the next few months. No big deal.

So, if I were required to give advice to Mia on how to handle this situation, it would be: don't think that I 'need' you without considering what it really means to 'need' something. You'd be surprised what you 'need' when it comes down to the bare bones of life.

Like social media. Who needs it? Really?

"Are we done?" I say to Mia, intending to sound harsh, but coming off a little too successful in that regard. I add, "Are we good?" to re-qualify the question and remove its hard edge.

"Yeah, we're good." Mia says. "In fact, maybe you're right. Why don't we try it tonight? Let's go see a movie, and I won't switch my phone on."

"It's Saturday," I say.

"Yeah," she says, "Saturday night, when people hang out with friends and stuff."

"I-" she's trapped me though, I've got nothing.

She waits. Finn smiles.

And I realise that it's not that I don't want to hang out with Mia. It's just that my knee-jerk reaction to any impromptu invite is to make an excuse and decline. I don't know why I do that and I don't even realise it's happening most of the time.

I can be such a dick.

"I'd love to," I say and get to my feet.

"You will?" she smiles.

I nod, "I will, it'll be fun."

"OK, I'll pick you up from yours at eight," she says, "If that's OK?"

"Perfect."

"I gotta go," Mia says and gets to her feet. "I need to go see my dad."

She wants to say more. Even I can see that, despite my lack of empathy. I should say, 'How is he?' or 'Are you OK?', but I don't say anything. I just nod. And smile. I have things to do and it's too easy to push these things to the forefront of my mind and the needs of my best-friend to the back.

Mia leaves. She does not look back.

I check my phone. 11:30.

I say to Finn, "Do you fancy a coffee? I'm buying!"

He watches Mia walk out of the door and shrugs. "Sure," he says, "I ain't gotta be anywhere."

"Cool," I say, "Let's go."

CHAPTER 5

The Ugly Mug is Bedworth's 'new' coffee shop, having deposed the previous 'new' Costa in what was the White Swan pub. It will probably stay 'new' for the next four or five years. Here, dignity is achieved by standing still and refusing to change. Time moves slowly and memories live long.

I like The Ugly Mug. They have wobbly tables outside and in. The beige walls have many pictures of cups of coffee and life-quotes about how important coffee is.

'I don't drink coffee to wake up, I wake up to drink coffee'

'Forget love, fall in coffee'

And my personal favourite 'I'm sorry for what I said before I had my coffee'

It's an independent business, not a franchise.

The Italian family that runs The Ugly Mug do so with a fusion of love and stress. The dad sets unachievably high-standards and the perfectly adequate and friendly staff, his two daughters, ignore him.

It's fun to watch.

Finn is drinking Latte, and I have an Americano. We have both gone for the Ugly Mug option, which means your coffee is served in a funky mug that is shaped like a monster or a hideous face or just a horrible design. I love the hideous face of the goblin on my cup with the sticky-out nose and wart-ridden chin. Finn has Frankenstein on his.

He's agitated and we're already back on 'the issue'.

"I'm not judging you, Hannah," Finn says, "but why are you doing this? What's the real problem?"

"I'm just sick of the fakery that we cling to like our lives depend on it. Instead of complaining about it I'm doing something about it. I want to make my life…simpler."

"A simpler time?" he says.

I nod.

"Hannah, this ain't the eighties, no matter how much you want it to be. We've progressed, whether we like it or not."

"But it's not compulsory Finn," I tell him. "We don't have to do what everyone else does. We do still have a choice."

"But why are you pushing us away? We care about you-"

"I don't mean to," I say, realising that is a pointless statement.

"You might think you don't need anyone, Hannah, but one day you'll find out that you do. And you might think you don't hurt anyone, but one day you'll find out that you do."

I don't know if he's talking about me and Mia or me and him.

"I do know that Finn, I don't do it on purpose, but I do need some space sometimes."

He puts his coffee down so he can use his hands to illustrate how important this issue is, which he does by running his hands through his hair. "But you seem to want more and more space, so much space that there's no room for anything else other than…space. And it doesn't work that way, and by the time you realise that, it's going to be too late."

"I get it, Finn. I do."

I want to tell him I do understand and appreciate his concern and I really do value his friendship, but he is going to have to accept I don't do things the way most other people do.

But I don't get the chance.

"Mia has a problem. A huge thing has happened to her family. A huge thing! And she needs someone to talk to," he says, "and that person is you. Sorry if that screws up your plans for creating all that space you need, but you need to put that aside for a while, OK?"

I can't believe what he's saying, and that this is Finn who is saying it and not making a joke about it and not disguising it as banter is frightening to me.

I thought I was perceptive, for Christ's sake.

I thought I could read people.

"What is it?" I ask.

"You're asking the wrong person," he says. "Ask her, tonight."

I nod.

"I will," I say.

CHAPTER 6

"You must be Hannah."

I turn to see who I presume to be SkyW@1kerOn£.

As I naturally expected, he's pushing forty, a little overweight and shave-averse, but the main give-away to his identity is his T-shirt, which I personally find offensive, which is Star Wars Episode IV- A New Hope. (The film is called Star Wars, end of.)

As far as I know, Leonardo da Vinci didn't go back to the Louvre to paint a moustache on the Mona Lisa .

However, business is business, and I doubt if SkyW@1kerOn£ is interested in me correcting him on such matters of historical importance.

I smile. "I am," I say, "and you must be…"

I very nearly say 'SkyWalkerOne', but something tells me that would be rude, so I leave some silence for him to declare his preferred means of being addressed.

"Simon," he says.

Finn has a startled look that soon turns to annoyance that he doesn't try to hide.

"Mind if I join you?" Simon asks and drags a chair to our table. He sits close to Finn, who is instantly repelled and slides his own chair away.

Simon doesn't seem to notice. To catch the shop owners' eye, he actually clicks his fingers and orders a "Large latte in a takeaway cup."

I imagine that he's spoken to his mother like this for so long it's become his standard M.O.

"Can I see it?" he asks me.

I'm glad that the social niceties are over and done with and Simon is immediately down to business.

I place the Gola Bag on the table and open the zip.

Finn looks at the bag even more disgusted than he did at Simon. "You knew this was happening? This is why you invited me?"

I ignore him. I'll explain later, it's a two-birds/one-stone situation.

I keep my eyes focused on Simon who is staring into the Gola bag like he's looking at the Holy Grail, or even Darth Vader's actual light sabre with a Certificate of Authenticity signed by George Lucas himself.

"I can't believe how pristine it is," Simon gasps aloud.

"I don't think there are degrees of pristine," I say. "There's pristine and not pristine."

"You're probably right," Simon says. "May I?" He gestures to the bag.

I nod, making sure that my nod implies he needs to be careful as he doesn't own it. Not yet. I carefully place the bag on the table.

Simon stands and rolls up his sleeves. He slips both hands into the bag for real, pauses for a second to be comfortable with his grip, and lifts out the box.

In a world of his own now, he holds the box like it's a fragile work of art, studying the top, sides and bottom of the box reading every printed word.

Then, to my horror, I notice that the price sticker is still on the side of the box. It's one of those thumb-nail size sticky paper labels that gets stuck on with those old pricing guns. Its got 'Stubbs' printed in tiny writing above the price marked '16.33'.

The problem here is that it's pretty obvious that the label wouldn't have lasted forty years without peeling off, even if it were kept away from prying hands for all of that time.

A more probable explanation would be that it's counterfeit, an accusation I would struggle to defend.

I can only hope that Simon, in his heightened state of excitement, doesn't notice it.

"I want it," he tells me, "but I need to see inside."

We both know the box is cello-taped shut and to break that seal effectively will devalue this pristine artefact.

However, I could be selling him a box of Lego bricks for all he knows.

But he needs to see what's inside.

"You have the money?" I ask. "Here and now?"

"I do."

I glance at Finn, who's sipping his coffee and looking both uninterested and repulsed at the same time. This is even better than I'd planned; Finn looking like my personal security guy.

Simon follows my glance, looks back at me, and nods.

"In cash?"

He nods and I wave my palm in a 'go ahead' motion.

Finn says to me, "This why you asked me here? As back up in case your dirty deal goes south?"

"It's not a dirty deal," God, he's ruining the burly-bodyguard-effect on purpose, but luckily Simon is in his own little Star Wars universe and hasn't noticed.

"Unbelievable!" Finn says. He looks extremely annoyed at me and I will need to pacify him once this is done.

Simon takes a retractable knife from his pocket and carefully slits the cello-tape on one side of the box, then hinges open the lid to inspect the contents. His expression is a picture of joy. "It's not even discoloured," he says.

"You happy?" Hannah says to Simon, who looks very happy indeed.

In reply, Simon places the box on the table and takes an envelope from his pocket. "For future reference," he says, "I prefer PayPal."

"I prefer cash," I tell him. "When you sell to me, we'll do PayPal."

He hands me the envelope. I open it and flick through the stack of notes, all twenties except a single fiver on top.

"Nine hundred and twenty-five pounds," Simon mutters, suddenly self-conscious, glancing nervously around at the Ugly Mug's clientèle. "It's all there."

Nobody was paying us any attention.

I slide the envelope into the secret seam of my Harrington , "I trust you."

This seam provides a hiding place for such things as cash envelopes and is sealed by Velcro.

Simon pulls out a large plastic bag and places the toy inside. The Falcon is perilously unprotected, but if no longer my problem.

"Pleasure doing business with you," he smiles.

"Like-wise."

"Can you get more stuff like this?"

"Sure," I tell him, turning my attention to the view through the window. "Anything you want."

Simon nods and goes to leave, but can't quite drag himself away. "You know," he says, "this is an amazing item, I'd love to know where-"

"A girl never tells," I tell him without looking away from the window.

Simon nods an understanding 'worth-a-try'.

"Large latte?" the woman on the till calls.

"Here!" Simon shouts. He turns back to me and says, "Thanks. Bye."

I don't bother to respond until he adds, "I'll be in touch for more."

Then I glance and nod in his direction.

Finn watches as Simon pays for his coffee and leaves.

"Sorry about that," I say, "Where were we?"

"Did that guy give you nine-hundred quid for a toy spaceship?"

"Nine hundred and twenty-five for a collectable vintage item of cultural memorabilia." I correct him.

"Jesus, Hannah!" Finn says, struggling to comprehend what happened. "That's more than two weeks plastering money for me. Why would he pay-"

"Market forces and the power of the nostalgia."

CHAPTER 7

Finn looks at me and sits back in his chair. "I can't believe you invited me here to cover your shady dealings."

"It's not shady," I tell him.

"Then where did you get that piece of collectable vintage cultural memorabilia that you sold for nine hundred quid?"

"Nine hundred and twenty-five," I correct him.

"OK, whatever, I thought you wanted to have a coffee with me," he sighs.

"I do," I say, "We're here, aren't we?"

I gesture at the table, but Finn can't look at me right now.

"OK," he says, "This is probably my fault because I stupidly thought you wanted to spend time with me, so-"

"I do want to spend time with you," I say. "I just had to do this thing, it took less than two minutes. I don't see the problem."

"You never do see the problem," he says. "You got what you wanted and that's all that matters to you."

I don't say anything.

I drink my coffee and stare at my Ugly Mug.

Finn raises his chin and looks away. He doesn't want to look at me, which, despite everything, I do feel is an overreaction, but choose not to say anything. If he says what he has to say, gets it off his chest, maybe then we can move on.

He continues to look away as he speaks. "You don't ask for help, you just take it by using people, and then you kid yourself that you didn't get any help. So you don't need to appreciate what anyone's done for you and definitely don't need to repay it."

"Its not like that."

"Why are you pushing your friends away ?" Finn demands.

"I'm not," I deflect.

"You are Hannah," Finn says, "Jesus, I should know, I'm one of them."

"I have things going on Finn, that's all."

"We all have things going on! The difference is good friends find the time," Finn says, "they're there for each other."

"Finn," I say and turn to address him. His face is overloaded with disappointment and it derails me for a second. I need to find new words.

"What?" he says.

"I'm trying to get something going," I tell him, "an income, I have a business model, I am making demands on myself to make this work."

Finn sighs and looks away.

"I just need time to get things started," I tell him. "We're not kids any more. I have to make a living, put some bread on the table."

"We all do," Finn tells me, "but what if you find the way and there's nothing else left?"

"It won't come to that," I assure him. I'm hoping that's what he wants to hear because I don't want to hit him with my unadulterated house-brick-shaped honesty.

Not now anyway.

Finn shoves his hands in his pockets and stares at the table. I think we're done. My phone vibrates.

I look at the screen; I have a WhatsApp.

Mother - we need to talk urgent

"It's my mum," I tell him.

"You'll regret this," he tells me. "Call me when you realise how shitty you've been."

"Finn, look, I'm kind of busy right now, I'm sorry I dragged you down here, but-"

"Tell someone who cares," Finn says, I genuinely cannot tell if he's serious or joking.

"And do not let Mia down tonight. She needs you right now."

"I'll talk to her," I say and nod my head, "tonight."

Finn gives me a disappointed glance, then leaves.

Sometimes it's best not to say any more, so I don't. I watch him go as my phone buzzes again.

CHAPTER 8

I call Finn back, but he's gone and I don't exactly plead with him. Point taken, however. I will take what he said on board.

I sip my Americano and wish I had gone for a cappuccino instead.

I turn to my phone, ready to engage in my mother's preferred means of communication (which I know is rich coming from me).

Mother - how are you honey

Me - im fine how r u

Mother - i worry about you x

Me - don't im fine

Mother - i cant not worry its my job im your mum

Me - OK thanks was there anything else

Mother - are you alone

I read the words again, searching for the hidden meaning - are you alone?

Me - im always alone

It's a half-cryptic head-melt response but all I can come up with on the spot.

Mother - i need to ask you something

Me - go ahead

Then I add - ask away :)

After a pause of a few infuriating seconds my phone rings.

Voice call - Mother.

I answer, "Hi."

"Hannah," her voice soothes, "how are you?"

"I'm fine," I say, "we've established that already." I refrain from adding 'Try to keep up' unsure whether a passive insult would be appropriate here or not.

"I know we did honey, I'm just-"

"You wanted to ask me something?"

"I did. I do," she says, "and you are alone, right?"

I look up and scan the room to assess whether my situation constitutes the state of 'being alone' and I believe that it does, or at least that I would not be lying to state that I believe I am.

So I say, "Yes, I am."

"OK, so, don't take this the wrong way because, honestly, it's not what you think, I just need a 'yes' or 'no' answer."

"Mum, just ask," I say, unable to disguise the frustration.

"Have you been going to the toy shop?"

I hold my breath.

My brain goes into overdrive, but the wheels are spinning in thick mud. With my focus momentarily elsewhere, my voice box murmurs, "errrrrr".

"I'm not mad," mother says, "but it's real, real, important Hannah. Real. Important."

There's something in her voice that confirms that importance and something I rarely sensed from my mum - fear. She seemed genuinely afraid of something and that fed fear to me, which I naturally ramped up a few notches.

I defaulted to Truth Mode. "Yes, I have," I tell her, "about once a week for the last few months."

"I need to talk to you Hanny," mother says."When can you get home?"

Normally I would refuse to enable her paranoid conspiracy methodology, but this time she's kind of got me on her side.

"Home?" I say.

Then I realise. "Mum, where are you?"

"I'm here," she says.

"I thought you were-"

"I was," she says, "now I'm here. At the airport."

"I'll be home in half an hour," I tell her.

"Good," she says. "We can talk more then."

There's no explanation, no concern for my well-being, just questions and demands. Annoyed, I'm determined to intend to use every one of those thirty minutes I quoted."

I finish my coffee and mooch around the charity shops before taking a slow stroll home.

CHAPTER 9

My flat, which technically belongs to my often absent mother, is a two-bed apartment above a converted garage. It's in a complex of houses and apartments designed to share the aesthetic of a hundred-foot-high brick-built water tower circa-1910. The thirty-eight properties are surrounded by an eight-foot wall that provides a reasonable layer of protection, although no property is impregnable. As such, I try to stay on top of security as best I can.

When I turn the corner at the bottom of the drive, I see my mother sitting on her suitcase with her arms folded. Her blonde hair in a ponytail, her casual-look beige sportswear is looking tired and lived-in, her trainers are white Nike with dark blue souls. She's been travelling.

"You're here!" I say.

She looks upset.

"My key doesn't work," she says.

I nod. "I changed the locks."

"Why?"

"No reason." Two can play at the 'No Explanation' game. I unlock the door and step aside to let her in.

She looks back at the suitcases and then to me.

"I'll get your cases the, shall I?" I say.

"What else have you changed?" she says as she passes me.

The main living-space is on the second floor; my room, the open-plan lounge-kitchen, bathroom and my mum's room, which I never go in. The ground floor is a converted garage, which I use as an office/storage room and this is where I head for.

This is my space. I claimed it and had it renovated into a den, or an office, depending on who's asking.

The walls are breeze-blocks painted dark grey and I've hung some framed pictures on each wall. I have a full size Moonraker movie foyer poster, a Madness 'One Step Beyond' with a photo-shopped bummer-conga (four time the original length) , and Conservative Party billboard poster with the head line 'Labour Isn't Working' which depicts a meandering dole queue (the poster is in top condition but the message didn't age well.)

I drop mothers suitcases on the floor and unsling the Gola bag from over my shoulder.

"Is that thing still here?" I hear my mum ask.

Without looking, I know that she's referring to Derek, my punch bag mannequin.

"I like someone to come home to," I tell her.

Derek is my work out buddy, I do my own freestyle boxercise and punch the crap out of him. Or on less aggressive days I'll dance to my 80s high-energy play-list. It's a small space, but it work for me and I never dance in public. Ever.

It's furnished with a writing desk and a leather chair, a reclining armchair, a ceiling height book case and a heavy-duty gun-metal grey cabinet that is essentially my safe. Not only is it hefty as hell, it's bolted to the floor, and double-locked with a combination locks and a padlock.

I place my new action figures on a shelf with their comrades of which I have now approximately forty, although a few are duplicates.

The Empire Strikes Back action figures were released in two waves, the first with twenty figures, and the next with nine. You could buy two Lukes, two Leias, two Han Solos, one Yoda, R2D2, C3PO, and an array of soldiers, guards, robots, aliens and even an AT-AT driver. I know! It's almost too much excitement, but unbelievably, someone at the Kenner Toy Company didn't know the difference between the 4-Lom and Zuckass, and both were produced with their names switched! However, thanks to this mind-blowing ignorance those two misnamed toys are worth their weight in gold, well almost.

I have two of each.

I also have an almost full set, an estimated value of £5k, but am missing that pesky Imperial Commander.

One of these days, I promise myself.

For the record, I also have two Evel Knievels both accompanied by a Scramble Van which is Evel's mobile workshop in a RV Van, very cool. Having sold these just a few weeks ago, these will have to wait a while so I don't draw unwanted attention.

I lock the cupboard and head upstairs.

Mum is in her room. No doubt engaged in exchanging communication with some clandestine fringe extremist.

It's weird having someone in the flat, even though it is my mother and we've lived here for years. I got used to being alone. I quite like it that way.

Luckily, for our relationship at least, I have changed little else, apart from the front door locks.

In the top kitchen cupboard, out of sight and halfway to the back of the shelf, I reach for a tin of chunky chicken soup. It's right where I left it, which it would be as no one else has been here, but all the same, it's reassuring.

I twist the top and it pops free. Inside are my two bankrolls; today's money and 1980 money.

All those old fivers, tenners and twenty-pound notes are obsolete now, so the exchange rate is extremely favourable. I buy hundreds of pounds for twenty quid or so. And the more used and creased they are, the cheaper they are. I have searches on Gum Tree, eBay, Shpock and Pre-loved. My current stash of cash runs into thousands. It's even more profitable than crypto.

But what about the 'responsibility'? I hear my conscience say.

Well, and this is just my opinion, I exercise discipline with what I do and have never manipulated the situation in any way outside of the transaction of purchasing goods for cash money. By that I mean I don't affect anything outside of that shop. In fact, I've never stepped outside of the shop.

I've never been across the road to Ladbrokes and bet on the Grand National, the FA Cup final, or for that matter to last Tuesday's third dog race at Hall Green, and I know the winner of all three. But that would be affecting things, putting an oar in the flow of time that could cause ripples that become whirlpools and devastate people's lives. Who knows? It could happen, but it won't happen because I discipline myself.

And don't forget, there is no one who would love to step out into that world more than me.

God knows it's a better time than now.

I add the change from Stubbs to the old-money roll, held loosely by an elastic band. I slip open the seam in my jacket and retrieve the thick wedge of notes in the envelope from Simon. Once added to the more considerable wedge of modern-day cash it's thicker than a deck of cards, clamped tight with an industrial-strength bulldog-clip. I don't count it, not yet. I replace the lid and replace the soup tin in the cupboard.

Mum doesn't like soup, but all the same, I'm going to need to change my security strategy.

Back in my room, I strip off my 80s clothes and throw them in the washing basket, and redress in a t-shirt, hoodie and trackie bottoms, all of which were manufactured in this millennium. I hate them!

When I get back upstairs, mum is sitting on the sofa, back straight, knees together, both palms cupped on her knees. Her posture makes it clear that she is waiting for me.

"I wasn't expecting you," I say.

She nods. "Yes, sorry, I've had to change my plans."

She looks stressed. She's usually smiling, but she's not smiling right now.

"Tea?"

"Can we talk first?" she says.

I feel my voice-box tightening as I think back to her original question, way back when she WhatsApped me in The Ugly Mug. "Is this about-"

"Please sit down," she says. Her grey eyes convey more than the words and I sit opposite her in the armchair and it feels like I'm in a dentist's surgery hearing the words 'needs root canal work'.

"Something has happened," mum tells me, "something important."

I nod. "OK."

"And there's consequences," she goes on, "or there will be."

"What does that mean?"

From across the room, I can see her eyes glazing over with tears. She looks away and composes herself.

I don't like to see my mother upset, no matter what the reason, but if the reason is me, then it's worse. "If this is about me going back to the toy shop, then I've only been going back about once a week, nobody has noticed anything and I never leave the shop, I swear, I have never affected anything."

"It's not about you," she smiles, looking back at me. A tear runs down her cheek unchecked. "But it is about the toy shop, and I need your help."

I am relieved, selfishly, that I am not the cause of her anguish, but my own fear rises from my chest into my head.

Mother adjusts herself in her seat and begins to explain. "Hannah, on the 27th of June 1980, I ran away from home. I was eighteen and, believe it or not, I was a bit of a drama queen. My family had my life planned out for me and I, basically, had other plans. I had shared my troubles, plus a little embellishment for effect, with my distant cousin Tina Evans. We hadn't met for over ten years but had been corresponding by letter fairly regularly. She had said I could move in with her for a week or so, and I arrived in Bedworth for the very first time on the agreed day, but I never made it to her flat."

I nodded. I had vague memories of picking up this story over the years.

"I think you know why that was?" she asked.

I nod again. "Jimmy," I say.

She nods back to me. "That was the night I met him for the first time," she says, "the night he showed me what he'd found in the toy shop."

This I also knew and had met my mother's boyfriend Jimmy a few times when I was very young, that I do remember.

"I know now that my not going to Tina's has caused consequences for Jimmy. Bad consequences."

I start to put things together. "So, I'm guessing that the date you mentioned, June 1980, is the day that you'd be taken to," I say, then add, "If you went back today."

I don't mention that I'd already been back this morning. I'm hoping it's not an issue.

"Yes," mum says, "27th of June 1980."

"So are you going back?" I ask. "It'll look a bit strange if you turn up and you're, well, you're not eighteen any more." I try to force a small laugh, but it comes out more of a dry cough.

"That's right," she smiles, "I can't really pass for eighteen any more, can I?" She says this as if there is a slight doubt about it. She's forty-seven.

"So, what's your plan?" I ask, "Push a note through her letter box?"

Mum shakes her head. "That's not going to work," she says. "I need to be there."

I'm such an idiot. "Mum!" I shake my head and get to my feet. "You can't be seriously considering this?"

"You can be me, Hannah," she says getting to her feet herself and crossing the room to stand in front of me. "I only briefly met Tina when we were ten years old, and I only need you to be there for a few days."

"Mum, I can't go back and pretend to be you. It's madness! No one will believe me."

"Nobody will know," she says and takes my hands in hers and lifts them to chest height. "Nobody knows me, nobody had ID, Tina has no photos of me at eighteen and anyway, you look exactly like me."

"Mum!" I say "I can't."

"And Tina is lovely. You'll have the time of your life sharing a flat with her. Just remember we share the same relatives in Lowestoft: various aunts, uncles, more cousins and others. Just nod if she mentions anyone."

"I have things to do here," I say, but as I look into my mother's eyes I know which way this is going to go. I can see how important this is to her and although I won't fully understand, I won't be able to deny her.

"You'll be back in a few days, Hannah," she says. "You just go, say 'Hi', keep your head down and come back."

If only my mother's plans were so simple.

"Hannah, this is really important," she's telling me. "I need you to do this one thing for me, OK?"

"Mum, this is the worst possible time for me," I tell her. "Mia's got a problem, I don't know what it is, but it's something big, I promised-"

"Honey, I assure you whatever that is, this is more important to us, to you and to me."

"So tell me what it is."

"You know I can't do that," she says. "There's things you cannot know. Sometimes knowing things can change things, and this is one of them. This is the biggest thing ever for me."

She lets that sink in for a second.

Then she adds, "You'll just have to trust me."

And I do trust her. I've never had a reason not to. Despite our perfectly normal mother/daughter conflicts, my trust in her has always been justified.

Whether I'm totally buying that 'things you can't know' malarkey is, however, a different story.

She knows she's got me. She says, "You'll go tonight, stay at Tina's place until Monday then come back. That's it."

"That's never it mum," I tell her, "there's always something more than 'that's it'."

"You tell her you've left home, where you live with your father, you're going to live with your mother. If anyone asks, you don't want to talk about it. Mum's coming to pick you up Monday, be vague on the time, say your 'goodbyes' and 'thank you's' and that's it."

She's won. I try to come up with something else, but we both know I'm defeated. Besides, I have always wanted to go back and experience more that 'life', it was on my mother's insistence that I didn't.

"Here," mum says and hands me a photograph, "this is Tina."

The picture is of a post-punk pre-goth girl, mid-scream/smile with spiky dark hair and darker, flourishing eye-shadow a la Siouxsie Sioux. She's wearing a studded motorcycle jacket and a t-shirt with wide black and white horizontal stripes. She looks incredible.

"Wow!" I say. "Who knew you had cool friends back in the day?"

"We weren't friends exactly," my mum says, not even granting my sarcasm a response. "She's my second cousin, we were pen-friends, basically. That's like being in a chat-room, but you put your comments in a letter, put that in a post-box and you get a letter back about two weeks later."

"Won't she know I'm not you?"

"She hasn't seen me in years, we wrote the odd letter to each other, and me and you are identical at eighteen."

"What kind of letters?"

"These letters," she says, magically producing a wad of opened envelopes held together with a rubber band.

She'd kept them, of course. She'd probably kept every letter she ever receive. Just in case.

"We were like pen friends," she says, "That was a thing back then, we just write about what was going on in school and with our friends."

"OK," I say, "I get it."

"You'll need to read them," she says.

"Why?"

"So you know what was said between you and her."

"Jesus!"

"That's all you've got to do," mum smiles, "read the letters and keep your head down."

I nod like, Oh yeah, that's easy enough, it's not rocket science, it's just time travel.

It's been part of my mum's life for so long that it's her 'normal', and mine too, but that doesn't stop me from playing the Sarcastic Teen card when the situation suits.

"Her address is on the back of the photo," mum says, "but we've arranged to meet in a pub."

I flip the photo over.

It reads,

I can't wait to see you!
160A Park Road.
Tina
X

"She lived in the Park Road flats," I say. I pass them every time I go into town. It's a four-storey block of council properties. Maybe she still lives there, but it's been forty years, so probably not.

"You'll meet in the Corner Pin," mum explains, "at 10:30 tonight, she'll be expecting you. The Corner Pin was next to the Ex-Servicemen's Club on the corner of the Rye Piece. You can't miss it. Well, you could today because it got burnt down, but back then you couldn't miss it."

I know where she means, but I didn't know there used to be a pub there. All that's there is a fenced price of waste ground waiting for an optimistic developer to build some cheap accommodation.

"And I come back Monday afternoon?"

"Monday night," she corrects me.

I shake my head. "The shop will be closed at night. I'll come back in the afternoon."

Mum is shaking her head more vigorously than I shook mine. "You can't be seen," she says, "people might see you in the daytime. Needs to be after nine o'clock."

"And how do I get in the shop? Break in?"

Her eyebrows raise minutely to confirm my assumption. I wish I hadn't suggested it so that she would've had to say it.

"So I'm breaking the law now?"

"It's not the Crime of the Century Han," she says, "there's a small window pane you'll need to break and you can reach the latch from there. It's collateral damage. The shopkeeper will bear the repair costs admittedly, but you are his biggest customer, after all."

This is how my mum wins arguments. She somehow convinces you that you can't win and then shows you all the ways you could've won by exposing all the weaknesses in her arguments, which you as the loser are now responsible for repairing. She always beats me at chess, Risk, Monopoly, and always using this tried and tested method. I have yet to develop a counter-strategy. Admittedly, it's a plan of action I have long since adopted myself to great effect.

I concede.

Whether I break into the shop or not remains to be seen, however.

I gather my photo and my letters and head to the bathroom. "I'm going to take a bath."

"Don't be too long," mum calls, but this time I don't deem her worthy of an answer.

Once the water is running, I sit on the loo and open the first letter, which is a carbon copy of a handwritten letter from my mum.

Dear Tina

I hope you are well and I'm so sorry to hear about you losing your job! I'm sure something will come up very soon.

If you're serious about putting me up for a few days, and I do think you're serious, then I would love to accept your invitation. (Of course, I must insist on paying my way.)

If you say 'Yes' then I will buy a train ticket straight away.

I am starting a new life. A brand new life.

I don't know where it will take me, but I can't stay here any longer. The sea is eroding the coastline and it's eroding me too.

And, I hope you don't think I'm crazy, but I feel something pulling me to Bedworth, I honestly feel it. Maybe because it's the centre of England and the furthest I can go from the sea.

I don't want to pressure you into anything, but please say yes, and I promise it will only be for a few days.

Yours sincerely
Laura

I take my time in the bath and read all of mum and Tina's letters. They're imbibed with the exact amount of teenage angst and innocence that I always associate with the finest of decades and times to be alive and young.

Mum definitely comes across as being the ambitious dreamer stuck in a remote dead-end town on the coast and seems to believe that Bedworth is some kind of urban metropolis, which Tina finds hysterical. Tina herself is more street-wise, cynical and tough, but her loving heart pulses with every word she writes.

But, by the time I've let the water soak into my skin and The Pretenders have soothed my ears, I've had time to think.

I can't let the details, the photos and the letters blind me to what might be really going on. My mum has been known to believe wholeheartedly in events previously that proved to be, in reality, a powerful and dangerous psychosis.

And Mia's need to talk to me tonight was real, and she deserved a friend better than me, but I was the basket she'd put all her eggs in.

I was prepared to let her down and make it up to her later, but I had to know, as much as that is possible, that my mother's crazy plan was in fact 'real'.

I found her in the kitchen, ironing my clothes.

"How do you know?" I asked.

"You know how I know," she tells me. "And anyway, it doesn't matter how I know."

"Mum," I say, "You know what this means to me-"

It wasn't that I didn't trust her, despite the obvious issue of her 'knowing' this stuff. She'd 'known' other things that she had no way of knowing and then there was the small matter of the toy shop, which was as much of my reality as the pain from a tattoo needle. I didn't understand it, and neither did she, but we both accepted it and used it and abused it.

Except for...the other thing.

"Hannah! We don't have enough time to-"

"We don't have time not to!" I say.

My mother is a truth seeker. More specifically, she has tried to find the truth about how we can travel like we do. And that's not something you can Google or look up in your local library. So she has been involved in some pretty far out stuff in pursuit of that truth. Although I am biased, I have to say that I do not believe my mother was ever unstable mentally or had any serious mental health issues. She was also susceptible to suggestion. Undoubtedly she would've been the first in the queue for the Jonestown Kool-Aid or to volunteer for dumpster duty for Tex and Charlie, but she knew what she was doing, and she knew the danger she was placing me in. It was just part of the process she had to follow to get to the truth. Hence, she has spent time with people who absolutely do have the most serious mental issues, and, in her own words, she 'had to blend in', which means partaking in the life-style and all that it encompasses. Hence her associations with Flat-Earthers, Dooms Day Preppers, Q-Anon and two Jesus Christs, doing what they do, thinking what they think and taking what they take. This is where the line gets a bit blurry between induced madness and the proper stuff. The broader debate continues, but I do believe that my mothers issues were due to drugs, and not her own brain chemistry. in the past, she'd been completely away with the fairies.

I busied myself as best I could but it was difficult to maintain any focus. Not for the first time with my mother, I didn't doubt what she believed, but I had to question her ability to differentiate fact from fantasy. Or psychotic delusion to give it a medical term.

Stress was known to trigger her episodes and the issues that stressed her ranged from personal problems to global issues. This Covid thing in China, which is on the news all the time it seems, would certainly raise her stress levels. Things could escalate rapidly.

But, like I say, I'm biased.

She also has the funds to get to where she needs to be with these people, and to pay for the lawyers to get her away from them if needs be.

I don't ask where the money comes from.

I also don't ask if she's found any 'truth' yet, although I suspect not.

Mum sits back and looks me in the eye. "I'm fine," she tells me, "I've been taking good care of myself."

"Mum," I say, "You know I have to ask: Is this real?"

"Yes."

"Is it real, mum?"

"Hannah, please," she pleads.

"No, mum," I insist, "If I am to do what you're asking, then I have to know how grounded you are."

She doesn't answer, but I can hear her breathing.

"How grounded are you, mum?"

She sobs, "Hannah, more than anything ever in my life, I need you to believe me. I am clear in my thinking. I am grounded in the real world, and I can tell the difference between this and psychosis."

My heart sinks. I almost wanted her to be wrong, to give me a sign that once again she had torn a hole in this reality and was experiencing an alternative version, one of her own making. But there were no signs. She was telling the truth. I can always tell.

"How much time do I have?"

"Hours," her mother whispers, "but you need to get ready."

CHAPTER 10

I have filled my Gola bag and an army surplus backpack and with all of my old clothes, dirty or clean. Nothing new can go in, not even underwear.

Mum said, as I'm supposed to be 'running away from home', I should take some of her 'stuff'.

She hands me a battered old record box full of singles.

I remember this box well, and am pleasantly surprise to see it again. As a kid I had played them all the time.

'Geno' by Dexy's and 'Mirror in the Bathroom' were personal favourites, closely followed by The Undertones, 'My Perfect Cousin', 'Call Me' by Blondie, and, of course, 'Rat Race' by The Specials, all of which were in the Top 40 in May 1980.

She also gives me money, old-money, and a lot of it. All crisp bank notes, all tens and twenties.

"Nearly a thousand pounds," Mum said, "just in case."

I don't count it.

I do however need to stash this cash somewhere safe, and, please don't think badly of me about this, but I have a pocket sewn into the lining of my Harrington. I'm quite proud of my handiwork. The money-belt is easily accessible, thanks to some late-20th Century Velcro, and is totally undetected and, as such, when I transfer the cash into the jacket,

Before I go, I fire up the laptop. I don't know why I feel such a huge compulsion to check my email and news feeds before I go, but I don't have time to analyse my psychology.

Covid is the only news story, BBC, CNN and Sky News, each one showing the same footage from Woohan; deserted streets, hazmat suited soldiers marshalling the whole town and lines of body bags outside hospitals. The first cases outside China were already being identified with dots on a map and then the ticker feed changed - the first deaths outside China were reported.

I shut down the lap top and shut the news out of my mind. There's always nightmare scenarios being foisted on us by 24 hour news cycles so it could all wait until I get back in a few days.

As I busied myself my mind continually went back to Mia.

After what Finn said, could I leave without speaking to her?

Could I ask her to come with me?

That wasn't going to work.

One thing I knew for sure was that I couldn't leave without talking to her.

I go to my room, shut the door and take out my phone.

I call her and prepare for what I'm going to say, which is, whether she answers or not, going to be me essentially dictating a voice-mail about what I need her to do.

Her phone rings three times, then picks up.

"Hannah?" she says.

"Hey Mia, listen, I'm sorry and I want to explain and I couldn't tell you before but I will explain everything, the thing is, I want you to come away with me for a few days, can you meet me in town in thirty minutes, you won't need to bring anything-"

"Stop! Hannah, what are you saying? We're going out later, you promised."

"I'm saying can you meet in town in thirty minutes?"

"Did you say you're going away for a few days?"

"Not me, us. We can go away, you don't need to bring anything-"

"You're not making any sense Hannah," Mia tells me, "Where are you going? Why are you going? We should just talk Hannah. I need you to-"

"Please Mia," I say, "I want to help you, just come with me. I know it doesn't make sense but I can explain everything when we get there."

"Hannah-"

"Please Mia, twenty minutes, meet me in town. I love you, bye."

I kill the call and switch off the phone. As it powers down, I drop it in my bedside drawer.

My mother is watching from the doorway. If she doesn't want me to know that she's been eves-dropping on my call, then she's not doing a very good job of it.

"Was that Mia?" she asks, all passive-aggressive.

"Yeah," I say and get to my feet.

I say nothing. but my mother is blocking the doorway.

"You can't tell her about this," she says.

"I do know that," I say, "but she asked to hang out tonight, she's got some problems she wanted to talk to me about, and I need to explain why I'm letting her down."

"And how are you going to do that?" mum says, shifting her weight on her feet as if she's getting out of my way, but not *actually* getting out of my way.

"What do you mean 'how am I going to tell her'?" I say.

"What I mean is," she says, "you can't tell her."

So condescending.

"I'm not going to tell her," I say, my voice raised and to hell with it. "I'm going to lie to her, like I always have done, like I always have done to every single person I've ever known on this planet, except you."

"Hannah-"

"You are the only person I have ever been able to be honest with, mum," I say. "Do you know what that's been like for me? I can never let anyone get close to me! And it's all because you demanded I trust you. And that's all I've ever done and I've sacrificed every other good thing in my life, OK? So don't tell me I can't talk to Mia, because I've never been able to talk to anyone."

Mother has stood aside and is looking at the floor, but now, although my path is clear, I don't want to leave the room.

"I'm sorry," she says, "I just got a little stressed about what's at stake."

"And what is at stake, mum?" I ask. I'm talking to the top of her head.

She says something I can't make out.

"I can't hear you," I say, "Can you look at me?"

She looks up and says, "Jimmy. Jimmy is at stake."

I'm glad I gave her a hard time, but I'm also glad it's over.

These role-reversal moments between us are rare, but I do accept as part of our relationship that mothers like mine do need mothering themselves sometimes. And that's OK.

We hug.

It's good.

We tell each other we love each other.

I know how much Jimmy means to my mother. I was raised on the stories of how they met and what they've been through. My mother would go back as many times as she could so they could be together. Who says long-distance relationships don't work? She even asked me once if I would like Jimmy to come back and live with us (we'd have to move again, obviously), which I said was fine. This was just days before 'the end' so it didn't happen. Their relationship ended in disaster, huge trauma for my mother and even worse for Jimmy.

I grab my Gola bag and rucksack.

"I'll see you in three days," I say.

"Do you want me to walk into town with you?" she asks.

"No thanks," I say.

"OK," mum says and brings her hand out of her pocket. "Here," she says, "this is for you."

She hands me a watch with a leather strap and Snoopy on the face. My favourite beagle is waving a big arm and a little arm and beaming with a smile.

"Thank you," I say to mum.

"Do you like it?" she asks. "It was mine, back then."

"I love it," I tell her. "It's cute as ducks."

Mum smiles.

She nods and says, "See you in a few days."

"I love you mum," I say.

"I love you too Hanny," Mum says.

Then I go.

CHAPTER 11

I don't remember walking into town, yet here I am.

I do remember getting more than a few strange looks carrying my rucksack and Gola bag and, no doubt, looking stressed.

I turn the corner into King Street and pray that Mia is there.

In my head, I'm still planning scenarios where I manage to convince Mia to travel back in time with me for a few days and then get back on with our lives, like it never really happened. All she would have to do is come to the ladies' loo with me, come in a cubicle with me, close her eyes and relax. And then, I'd explain what just happened and-

Knowing that is impossible is something I can easily push aside or file under "To Do" because the alternative is having to plan how I am going to tell Mia that I am not going to meet her tonight as I promised.

My heart leaps the second I spot her, but it immediately sinks when I see that she is with Finn.

Even worse is the look on her face.

Anger.

Pity.

Frustration.

It was all there.

I knew it was hopeless. I would've turned around and fled, but there was no way around it.

As I approached her, she spread her arms to either hug me or tackle me to the floor.

"Where are you going?" she asks.

"I'm going away for a few days," I tell her and try to sidestep her outstretched arms. I succeed. For a second I thought she was going to grab my arm, but she lets me pass.

"Hannah stop!" she says. "Talk to me."

"I can't," I say, "I'm sorry. When I get back, I'll do anything you want-"

That came out wrong.

"Your mother is not well," Mia calls. "She needs help."

"What?"

"A soon as your mother is back you're acting weird," Mia says, "and 'going away for a few days', What is that about? Why does she have this control over you?"

I turn to her, trying to convey something not possible in words, not in the time we have left.

"My dad's had a stroke," Mia tells me. "He's in hospital and I don't know when he's coming out or if he's going to be OK."

I can feel my heart is breaking, and I hope it is being conveyed in my expression, but I know, without a shadow of a doubt, that the best for both of us is that I go. Now.

"Mia," I say, "I love you. I will be by your side and we will get through this, but I have to go. There's something I have to do."

I have nothing else to say, so I turn and go.

Then a body-slam of a bear hug stopped in my tracks. I try to take a step back but I'm held tight. Finn has both his arms around me, he's saying something into my ear, but I can't hear him over the words in my own head.

I don't like being held and I don't understand why it's happening, so I panic. I can't move my arms. I butt my head into his cheek and wrestle my arms free.

Finn lets out a loud 'Ugh', and I push him away.

"Hannah!"

"Let her go," Mia shouts.

"I'm sorry," I call back to them as I dash to the pub, "I can't explain, but I have to go."

There are tears in my eyes as I push through a small crowd at the entrance to the pub.

"Are you alright love?" one of them asks.

I don't answer him. I head to the toilet and it's at this point I realise that a teenage girl carrying two travel bags with tears in her eyes is hardly the most inconspicuous of people to be hurrying through a crowded pub.

Luckily for me, I don't have time to worry about it.

A glance behind me confirms that Mia and Finn have not given up the chase and are moving through the crowd in dogged pursuit of their friend.

I get to the loos and, prayers answered, the cubicles are all empty. I cram myself and my bags into the third from the left and sit on the seat.

Then I close my eyes, clutch my bags to my chest and try to regulate my breathing.

I think nice thoughts. Or try to.

I manage to slow my breathing to a four-count.

Then a five-count.

I open my eyes.

I see the familiar graffiti written in black sharpie pen on the door in front of me.

How much does a media whore weigh?

An Instagram

And

Question everything.

Why?

OK, I'm still here.

But I am relaxing, my heart rate is down, and my breathing is under control.

My eyes closed again and I can feel the air temperature around me fluctuate from a comfortable warmth to something distinctly cooler and fresher. This cycling from one environment to the other is super-relaxing, I let it wash over me and start to forget myself.

I know this feeling. I love this feeling.

I'm going.

I don't know why, but I am going to the other place.

I open my eyes, just a tiny bit, and I can see the toilet door dissolve into a darkened cupboard door, the only light is the shroud that surrounds it. Even in the dark, it's vivid.

I smile.

Then it fades again and the toiler door replaces it, but it's nowhere near as vivid, nowhere near as real and I know from experience that I won't see it again.

As it fades, I hear the toilet door open and footsteps enter the room.

"Hannah! Are you in here?"

I hear Mia's voice but I can't answer her.

I want to tell her I'm sorry.

I want to tell her I love her and I will be back soon.

But I'm breathing so slowly that by the time I am able to form the words in my throat, I am gone.

CHAPTER 12

Laura had positioned herself outside an estate agent's and used the reflection in the glass shop window to keep an eye on the entrance. From that safe distance, Laura had watched Hannah enter The Bear and Ragged Staff, followed by Mia and Finn. Hopefully, Hannah had enough of a head-start to travel before Mia caught up with her.

Laura didn't move although she was quite sure her bug-eye shades would disguise her face sufficiently should she bump into Mia and Finn, but why take the chance?

Patience was the best tactic, Laura knew and was rewarded when she saw Mia and Finn emerge looking bemused. Mia used the universal hand-signal for 'disappeared in a puff of smoke'.

It was a good sign, but all the same, Laura has to be sure. She crosses the road and entered the pub.

The place was crowded, which was good as it provided me with enough cover to head straight to the ladies' loo without looking conspicuous. She received a few glances and there was no denying she stood out from the usual female customers who frequented the place.

A step closer triggered memories from the years gone by; her meetings with Jimmy, bringing Hannah here when this was Stubbs and, (as the plumbing dictated) the store-room loo was in the exact same place as the ladies loo is now, and, although she tried to push it away, from her mind, when she had staggered away, shell-shocked and devastated, carrying her daughter and knowing that she would never see Jimmy again. Or so she had thought at the time.

All the years of guilt that has brought her back here and this time she was determined to put things right, whatever the consequences.

Laura shook her head to concentrate on the task at hand.

She pushed the Ladies' door open and stepped inside.

A young woman was inspecting herself in the mirror above the sinks and stroking her long brown hair into place. Her eyes met Laura's in the reflection, but with no recognition, she looked away instantly.

The doors were all open.

Laura took two steps forward, saw the empty stall and smelt the sweetness.

Her daughter was now back in 1980.

And safe.

She hoped so, anyway.

Partly from the relief, Laura allowed herself the small reward of reminiscence. It was, after all this very spot, where she had seen Jimmy disappear before her very eyes. And where, thank God, Jimmy had the presence of mind to throw her his ID card, that small bound book, like a tiny passport, that she had promised to, one day, return to him.

It had taken months, but she found him.

The police hadn't arrested her that night, although they had threatened if she didn't call her father, she would be charged with breaking and entering and burglary. He had driven through the night from Lowestoft to 'pick her up'. She had protested that she was eighteen and did not need 'picking up'. She wasn't a child, she insisted, but her father and the police disagreed.

So did her father, who had repeatedly explained exactly how much he disagreed and how things were going to change from now, but Laura wasn't listening. She knew with a concrete certainty that nothing was going to change, which is why she left in the first place.

Instead she had brain-stormed the ways she could research the ID card that she had tucked into her knicker line before the long arm of the law had been placed on her shoulder.

Four months later she had conclusive proof of who he was, and is. She had his national service record, she knew his birthday, he has indeed lived in a now derelict cottage on Nuneaton Road, everything she knew about him was true.

But...

There was one thing that didn't make sense. He was born in 1922 and is fifty-eight years old.

The facts, however, spoke for themselves, and when Laura had seen him with her own eyes, he was decidedly younger. So she continued her pursuit of him and, eventually, found him.

The woman in the mirror was staring at Laura.

"You alright?" the reflection asked.

"I'm fine," Laura answered.

"Had a drink have you?" the woman smirked.

Laura didn't answer.

Ten minutes later, Laura pulled her BMW 3 away from the traffic lights beneath the M6 Junction 3 and hit the southbound slip road bound for Rugby.

Hannah had gone through, and that was clear by the smell in the air.

There was a big part of Laura that hated herself for coercing her daughter into doing something so immense under false pretences, but the alternative of staying here was simply unthinkable. The thought that she could lose, or never have known, her daughter, haunted her.

She said a silent prayer for her daughter, then allowed her thoughts to turn to Jimmy.

10:35pm
Friday
27th June
1980

CHAPTER 13

I'm back in the darkness of Stubbs toy shop store room. It smells of sweet Blue Tac. I'm not feeling as relaxed as I usually do, and I'm certainly not feeling elated. My mind and body are frantically occupied with planning my next move. And I'm trying not to think about Mia. Or Mia's dad. Or what Mia thinks of me.

I need to calm myself, but first, I need to get out of here.

I look at my Snoopy watch. it's 10:35 at night.

I get to my feet, sort my bags which feel heavier now, and step out of the stall. I can't see a thing. Arms out, I turn right and feel for the fresh air that lies between me and the door. I know from memory where to head to, but I take small steps. My eyes adjust, but I can only make out vague shapes and it doesn't help much.

My rucksack scrapes along something to my left and I spin away, but nothing leaps out of the darkness, alive or otherwise.

I reach out and after another two steps, I'm relieved to feel the surface of the door at my fingertips. I fumble for the latch, slip the handle down and open the door, which complies with a quiet creak.

I step into the back room of the shop, or rather, a darker and therefore very sinister version of it. What is it about toys that make them so scary in the dark?

Although there's no one here, at least there shouldn't be. I'm very conscious of not making a noise.

I tell myself I'm being ridiculous; I know my surroundings perfectly well and I know there isn't a single threat here, but then there are the eyes, thousands of them, the Action Men, the Barbies, an army of Six Million Dollar

Men, even the Subbuteo players were staring at the intruder.

I'm scaring the toys.

My heart is racing.

I'm trespassing.

This isn't right.

I have to get out.

Mother had said that the back door would be unlocked.

For the first time I wonder; How does she know that?

And what if she's wrong?

I reach out for the door handle, and it swings open at my touch.

Cool night air rushes in. It smells of nothing, but it smells beautiful.

I step outside, close the door behind me, and adjust my bags on my shoulder. The backyard is partially lit by a street-light and then some cloud-free moonlight. I can see the ground before me and I take confident steps to the gate, which, I'm pleased to find, is only secured by a sliding bolt.

There's an alley that connects the back of the shop to its King Street frontage. The steps I take are the first I've ever taken outside the shop in this time and place. I don't mark the moment with a fist-pump, I'm too scared and have too much to do.

The Corner Pin is standing where it was supposed to be (which is such a strange thought, but this is a strange situation) on the corner of the Rye Piece crossroads. I'd read that it had become derelict in 1996 after it was closed down due to a series of scandals; fighting, gambling, under-age drinking, disturbing the peace, and more. There were rumours that the Hell's Angels had used it as an HQ and the basement was a "knocking shop". In 2004, after standing empty for eight years, a fire was started on the ground floor that rapidly spread to the second and third and collapsed the roof. Structurally damaged, the building was condemned and knocked down.

And this was the place I was supposed to meet Tina?

It was bad enough I'd be walking in there on my own, but a girl carrying two bags over her shoulder is bound to attract attention and not the good kind.

As I approach the door, the first thing I notice is that the murmur of the crowd is louder than the music on the jukebox, which is Led Zeppelin's Black Dog.

The double doors are propped open by a two halves a house brick. There's no one hanging around the doorway itself and from there I can survey the scene without stepping inside, which I am definitely not going to do. Not until I see Tina, even then, maybe not.

She isn't here. There is nobody even closely matching Tina's description and photo.

I've been standing here for about ten seconds and already more than half of the men have turned to stare at me. They're like a wolf pack, picking up on silent signals as they identify potential prey.

It wasn't a feeing I enjoyed. There wasn't a single person here I would be comfortable holding eye-contact with for more than a second. I certainly wasn't going to explain how I'm new In town and looking for someone I hadn't actually met.

This was madness.

How could my mother put me in this position? And how could she know that a particular person would be at a particular place at a particular time?

I step away from the door and make my way back to King Street.

Scared that I was being followed. I try to look casual, but there's nothing casual about checking behind you every three seconds.

Nobody was there, but still, I picked up my pace as I weighed up my options: go to Tina's flat or go home.

I have Tina's address and I know the place well. I had passed it this morning twice already. My Snoopy watch tells me that it is now ten forty-five and I could wait outside for Tina to return and explain that I couldn't find her in The Corner Pin, where we'd agreed to meet. I was sure she'd understand, even if she'd be a little annoyed. But what if she didn't turn up? What if she stayed out for the night? Or if it wasn't even her flat? I'd be stranded there. Creeping around the town in the early hours to get back into the toy shop would look a bit dodgy and take some explaining should I get caught.

The possibility of sleeping rough for the night was a realistic proposition if things went south.

The other alternative, the more appealing one, was to go home. Right now.

This whole thing was crazy, even by my mum's crazy standards. Coming here, where I don't know anyone, with no backup plan if things went wrong, was just stupid and I should never have agreed to it.

In less than a minute I'm outside Stubbs toy shop again.

I peer into the darkness of the alley, knowing that the back door is unlocked. I could go back now and there'd be no harm done to me or anyone else. I'd tell my mum that her plan sucked, and Tina didn't show, and before she gives me that disappointed look, she needs to know I'm way more disappointment in her for sending me on this wild goose chase, but then I heard someone say, "Are you Laura?"

"Yes!" I say before I've even turned to see who is asking.

Of course, it had to be Tina. No one else knew my name or my mother's name I should say, but immediately I know that jumping round shouting 'Yes' was such a dorky first impression.

"I'm Tina," she smiles.

She is more beautiful than the photo that mum gave me. Her spiky black hair reaches out in all directions and her dark eye-shadow highlights her bright green eyes. She's wearing a Clash T-shirt, the tightest faded jeans and sky-blue stilettos with black leopard-print.

I can't help but smile back. "You're here!" I say.

"I am!" she beams.

I try to sort my hair out as Tina strides toward me. I don't know whether to expect a full-on bear hug, a tender embrace or a firm handshake. I have a whole new social etiquette to learn and already I'm determined to actually participate in society this time!

Tina opens her arms and wraps them around me. She smells of perfume, cigarette smoke and beer.

"I'm so sorry I wasn't there when you got here," she tells her as she lets me go.

"No problem," I say. "Thanks for letting me crash."

"Crash?"

"I mean, stay here. It's super-kind of you."

Tina shakes her head, "It's my pleasure, we're going to have so much fun!"

I laugh. It's my first genuine laugh in a long time. My face feels strained as it's responding pleasurably and not using the sarcasm-assigned-muscles.

"Oh, my God!" Tina gasps. "You won't believe what happened to us tonight!"

"To us?"

"To Terry," Tina explained. "I was in the pub and this guy tried to rob the pub!"

This doesn't really register with me at first, as I'm disturbed by Terry. He looks like a borderline skinhead with his half-mast bleach-splashed Levis,
brown docs, and short hair, but not that short, more like a No.3 plus two weeks' growth. He also has a Fred Perry, but no braces which, to my mind, equates to skinhead-aspirations, which is despicable, but doesn't even have the conviction to do it properly.

A wannabe, basically.

I know I'm being judgemental and I absolutely shouldn't be, but I don't like him.

I don't know if he and Tina are a couple or anything; I hope not, but it's none of my business.

Tina is staring at me, her eyebrows raised high on her forehead. "He tried to rob the pub!" she says.

What she says finally registers with me, "Oh my God! Are you kidding me?"

"I'm serious," she insists. "Terry and the Landlord went after him but he had a taxi waiting."

"He won't get away with it," Terry says, "We'll get where he went from the taxi firm. There gonna be repercussions."

The way he stressed the word 'repercussions' indicated that the matter was far from closed, but Terry didn't seem the type to be dealing out justice, at least not on his own.

In fact, maybe the whole thing was BS.

"Laura, don't think this happens here all the time," Tina says. "It's not exactly The Woodentops, but, you know."

"Tina!" Terry says, harsh enough to stop her from talking. He gives her a look to say 'that's enough'..

"Sorry," she says, takes a breath, and then says, "Terry, this is Laura. Laura, this is Terry."

"Hi," Terry says.

"Hi," I say, thinking too hard to force a smile. "And," I say, "if it's OK, can you call me by my middle name, Hannah? Is that OK? It's a new life, new name kind of thing."

"Hannah?" Tina says.

"Yes, Hannah, if that's OK? I'm trying to put my past behind me."

"Sure," she smiles.

"So did he get away with anything?" I ask in a hushed voice. "The guy who robbed the pub?"

I don't want to ask Terry anything, as there's just something I already dislike about him, but I firmly believe that there's no such thing as a coincidence. Being told to meet at a pub just after its been robbed is a definitely a coincidence. And I don't believe in coincidences.

Terry chuckles at my question. "He was never going to get anything," he sneers, "except a good-hiding, which he will still get when we find him."

"Anyway, forget that," Tina says. "You must be exhausted. How was your journey?"

"It was OK," I smile. "I came on the train in the end."

"Do they know you're here?"

I don't answer. It's clear I need to catch up quick or I'll dig myself a hole before I really get started, but I'm not sure who she means.

"Your dad and boyfriend and that," Tina says. "Is anyone going to come looking for you?"

"Oh, no," I say, "there's no chance of that, I promise."

"Wouldn't be a problem," Terry says, "just good to know. Forewarned is forearmed and all that."

I shake my head. I know I'm supposed to have ran away from home, but again, I don't have any details. "I'll call my dad tomorrow and tell him I'm fine, but none of them know where I am and they never will."

"You're so brave," Tina beams. "We'll look after you here. Me and my mates, we're like a family. You can be my new sister!"

"I'd love that," Hannah smiled. "I really would."

She hugs me again.

I know that I'm smiling and can't seem to stop. Tina hooks her hand on my elbow. She's walking extremely close to me, rubbing shoulders and the long spikes of her hair touch me as she leans in. Normally, I would hate this. I wouldn't even allow Mia to do this, but here and now it feels 'right'. I actually like it.

I try not to allow my thoughts to dwell on Mia. I have vowed to make it up to her when I get back, but there's no point in it occupying my mind here and I need to keep my wits about me and focus on the here and now.

"How long are you staying?" Tina asks me.

"Until Monday night, if that's OK with you?" I say, still bloody smiling. She must think I'm insane or something.

"Of course," Tina says, "You can stay as long as you like."

9:30am
Saturday
28th June
1980

CHAPTER 14

"As soon as you're ready, we can go out and doss round town for a bit. You have to meet my mates," Tina explains, "I've told them all about you."

We're in the kitchen, it's nine o'clock, and she's making a fry-up; sausages, baked beans, scrambled eggs, black-pudding, tomatoes, fried bread and a lot of lard (like half of the pack seems to have gone into three pans already). It looks stodgy, dripping with fat and contains calories in the thousands, but it smells delicious.

Last night Terry 'walked us home' and came in for a drink, but didn't stay, much to my relief, to be honest. I still don't know if he and Tina are an item, but I do hope not. There's something about him I just can't warm to.

Everything felt so weird, like panic-inducingly weird. I walk past these flats every day. back at what I'm going to refer to as 'home'. I know people who live here, although not well enough to have been inside. And the flats have hardly changed. Everything is familiar yet I'm a long way from 'home'. Although I'm only a two-minute walk from where I live, I'm forty years away.

Tina must've sensed my panic, and we talked into the night, mostly just friendly chat about music, movies, TV shows. I held my own on those subjects without making any major boo-boos or contradictions to my backstory, but when she spoke about her friends, family and the people she knew, I had nothing to contribute. All I could do was allude to Mia and Finn whilst keeping things vague and as general as possible. Tina sensed this too and was happy to do the talking and not ask too many questions. She told me about how she's having a hard time as she and has lost her job. When I asked her why, she said she didn't actually know and I didn't push her as it's none of my business at the end of the day. Mostly though, we spoke about music, her mates, what they get up to and how boring her life is, which seems an impossibility to me.

She is my soul-sister, I really think we connected. We laughed so much my face hurt.

At about half-past-one I was yawning like a very tired Cheshire Cat and Tina showed me to my room.

I'm in what you'd call the box room. There's a small single bed, a chest of drawers, and not much else, but it's fine. The bed itself was incredible, a perfect combination of soft and firm, like a cloud of cotton wool. I had blankets instead of a quilt, and I remember hoping that I'd get used to them and the next thing I'm aware is the smell of fried bacon.

I'd slept so deeply that waking up was a slow process and everything else was vague. I knew that it was Saturday morning, but then I realised I wasn't in my bed. I tried to open one eye, but it was all too much.

Where was I?

Mia's house? I've slept there twice before, but I don't think so.

Finn's place? I've stopped there more than twice, but Finn's bed was tiny and as comfortable as a bottom bunk in Alcatraz.

This bed was extremely comfortable.

And there was no Finn snoring beside me.

As my brain cleared and I realised that the way to resolve this riddle is to access my memory banks, and it is then that I remember that I'm in Tina's flat and-

Yeah.

I'm in 1980.

And that woke me up.

A big part of me was super-excited, and the other part was more-than-super-terrified.

What have I done?

How could I be so stupid?

I should go 'home' before something happens that-

"Morning," someone sang in a low drone. Her voice was like a cat's purring.

I felt obliged to open both eyes and say something, but without an instruction from my brain, my mouth says, "What time is it?"

No, wait. Rude! I say, "Sorry."

I sit up and through my blurry eyes, I see Tina smiling in the doorway.

I say, "Good morning. How are you?"

"I'm OK, thank you," Tina told me. "Breakfast?"

I nodded and felt my smile grow, not just because I was hungry, but because there's something about being with Tina that tells me things will be alright. Or even better than alright. Possibly even 'great'. Or maybe even 'hyper-great'.

I was starving, I was awake and I wanted to help my host with the cooking.

I didn't think of home. I'd be back there soon enough, but for the next few days I wanted to enjoy every moment of my here and now.

I contort my body into a day-starting stretch from my hands to my feet and I decide that today is a special day and as such I shall be wearing my Madness t-shirt.

Once dressed, I crossed the hallway to the kitchen.

"Good morning," I say. "What can I help you with?"

"Good morning," Tina smiles, "I think everything's under control. How did you sleep?"

Tina is wearing on over-sized red t-shirt that's mid-thigh length, like a mini-dress. She is barefoot and her hair is scrunched on top of her head with an elastic band.

"On Saturdays, I normally wander round the shops and the market. There's not much here though, but if you want, we can get the bus into Coventry," she tells me.

"I'll be happy doing whatever you want to do," I say,

Tina's kitchen has a breakfast bar and two tall stools sat opposite each other. The room isn't really big enough and much of the workspace had been sacrificed, but it was worth it. There was an oven and a cooker top and an equal-sized space on either side of it, .

'Keep a low profile'. My mother's words come to me.

I tell myself I should make an excuse and say I can't go out, but what kind of excuse is going to fly? I'm here to hang out with Tina. I can't now say that's not going to happen. This is undoubtedly another flaw in my mother's plan, has got more holes in it than a tramps vest.

Besides, I have the once-in-a-lifetime chance to hang out with fun people in one of the best times to be alive, so staying in was never going to happen.

The kettle is boiling on the electric cooker hob. I know this because it has a spout and a nozzle that is also a whistle, which I've never seen before. The steam rushes out of the nozzle and the whistle screams with a high-pitch continuous wail. It gets louder and louder until we can't hear ourselves speak.

Tina, poking the fry up around the frying pan, glances over her shoulder at me. I smile and wait for the kettle to turn itself off.

After a few seconds, I realise that it's not going to happen by itself. Of course, it isn't. It's just a pot sitting on a heat source. There is no thermostat or cut-off switch.

I jump up and turn the dial on the cooker. Immediately, the whistling dies.

I set about trying to make two cups of tea, and get as far as placing two cups on the kitchen top.

"Tea's in the caddy," Tina tells me, pointing to a metal cannister.

I open it expecting to see tea-bags but instead I find it full of tiny brown grains of some kind, which I realise are ground tea leaves. Despite this discovery, I still don't know what to do.

"Tea pot," Tina says and points this time to the more obvious item.

I pick it up and place it next to the tea caddy.

Tina hands me a spoon, which is another clue, but I can't quite figure out the process.

"How do I-"

"Four," she explains, "three people and one for the pot."

"I don't..." Four what? Three people? One for the pot? I'm more confused, if that were possible.

"Don't you know how to make tea?" Tina smiles.

"We have tea bags," I say.

Tina wrinkles her nose. "Well we have proper tea here!" she says. "Put four tea spoons into the pot and fill it to the top."

I manage to get the tea leaves into the pot, but I don't know how to get the nozzle off the kettle. It kind of has a little handle on the end, but I hope I'm not expected to touch it as it's boiling hot.

Tina spots my hesitancy and using a tea towel to hold the big handle, she jiggles the nozzle free.

She smiles. "It gets stuck sometimes."

I smile back and use the same tea towel as I pour the water.

It's embarrassing being so domestically useless, but this whole operation seems fraught with danger. The risk of scolding myself seems disproportionately high to the reward of a cup of tea, but I figure she who dares and all that.

After the regulation three minutes of 'mashing time', as mandated by Tina, I am introduced to a utensil known as a 'tea strainer', which is a kind of filter that sits on top of the cup to catch the leaves as the tea is poured. Ingenious.

By the time I set the three cups on the table, Tina is dishing up.

"Who's the third person?" I ask.

"My mum," she says.

"Call me Barbara," says a voice behind me.

"Oh, hi!" I say, similarly startled to when I met Tina last night.

Barbara is smoking, wearing a quilted dressing gown and high-heeled fluffy slippers. Her resemblance to her daughter is almost perfect, except her hair is a dirty blonde, long and lank, with lots of split ends and dark roots.

"Good morning," she says, as she rushes toward me, "you must be Laura."

She embraces me in a tight hug and hums a satisfying groan.

She stands back, takes a deep drag on her cigarette and asks, "Did you sleep OK?"

"I did," I say, "thank you."

Tina puts two plates on the table.

"And thank you for letting me stay," I say to Barbara. "You're very kind. Please let me know if there's anything I can do while I'm here."

Tina says, "As long as it's not making tea."

Barbara smiles again. The smoker's lines on her lip disappear when she does.

"Here's your tea and toast, mum," Tina says, conjuring a plate of toast from somewhere. "I'll bring your tea through once it's mashed."

Barbara shakes her head and takes the plate. "Don't worry, I'm not staying. Speak soon Laura."

"Oh, Barbara," I say, "It's Hannah."

She frowns, "I thought-"

"It was Laura," I explain. "I changed it. Now it's Hannah."

"OK," she says, "you're not on the run from the law, are you?"

"No," I say, shaking my head, "nothing like that."

Barbara is amused that I took her joke a little too seriously and I feel my face redden.

"Well, have fun," she says as she leaves.

I sit down and admire my breakfast. It looks and smells incredible. Tina adds salt and red sauce, which she applies by squeezing a plastic tomato the size of a cricket ball. I love it. I pass on the salt and add both red and brown sauce.

"Oh, my God!" Tina grins. "Red *and* brown?"

I nod. "Why choose when you can have both?"

Tina's eyes marvel at my ingenuity.

We eat.

The fry-up is delicious.

And the tea is not bad either.

"It sounds great," I say. "Thanks for doing this for me Tina-"

"It's OK," she says, "you don't need to keep thanking me all the time."

"Sorry," I say. I'm getting predictable.

I need to come up with something to contribute to the conversation.

I look out the window for inspiration and see the market. It's a hive of activity already: stalls have been set up, I can see five rows of canvas canopies and plenty of shoppers are milling around them. The legend of the market, as told by the oldies back home, is that you could buy whatever you wanted from Bedworth market. Obviously, that's a bit of an exaggeration, it ain't Amazon, but I get the point.

I remind myself that I'm not supposed to know any of this so I decide to ask, "How big is the market?"

"We walked past it last night," Tina says, "There's loads of stalls, all of them crap!"

I laugh.

"My mum used to have a clothes stall there," she says. "I used to work for her."

"Why did she stop?" I ask her.

Tina doesn't answer, instead she says, "You can see it from here, it's opposite the HyperMarket."

"So it's like the Not-Hyper-Market?" I say.

Tina laughs, a big shoulder-jiggling giggle. She has a fork loaded with baked beans, which she returns to the plate. "Did you say the 'Not-Hyper-Market'?"

"I did," I say and laugh myself. "That's what it is though, right?"

I've never been more relieved that a joke of mine landed, although that's not a high bar, as I don't usually make jokes and I'm not usually concerned about the reaction when I do.

"We can do something else if you want," Tina says.

"Something else?" I ask. I'm confused.

"If you don't want to go into town."

"Oh, no," I say, "I'm down for that."

"You're 'down for that'?" Tina smirks, emphasis on the 'down'.

"I mean, yes, I'd love to go into town."

"You make me laugh the way you say things."

It's a stark reminder of my situation. No matter how much I try, I don't speak the lingo here. Every time I speak, I'm going to sound different. I hope people will put this down to me not being from 'around here'. One thing for certain is that they will not guess the actual reason.

I make a note to pick up a few phrases today and blend in as much as I can.

CHAPTER 15

We're in town.

It's eleven o'clock and already I've lost count of the people I've been introduced to and Tina has dropped in my 'Not-Hyper-Market' gag to every one of them. We've been in Woolworths, WH Smiths, Taylors Record Shop and the market itself. And although I always knew it, the biggest impression I've got from this social whirlwind is just how tribal things are. I've met Dave the skinhead, Pete the punk, Roger the Rudeboy, Rod the mod (I'm making up the last two names because I've lost track of people) but everyone is something, including the people we don't speak to: the greebos, new wavers (arty kids who are not punks), and what I'll politely call 'the normal kids'.

I've never seen the town-centre so busy, it seems like everyone within a mile radius is in town this Saturday morning. It is literally 'heaving' with people and twice I've bumped into unsuspecting shoppers.

There's also a reminder of how there's been hardly any development in Bedworth town centre over the last forty years, the shops have changed but the buildings are exactly the same. Only the pavement has been updated in that time, and the market.

The market in 2020 is an open space covered with a high roof. The stalls are set up on either temporary tables or within permanent rooms on two opposing sides.

The market of 1980 takes up the same space, has no roof, and is made up of rows of stalls with huge displays, overhanging canvas awnings and each with their own individual sound and aroma. The market sellers stand on raised duckboards and the more animated ones give the full sales pitch, 'Half price to you my love but don't tell no one else!'

The tales the old folk told me back home are also true, 'Whatever you wanted, you could find it on the market'. Provided you didn't want much, they've got it here.

A stall selling curtains sits beside a stall selling jeans which sits beside one selling electric lights: we wander past them all. There's me, Tina and an hundred other kids who come and go and come back again and there's always something going on. We're like an army of ants, working together, moving as one and passing messages through the ranks.

I catch bits of conversation from within this whirlwind of stuff that happens.

Someone has been caught shop-lifting - Why would he even try to rob a cricket bat?

Someone is starting a band - We're going to be bigger than Bad Manners.

Someone is pregnant - That's the last time I play Naked Twister with him.

I'm overwhelmed, there's a lot to take in. I'm definitely feeling out of place due to my appearance. Nothing is said, but there no shortage of dismissive looks.

Tina is now saying that she is 'down' for a pot of tea at Harry's Bakery and Cafe.

As we enter the cafe, I'm looking forward to a sit-down where I can take a breath and compose myself, but that the anarchy doesn't subside, it increases. There's twelve of us and six chairs and the pushing and shoving has kicked off big time. Lads are dragged from seats and no-hold-barred wrestling matches break-out everywhere. Finally the hierarchy is established leaving those with seats grinning and there's without dusting themselves off.

I stand back, staying well out of it, until Tina announces that as a guest I should be given a seat, and as a host, so should she.

Surprisingly, or maybe not, no one argues and Sharpie and Johnny, the two punks in the group, surrender their hard fought prizes and announce that they are leaving anyway.

I've forgotten all about my problems and worries. There's been too much music to take in: the boom-boxes at the market cycling through a mix-tape of Specials, Selector, Madness and the Bodysnatchers, a works van playing Suicide Is Painless, and, in our current location Harry's Bakery and Cafe, Radio One which has too much talking, I assume as it's Saturday, interspersed with a play-list of chart hits.

Then, as quickly as we arrive, there's an exodus.

The leaders of the boys group is Banjacks, aka Ben Jackson, and Twin-Tub, aka I don't know who. Both are big lads, but Twin-Tub is a mountain of muscle. Apparently at twelve years old he was ridiculed for being overweight and quiet, at sixteen no one is going to ridicule him ever again, with the exception of nickname.

Banjacks spots something outside and announces, "Bloody hell! There's Bloodline!"

"Where?" Twin-Tub snaps.

"There!" Banjacks points.

I look but see nothing unusual, and in seconds all the lads fly out of the cafe and sprint towards the market. I hear car horns and shoppers shouting, then nothing.

It's like they've created a vacuum and I miss them already.

"Here's Clair," Tina says.

We're sat at a table beside the front window. I'm so enthralled by the view across the precinct at the people milling around; their clothes, their mood, their body language, all fascinates me.

I follow Tina's gaze and immediately pick out Clair; she's a Rude Girl extraordinaire. She has the gorgeous good looks to match any of Charlie's Angels, with perfect use of minimal eye-liner, framed with a blonde fringe/long sides or dog-ears as they are known. She is sticking closely to the uniform specification of Fred Perry, Harrington, tight jeans and pointy flat shoes, but she stands out purely because of who she is. Everything about her expression and style says fun to me.

"She looks great," I say.

"She's a hairdresser," Tina says, "at college."

Walter is a rudeboy and the first genuine article that I've ever met in person. He's pure Afro-Caribbean with the darkest skin and a modest yet pronounced swagger to his walk. He's wearing a suit, a real suit, so authentic it looks to me like it was bought in a Trench Town tailor shop. His shirt is pure white, his tie is chequered black and white, as are the tops of his loafers and his whole look is topped off, of course, with a black trilby.

I'm in awe of them both as they join us at the table.

After we all say Hi, Tina introduces me, "This is Hannah, previously known as Laura."

Clair smiles and her eyes sparkle beneath her perfect blonde fringe, "Hi Hannah, I'm Clair, this is Walter."

"Hi Clair," I manage to blurt out, "It's great to meet you."

I realise I'm being a complete fan-girl, but I can't help it, these are the kind of people I've wanted to meet all my life. And here they are. But they are just normal people and I'm aware that if I treat them like rock-stars it's going to look a bit weird.

Walter extends his hand across the table, "Hi, everyone calls me Walter." He may look like a Jamaican gangster but his accent is pure-Coventry, there's hardly any 'T' in the pronunciation of his own name.

I shake his hand and say, "Walter, as in Jabsco?"

His eyebrows rise up and lift his smile with them. "I'm impressed, you must be a proper Specials fan."

"Isn't everyone?" I say.

"What's Jabsco?" Tina asks, looking bemused.

"The guy on The Specials logo," Walter explains, "That's based on a guy named Walter Jabsco, and some say he and I have a resemblance. Hence my nickname."

"Oh," says Tina, "So your name's not Walter?"

"No," Walter smiles, "its Jerome, which is why I prefer Walter."

The four of us laugh and I think my heart might burst.

"So where are you from?" Clair asks.

"Lowestoft," I say, pleased at my rapid response time.

"Is that by the sea?" says Clair.

I nod. "Norfolk," I say. "Near Great Yarmouth."

I've decided that the best bullshitting tactic is to offer the absolute minimum amount of actual information. It pains me but I tend to give single-word answers to questions, then go heavy on the mindless chat to balance it out. That way there is less to remember and less chance of contradicting myself.

"Oh, I've been there," Clair says.

"Lowestoft?" I ask, a trace of concern showing in my voice.

"No," she says, "Great Yarmouth. To a caravan site, a few years ago."

"Small world," Tina comments, her attention somewhere outside the window.

"It is," I say, "until you try to walk around it."

"What?" Clair says.

Walter bursts out with a boom of hysterical laughter, "Oh my God! Where did you get that?"

"You mean-"Clair's expression melts into a cringing laugh that makes her look even more stunningly beautiful. She grins at me across the table, "I like you, you're funny."

Tina is laughing too. "She is funny," she says, "do you know what she said when I said the market was opposite the HyperMarket?"

"What did she say?" Walter asks, looking totally enthralled by what is coming.

Tina explains.

The howling laughter is now the prime source of my embarrassment. People are staring at us. We must be having too much fun for people our age.

We sit there for an hour; talking, laughing, exchanging looks and smiles and scowls and someone has really bad body odour and some people talk too much and some don't talk at all and I love every minute and everyone. Even the one who smells rank.

It's a continuous blur of people coming and going, intoxicated by this comraderie to the extent that I supped coke from a can that had at least five sets of lips on it before mine, but with friends like these, who needs hygiene?

More names are given, more nicknames; Cock-Womble, Dog-Botherer, Window-Licker.

Tina explains some of the associated mythology, my personal favourite being a lad known as 'Hong Kong Fooey'. Legend has it that in a case of criminal mistaken identity the police raided his house in the early hours, dragged him out in handcuffs and he was wearing Hong Kong Fooey pyjamas. Things like that tend to stick.

One plate of chips is shared between eight people and I'm offered at least seven cigarettes, each time I decline and twice I'm asked if I'm OK.

Our table was at the centre of it all. At one time I counted twenty people, our people, in the cafe, everyone knew everyone, and I, in turn, got introduced to them. I made more friends in those few hours than I had in my whole life, literally, and wished I could sit down with each individual and talk for hours about their lives and thoughts and hopes and regrets and loves and hates, but there were just too many people and too much life.

When Banjacks and Twin-Tub return they have gained another crew of lads from somewhere. More people, more names, more talking shouting, laughing.

One of them, Steeple, spotty, skinny, and standard issue in his stai-prest and Fred Perry knock-off, is rounded on by the rest and hunted like a fox.

(When I discretely ask Tina why he's called Steeple, she makes a steeple with her fingers. I have no idea what that means and decide I don't want to know).

"How's Mandy Connor, mate?" Twin Tub asks.

Steeple answer is a little too snappy. "How should I know?"

The pack smell blood. Heads turn and elbows nudge neighbouring ribs.

Twin Tub presses on, "Don't get stroppy mate, I was only askin'."

Now a rabbit in the headlights, Steeple tries to back pedal. "I'm just sayin', I haven't seen her for yonks."

"I thought you said you was going round hers last week?"

Banjacks points at Steeple sandwich and says, "You was playing with *her* bacon batch, I heard"

"No I weren't!"

"Sorry Lawrence! Don't bite my head off!"

"I never even fancied her that much-"

"Fa-garf! You was chuffed to bits last week, happy as a dog with two dicks."

"Yeah, well-"

"I heard she gave you the arse, mate," someone says. "You must've been well-gutted."

"You went Radio Rental, Steeple! Chasin' after her, we all saw it mate!"

"It weren't like that," Steeple insists, "and anyway, I'm not bothered, honest."

"Oh no, not much, you've had a monk on ever since she blew you out."

"No way! I swear, I'm not bothered."

Banjacks strokes his chin and the whole table joins in.

"Chinny chin, do you reckon?"

"Chin-neeee."

"Jimmy Hill!"

"Chinny-chin!"

"Jiiii-mmmmy!"

"You lot can swivel."

"Your mum can swivel, mate."

"Mandy Connor can swivel; proper swivel, so I heard."

"Its no good asking, Steeple is it?"

"He wouldn't know."

"He's the only one who wouldn't know."

This goes on until the pack get tired or identify another victim.

Its vicious and fascinating and brutal.

I'm so jealous of all these people, of the lives they've shared from school days to Saturday nights. They have something that I will never have: each other, mates they have known all of their lives, since they started school or before.

As close a group as yo could possibly get.

And I was the new kid, but, although I say it myself, I was a hit!

Nobody tired of the repeated tellings of my Not-Hyper-Market and Small World quips and I also added a few more to my repertoire.

As we were leaving, a girl in a pencil skirt and leather jacket, I only know as 'Pricey', says to Tina, "There's a singles party at Boogie's tonight."

"Cool," Tina grins, "we'll be there."

"About nine," Pricey says, sliding her smooth auburn hair behind an ear.

I'm not sure about this. A singles party? At Boogies? Was this some kind of dating-thing at a nightclub?

As we left, Tina was practically buzzing with this piece of news. She yells, 'Singles party!' in my ear.

"I'm not looking for...you know," I say and shrug awkwardly.

"Looking for what?"

"You know, the whole single thing."

"What do you mean?"

"Dating, boys, nightclubs," I say, "all that stuff is not me right now-"

"You've lost me," Tina says.

"Well, I don't really want to go to a singles night," I tell her, hoping I hadn't somehow insulted or disrespected her.

"I don't know why you'd think that," she smiles. "It's a singles party, singles as in records, everyone brings records, it's a dance party."

"Oh," is all I can say. This singles party does sound very much like my kind of thing.

"And," Tina adds, then bursts into laughter yet again, "Boogie is a mate, not a night club owner."

"No?"

"No," she smiles, "Although, he'll love that when I tell him."

Embarrassed, I offer a smile.

Tina hooks her arm under mine as she does and explains, "Boogie is a friend who has parties at his house."

"OK," I say and repeat, "Singles party at Boogies. I'm down for that."

CHAPTER 16

"Who's your favourite band?" Tina asks.

I love this question, but I need to tread carefully with my chronology. Where I am now, just ten years ago, The Beatles were still together. Back home, twenty years ago (before I was born), Eminem was asking for the real Slim Shady to please stand up. I have sixty years of music history in my memory banks, but I can only reference the first third of it. I need to draw a line in mid-1980 and pretend nothing after that has happened. Because it hasn't.

We're walking home after a visit to Taylor's Record Shop which is brilliant. And it's a good job I didn't know of its existence before as the temptation to leave Stubbs may have proven too difficult to ignore.

It has literally every album from the punk and post-punk era, all brand spanking new. It also has every single in the Top 40, plus many beyond that, and a bargain of reduced singles that are now "old hat", but will, in time, become absolute classic songs that defined major turning points in musical history, and, naturally, collector's items worth a fortune in mint condition. All for twenty-pence each.

When I get home next week I will investigate how much profit there is to make in the vinyl market. I suspect that it is considerable and I already have the pre-requisite knowledge to take full advantage.

I've bought 'Messages' by OMD, 'We Are Glass' by Gary Numan and 'Police and Thieves' by Junior Murvin, all of which are in the charts this week.

Pondering Tina's question is troublesome, not in defining my musical taste, just in getting the answer to precisely fit the era.

I give the measured answer of, "I like all the Two-tone stuff."

Tina nods approval and says, "The Specials."

I want to add that the Two-tone label also included The Bodysnatchers and The Selector, but of course, I hold back. No one likes a smart-arse, especially those with an unfair advantage.

"Madness," I add, exposing my t-shirt for comic effect and staying on safe ground, but disappointing myself that my music taste is so boring and predictable. I get very, very close to citing one of my top ten LPs of all time: Nah Poo: The Art of Bluff by Wah. I found this album in my mother's collection, but she insisted she didn't know where it came from, who they were and can't remember any of the tracks.

It was the album cover that reached out to me. Its white and green text on the black background is simple but outstanding in its brilliance. Inside was a picture of the band, just two guys, Pete Wylie in a face mask and Carl Washington, and a 'call to arms' diatribe extolling the beauty and power of Wah, no doubt written by Wylie in a poetic mood. The band later shot to fame with The Story of the Blues. Then, just as quickly, they shot from fame to cult status before breaking-up. But that strangely titled first album was, in my humble opinion, the best debut album of the entire 1980s.

But I'm sure it was released in 1981. Therefore it's barred.

To fill in a gap before my silence becomes conspicuous, I say, "I kinda like old stuff too, like Bowie and Iggy Pop."

Tina continues to nod her approval but I need to buy time to think, so I say, "And you?"

"Well," she says, "my idol is Siouxsie Sioux, obviously, but I'm into The Pretenders, Blondie, stuff like that. Music means everything to me. I want to go to more gigs and see more bands. I saw Siouxsie and the Banshees at Birmingham Odeon and they were supported by this band called The Cure. Have you heard of them?"

"Yes, I've heard of them," I say. I love The Cure, but I'm not entirely certain where we are on their timeline: their second album Seventeen Seconds came out in 1980, but I don't know if it's out yet. This is frustrating.

"The lead singer is like a male Siouxsie Sioux," Tina says.

"Robert Smith," I smile.

"Is that his name?" she asks.

I nod, and add, "I think so."

Back in the box-room at the flat, me and Tina sit on the bed and I pop open my mum's singles box which is battered from years of use and is literally falling apart. It had once been a blue vinyl-covered cube with a lid a handle and a latch. Each of the six sides has since aged indelibly. Its once supple vinyl skin now brittle and cracked. The hardboard beneath was battered and bloated from water damage. The only part that looked likely to survive much longer was the handle, which the lid clung to with a loosening grip.

A loyal servant, I thought to myself, It had safely protected its valuable cargo.

As a kid I had often thumbed through the thirty or so 7" records, loving the artwork of the cover and label, but unable to marry the object itself with the sounds contained with the vinyl's groove as we didn't have a record player.

Instead, I would search for and play the songs on-line. Within a short time, I knew each of them off-by-heart, including the B-sides. From there I spread out to other songs by my treasured artists, their peers, and eventually their albums.

From the age of twelve to fourteen, I fell totally and utterly in love with the music of the early-80s and pestered my mother to buy me a second-hand record player (specifically not one that had been manufactured in that current millennium).

Why do I love the era so much? If you have to ask, you'll probably never know.

For some reason there are three cassettes in the box too, taking up valuable space for singles in my opinion.

There were two pre-recorded tapes in their original boxes, 'I Just Can't Stop It' by The Beat and 'Regatta de Blanc' by The Police, and there was a Memorex C90 with just a date written on it - 10/10/78.

"Which ones should I take to the party?" I ask.

Tina uses her forefinger to flick through the records without taking them from the box and gives an approving "Yep" to the vast majority and the occasional "Wow!" to some.

There's:

'Dreaming'

'Can't Stand Losing You' (with the banned suicide sleeve)

'It's Different For Girls'

'Three Minute Hero'

'Nice n Sleazy'

'David Watts'

'Teenage Kicks'

'Brass In Pocket'

Even 'Hersham Boys' has a time and a place, right?

At the end of the run-through, Tina sits back, smiles and says, "Take the whole box."

I'm pleased with this seal of approval.

Tina jumps to her feet and disappears for a second, then returns with a thick black marker pen.

She pulls the top of the nib, holds it to her nose and breaths in sharply.

"Love that smell," she smiles. "You can get high if inhale enough."

"I'll take your word for it," I say.

She hands me the marker. "Write your name or initials on your records," she says, "so you can get them back."

I nod. It makes sense, there'll be a lot of people bringing their records too, but there's something about defiling the sleeves that goes against principles.

To hell with principles, I tell me myself, and get to work writing HO on the back of each single.

"Didn't you bring any LPs?" Tina asks.

"No," I say. "I've got loads, I just didn't bring them."

"So," she looks away as she asks the questions, "are you going back to get them?"

The question is a bit of a left turn from our discussion on our musical taste. Intentionally or not, she's put me on the spot.

"No, I'm not going back, they're just records," I say.

"I don't mean to stick my nose in," Tina says, still watching the TV, "but you didn't bring much stuff and I wondered if you were planning to stay or going back."

I don't answer. I don't know what to say.

When Tina looks back at me, I think there might be a tear forming in her eye.

She says, "We have a good laugh don't we? I just want you to stay."

I smile and I feel myself blush, and gush out the words, "Thank you."

We do have a good laugh, the time of my life in fact, but for the first time I'm seeing a deeper sadness to Tina and it breaks my heart that I might add to that when I, inevitably, leave.

As if reading my mind, Tina asks me, "So, all I'm saying is, you can stay as long as you like. Me and mum both like having you here."

I can't stay though, much as I want to, and the right thing to do id to get Tina used to the idea. "Thank you so much," I say to her. "That means the world to me. I don't want to be a burden on you. I want to get my own place-"

Tina laughed. "Get you're own place? Maybe in nine months if you get to play Naked Twister soon enough."

"No, I mean-"

"It's OK, I know what you mean," Tina says, "but nobody gets their own place round here unless they have a kid. Loads of my mates had a kid just to get a house."

"There's a first time for everything, though, right?"

"I admire your optimism," Tina smiled.

"All I'm saying is if we put our minds to it and work hard, we could make some money-"

"I don't wanna get involved in anything ropey," Tina sighs.

"I'm talking about doing something legit," I say.

"Legit?" Tina frowns. "You've been watching too much Sweeney."

"Why can't we?" I say.

Tina shakes her head, "Forget it, whatever it was like where you're from, it ain't like that here."

"Just bear with me," I tell her. "There's always a way."

"Like what?"

"Didn't you say your mum used to run a market stall?"

She frowns. "She did. Well she still does, technically, but there's problems."

"Yeah, but," I say, rolling an arm forward for Tina to fill in the blanks. "Things don't always have to end badly. Right?"

Tina goes quiet and I know instantly I've overstepped a line when I didn't know it existed. Or maybe I should've but I missed it. Something about her mother, but I don't know what.

When she looked up, she was smiling like someone resigned to fate. "Technically, she still owns it, but then she got ill."

For the first time, I could sense the deep sadness that Tina was dealing with beneath her scary-hair and feline black eye-shadow. I didn't want to dwell on her mother's illness, whatever it is, but to me, the biggest tragedy was her acceptance that she had no future and that everything was going to turn out badly.

All I can think to say is, "Things don't always have to end that way."

She smiles, then smirks and says, "We'll see."

Tina is without a doubt an amazing person. She's such a free spirit, but a fighter, too. She lacks the underlying optimism that future generations have been blessed with, even in the toughest times, but I can't blame her for being protectively pessimistic about the future. Millions of people are unemployed, many with jobs are not many rungs above those of modern slavery and there's nothing on the horizon that suggests the next few years will be any different.

And I could tell her exactly what those years will be like and exactly what to do to come out of them on top. I just know I could help her a lot if she'd believe me.

But can I?

The truth is, I can't. At least, I shouldn't.

And it tears me up inside that I won't help someone who's helping me massively.

All I can do is help her in every other way I can.

That I promise to do.

I finish initialling the records then gather them up and drop them into the box. I drop the lid, slide in the worn chrome clasp, and it's good to go. I just hope it survives the journey.

CHAPTER 17

As we get ready for the party, I'm in a heightened sense of anxiety/excitement. I've never done dress-up with the girls before, never done sleep-overs, never done (much) make-up, yet here I am with Tina, Clair and Sarita doing exactly that and loving it.

In 2020, after much social analysis and deep thought, mostly by marketing people, they came up with the word 'Tribes'.

In 1980 there actually were very clear 'Tribes' in a social sense.

I am a punk.

I am a rude boy.

I am a soul girl.

It's an identity, it's one of the few expressions of individualism that young people have got left.

Nobody here is identifying themselves as a postman, a bricklayer, a labourer: those are unobtainable aspirations.

I am yet to meet anyone who has a job,

I have a newfound respect for these kids who are facing this adversity every day.

To them, 'No future' isn't a chorus in a song, it's a fact of life.

And I am overwhelmed with a burning desire to show solidarity, even if I can't show full commitment.

And that is why I'm in Tina's bedroom, sitting in a chair with a towel around my shoulders and the top scalp of my hair separated from the sides by hairpins. Clair is at my side with an electric shaver in her raised hand.

"Are we doing this?" Clair asks.

Tina and Sarita are watching and no one is saying a word.

I look at them both and grin.

Tina is resplendent with hair not only spiked to a towering extent but crimped for good measure. She is the archetypal Banshee and will rightfully become Bedworth's God-mother of Goth. A grey, once black, Joy Division t-shirt nearly covers her leather mini-skirt which in turn is matched with holey fishnets.

Sarita is our rude-girl butterfly who arrived in her college clothes and is now a two-tone Cinderella with her sky blue Harrington, Specials t-shirt, black pencil skirt and black and white check leggings. Tina has teased her hair into a loose but sturdy bee-hive and she is hot to trot.

Clair is wearing her best Fred Perry (her words), spray-on white Stai-Prest and spotless Lonsdale boxing shoes just like Paul Weller's. 'Nice trainers!' I told her, hoping for a back-story of how and where she got them, 'Thanks!' she smile, and says 'Joe Davis', which I now know is a sports shop opposite Harry's Cafe.

(I make a mental note to check in there if I get time.)

Tina looks worried, "Hannah, you don't have to do this if you don't want-"

"I want to!" I announce. "Let's do it."

I want a Mohican like Joe Strummer when he came back from Paris, Annabella Lwin (soon to be) of Bow Wow Wow, and Pete Burns, wherever he may be, but of course, I can't say that. Hopefully, I have described it sufficiently in words.

"Are you sure about this?" Clair asks, way more nervous than me.

"Deffo," I say, then clarify with, "I'm sure."

"OK, it's your funeral," Clair smiles.

I smile to reassure the and she fires the razor into life. I feel the blades slashing through the roots of my hair at the side of my head.

Sarita says, " Oh my God!"

I smile.

No going back now.

Mother told me to keep my head down, but she didn't say don't shave the sides.

I close my eyes and tell myself it'll look great.

Then I wait.

It takes about three minutes.

"Finished," Clair announces.

There is absolute silence from everyone in the room.

I go to the mirror and stare.

Then, for the first time in my life, I squeal in delight at my own reflection.

I am pleased to say, and to hell with false modesty, I look ace.

Once my friends are certain my screams are not ones of anguish, they join me in celebration.

Clair finishes my look by piling up my remaining scalp of hair into a spiky high top and I'm done.

Again, I look in the mirror and admire what I see.

Tina throws her leather motorcycle jacket on the back of the chair and my head churns like heavy machinery mangling and literally tearing itself apart. I recognise the garment instantly as the one that Tina is wearing in the photograph my mother showed me.

But my brain is not believing what my eyes are seeing.

Which is: JJ Brunel, bass player of The Stranglers, in full flow, knee raised shoulder high in preparation for a karate kick, bass in hand, all captured in a perfect black-and-white image.

But it's not a photo. It's better. This is a painting. It's more detailed and is beyond real. It's a piece of art.

A *beautiful* piece of art.

I'm drawn to it, moth/candle-like, and I swear I can hear JJ singing to me. He's smiling, and I'm not sure if he's going to kiss me or stomp on my head with the sole of a Doc Martin.

"Do you like it?" Clair says.

Even though I know she's stating the obvious, I respond anyway. "It's incredible."

Clair laughs at my display of joy.

"Tina did it," she says.

I don't quite comprehend this, and I stare at JJ for an interpretation of the words 'Tina did it' and he says 'Yes, she painted me on the jacket'.

The only word I can form with my mouth and my brain is, "No."

"Yes," Clair says.

"Do you want to wear it?"

Do I *want* to wear it?

Do *I* want to *wear* it?

What kind of question is that?

"Can I?" I ask. Am I actually within a realm of reality where that is possible?

I equate slipping my arms into the sleeves and dropping that jacket onto my shoulders with some form of coronation: it doesn't seem at all plausible.

And yet...

...Tina, with mock impatience, has the jacket in her hands and is guiding my left arm then my right arm into it. The jacket hugs me, weighing on my shoulders like the World Heavyweight Boxing Championship Belt.

I am the Champion of the World.

My body exalts at my very being.

I spread my arms in a crucifix and throw my head back.

With this jacket, I am the resurrection of rock n roll.

Except it's only seven o'clock, so we have decamped outside to the balcony. The night belongs to us as we survey the scene of Bedworth town on a hot summer night.

Park Road has been buzzing with people milling everywhere, but now that the pubs are open they are doing so with more purpose and direction.

Clair announces that she is going to 'dance myself dizzy' tonight and does so in silence, seemingly to the music in her head. She is a natural, her moves are the smoothest a human is capable of and she never repeats the same one twice. She's a constant flow of innovation, twirling and swooning and always smiling.

I imagine I can hear her music, put my record box on the floor and start to shuffle on the spot, trying to appear like it's an unconscious act, but every ounce of concentration I have is being poured into my performance.

To my delight Clair joins me, our moves locking together until, like two ballooning bubbles, we burst into a fit of laughter.

A voice behind me says, "Someone's having fun."

I spin around to see Barbara standing in the doorway. She's in jeans and a t-shirt, smiling and smoking.

"Good evening, Mrs Evans," Sarita sings in her politer-than-normal voice.

"Evening Sarita," Barbara replies. "Does your mum know you're out?"

Sarita smirks and pokes her tongue out.

"Don't worry, your secrets safe with me," Barbara smiles, "and call me Barbara. Mrs Evans makes me sound old."

"You are old," Tina says without turning from the balcony.

I'm smiling at Barbara, but for some reason, she hasn't acknowledged me. Do I look that different in my party clothes and make-up? Or, more likely, my new hair-do has transformed my appearance?

"Hi, Barbara," I say, as respectfully as I can with such an informal greeting.

"You must be Laura," she says to me, ignoring her daughter.

"I am," I say, but I'm confused it seems that she doesn't know me. I should cross the balcony and shake her hand, like we've never met, but instead, I offer what I hope is a warm smile.

"I thought your name was Hannah," Clair says.

"It is," I say, "Long story."

Clair seems to realise something, nods her understanding and looks down at the floor.

"Did you have an accident?" Barbara asks me.

"Sorry?" I say.

She gestures with her hands to the sides of her head.

"Oh, this?" I say doing the same. "Do you like it?"

"No," she says.

I wait to see if there's a punchline, but there isn't.

"Enjoy the party," Barbara smiles and lifts her hand to wave us goodbye. Her cigarette is thrown onto the balcony and the door shuts behind her.

None of the girls say anything. Tina looks out at the skyline and for the first time since we met she's quiet.

CHAPTER 18

Boogie is what might be called a congenial host; generous, well-liked, and respected. An equally accurate description would be an eccentric hedonist, or, colloquially, as mad as a box of frogs. However, all of these descriptions, although accurate, are inadequate.

He describes himself as a 'roadie by trade, DJ by necessity', but I suspect that he may be missing the word 'ex' and DJ is applied in the olde-worldy sense (I was once told that, in the 80s, a DJ is defined as having a large record collection and a microphone). He does appear to own a large amount of musical equipment; every room of his house is stuffed with amps, speakers, cables, mike stands and lighting rig frames. There's quantity, not so much quality.

He is wearing something that I've not seen before, which I later find out to be a British Army Parachute suit, a huge baggy white canvas 'onesy' with elastic cuffs, Paratroop Regiment badges and padded elbows and knees. On the back is some two-tone artwork and across the shoulders is written, 'My neighbours listen to Ska Music all night' and at the bottom, 'whether they want to or not'. He tops this off with a pair of goggles which stay on the top of this forehead for most the evening. Apparently this attire is not unusual for Boogie and is not restricted to indoor usage alone. My guess is that he is in his mid-twenties, much older than the rest of us. He has a lean and mean build, no doubt from lugging those amps from vans to stages and back for years. I'm dying to ask him divulge his 'Confessions of a New Wave Roadie', first-hand accounts from behind the scenes of the most innovative musical and cultural moments in time ever. But I can't pin him down, he's constantly on the move and doesn't seem to notice me.

He is cute, in a gnarly way, but he's out of my league, or maybe I'm playing a different game. Not that I want to hook up with anyone, it's just that there are people I'd really like to get to know.

He does, of course, have a record player and that record player does have the single greatest audio invention of the 20th Century, (which sadly became obsolete before the 21st century): the extended spindle. This enables as many as six singles to be stacked onto the spindle, which then plays each one in turn. It's a 1980s version of a Spotify Play List, only better.

I manage to remember a few names of the people I met earlier and everyone says 'Hello' and asks how I am.

And everyone is bringing records. They are piling up on Boogies side table with some spilling over the sound system cabinets which look like they house some more than adequate 12" speakers.

Half an hour after we arrive, having stood chatting to people I recognise from earlier, Boogie finally talks to me.

"Records?" he says and points at my belly.

I'm thrown for a second and look down, and then realise I've been carrying my singles box around with me for so long I've forgotten about it.

"Yes!" I say.

Boogie puts his hand out like he's inviting me to dance.

But he wants the record box.

I hand it to him and he smiles as he flips open the lid and flicks through my 45s.

He nods an approval at each successive disc and then breaks into a beaming smile. "I'm impressed," he says, "you know your music."

"Thank you," I gush.

"We," he says, his eyes full of excitement, "are going to be great friends."

Then he was gone.

With my records.

I have always believed in the power of music and its connection to our soul. It does something to me, it creates reactions; emotional and physical. It enables deep and meaningful thought, and it enables my body to communicate in ways otherwise impossible.

I have never tired of music and I cannot ignore it, the good and the bad.

And yet, for me, enjoying music has rarely been a shared experience. It's easy to blame social, or tribal, norms in my case, me being born out of time and everything. People my age back home are happy to dance at an 80s night, laugh at viral Rick Astley memes or watch Boy George do reality TV, but it's all tinged with Irony and it evaporates when the discussion turns to the merits of The Jam's 'Setting Sons' LP or Dexy's Midnight Runners 'Searching for the young soul rebels'.

What I'm trying to say is, back 'home' I dance alone, in my converted garage, to my personal play-lists, but never in public.

And now. Here. Amongst these people I have known for two days, I feel different.

Everything feels different.

As we chat and laugh and nod to each other and communicate without speaking, we are somehow connected, and I become aware that we are about to engage in a shared-experience.

And when the music starts, it happens.

We hear the heavily muted melody of an electric guitar:

Dum-de-dum dum dee-da da-da.

It's a countdown.

It repeats.

Everybody in the room stops what they're saying, drops what they're doing and turns to face the speakers.

Boogie, the widest smile slicing his face in two, is already dancing.

The riff repeats twice more and by that time we have flooded the 'dance floor' and already skanking as The

Wailers kick-in and Bob Marley asks 'Could you be loooooooooved'.

It happened in an instant, but the entire house is bouncing on the offbeat, swaying to the rhythm and singing back to Bob, 'Oh ohhh yeah!'

Every line of the song is a 'call and response', and some sing with Bob, the rest sing the refrains. In music, as in life, sometimes you're Bob Marley and sometimes you're a Wailer, either way, you're beautiful.

In this world, I have no inhibitions, no self-consciousness, we have a group conscience. We love and laugh together, we dance and sing as one.

The reggae begins to fade and we beg it not to, but end it does. There's a buzz on the dance floor as the record ends and the next one drops.

A crackling hiss of the needle meeting the vinyl breaks the silence, and there's an agonising two seconds as the weight of anticipation threatens to crush us, but then two hits of a snare drum save us and there's a deluge of power chords that fall from heaven.

Teenage Kicks.

We wanna hold her, wanna hold her tight, but we also wanna pogo to the thumping bass and those slabs of sonic concrete that the guitar drops on us. Its sheer hysteria, a leaping, screaming monster of a dance floor goes berserk.

And, as the next record drops, I have a premonition. I just know that the next record is 'Three Minute Hero', everyone's favourite track by The Selecter.

Somehow, it is, and we are off to the races again. The jittery-drums intro is joined by the punchy bass line and stabbing guitar chords. The tempo has gone up a notch and so has the atmosphere. Some dance to the beat, some double-time it, shadow-boxing on the balls of their feet. There's a lot of sweat forming, and every inch of the floor being utilised. Tina and Sarita are winning all the accolades for this one. Their moves are ultra-relaxed and carefree, but dripping in elegance and grace.

'Going Underground', The Jam with a teenage Paul Weller, is a call to arms from the opening riff to the key change at the outro. It's a solid gold classic and is treated as such, although it topped the charts only two months ago.

Twin-Tub is centre-stage for the sixth and final song of this batch of these 45s and he's mobbed as the jangling guitar riff of 'Lip Up Fatty' fills the room. Much insanity ensues. There's a mass of limbs and some rough and tumble, but it's so high spirited that when I get bumped I feel no pain.

People are flagging, but no one is sitting down. Not yet. During the brief breakdown of the song, a few dancers stop for a breather, but it's a brief respite. We resume with double the energy for the last verses of the song and wring out every last ounce of fun to be had.

The breaks between the records are spent grabbing a drink or finding your friends or making new ones, but the excitement never lets up. Boogie, as the Master of Ceremonies, does an amazing job sequencing the songs, varying things enough for maximum anticipation, but delivering what we want, almost always when we want it.

We chant to 'Geno' and 'Eton Rifles', jitterbug like Debbie Harry to 'Hanging on the Telephone', and sing every word to 'Too Much Too Young' and 'My Girl'.

The girls had the floor for 'Christine' and this was maintained by 'Hong Kong Garden' and 'Brass in Pocket'.

The boys turn was heralded by 'Hersham Boys' and 'Kids are United', (what else), then 'Staring at the Rude Boys', "David Watts', 'Rude Boys Outta Jail' and 'London Calling'. it was pretty frenetic for the first few numbers, but I joined them for the last two and enjoyed bouncing around with the lads.

For variety we had 'Funky Town', 'Le Freak' and something by the Nolans, amongst a few others, all of which were met with a chorus of 'Who bought this!', sometimes the culprit was unveiled by Boogie and some times not.

The highlight for me was the mammoth marathon of six copies of 'One Step Beyond' stacked in one go and, I swear, the volume cranked up to eleven. Six times we shouted the intro and six times we launched everything we had to the landslide of joy that is the saxophone and guitar led instrumental of pure Madness, Limbs and bodies were flying across the room and more than 'bummer-train' was formed, circled the room and inevitably crashed and burned. Two minutes and eighteen seconds of ecstatic rhythm, multiplied by six.

CHAPTER 19

Tina grabs my arm and, the two of us are in hysterics, and she more or less drags me to the kitchen.

"Oh my God," she gasps. "I've never danced so much in my life."

"That was kinda fun!" I say, my whole body still giggling with excitement.

Tina finds a solitary glass in the cupboard and fills it with tap water.

"I'm spitting feathers!" She drinks half the glass then hands the rest to me.

I'm well thirsty and in way too deep to insist on a clean glass, if there is such a thing in Boogie's house, so I take the glass and drink the water.

"You're not really going to leave, are you?" she asks. "I haven't had this much fun in ages."

I laugh, "I've only been here for one day."

"I know, but we did know each other before, didn't we?"

"Did we?" I say, with a comical frown. I regret my choice of words immediately and gloss it over with a smile. I'm still holding the glass. Tina takes it from my hand and places it on the side. She doesn't seem to have noticed by faux pa.

She takes my hand and we go outside. Boogie has a back garden, but doesn't do much gardening. Some of the weeds are nearly a tall as me.

He also has open views of the park, although there's nothing to see at night time, just deep darkness beyond an iron fence.

As the back door closes the music almost disappears. It's peaceful. I can feel myself recharge.

"It would be great if you stay," Tina says, "we could knock around together, you know, you can stay in the flat for as long as you like."

"It would be *so* great," I say. And it would. There's no doubt about that, but it's not that simple. In so many ways!

"I need you," Tina says and the words hang in the air.

I try to make out her expression but beneath her huge plume of hair, all that's visible in the twilight are the wings of her black eye-shadow.

"I need you too," I say, not sure what she meant, but knowing what I mean. I've never felt a friendship like this one, nothing even close.

Tina doesn't answer, but I'm fairly sure she's looking at me.

"I can't make any promises," I say. "But I'll try to work it so I can stay. I've just got some stuff to sort out."

"OK, thanks."

"But if I have to go," I say, and I know I shouldn't say this, I know that this is wrong and will probably cause God knows what to happen in the future, literally, but I say it anyway because I mean it, "I'll come back. I'll come back very soon. I promise."

"Really?" she says, "You'll come back? And stay?"

And I can't answer, not in words, but I do nod my head. And I smile.

And I mean it.

CHAPTER 20

As life is a roller-coaster of highs and lows, the close moment between Tina and me had to be interrupted by the worst possible person: Terry.

Coincidentally, as if we're in a movie, the music has stopped.

"Charlie wants to see you," he says as he steps through the door. He nods his head backwards, a command for Tina to follow him.

He never looks my way. It's as if I'm not there, which is fine. It's not that he's done anything but I still can't warm to him and it seems the feeling is mutual.

"He wants to see me?" Tina says.

"Yeah."

"What about?" Tina sounds scared.

"Ask him," Terry says and does the nod of the head thing again.

"He's here?" Tina says. She seems genuinely scared by the prospect.

"Who is this guy?" I ask.

But once Terry had nodded that 'yes, he is here in this very house', Tina was already on her way back inside.

I follow the two of them and Terry tries to shut the door on me but I see it coming, block it and push it back open.

He scowls.

I smile.

I don't like this set up and whoever this Charlie is, I don't like how he can make Tina jump out of her skin at the mention of his name.

From the hallway, I hear the music come back on and a booming voice commanding, "I said turn it off!"

The music stops instantly.

"Boogie, I don't want to fall out with you again," the voice says, "but I have to then I will!"

Everyone in the living room has formed a circle, each one trying to get as close to one of the four walls as possible, but no one is actually brave enough to leave.

I walk in behind Tina. Boogie is at the controls of his hifi looking furious and petrified. Tina stops when she sees a tall man at the centre of this circle. He's heavyset, stocky yet tall, well over six foot four, in his fifties at a guess but that's hard to call. His face is both expressionless and sinister. He has short brown hair, sharp grey eyes and a jaw-line square enough to impress, but not enough to detract from the mercenary menace that he exudes.

"Tina Evans," he says and raises his chin. "May I have a word?"

Tina nods, she doesn't seem capable of speech. To be honest, she looks like she might wet herself.

"I've been thinking," he says, "maybe you're ready for a second chance."

Tina nods again, and almost smiles but then realises this might be a cruel trick and holds her expression rock solid.

"So if you feel that you have learnt your lesson," the man goes on, "you can come back to work."

"Thank you," Tina says and allows that smile to surface, albeit forced through the fear.

"Do you think you've learnt your lesson?" he asks.

Tina nods. "Yes," she says, "what happened... won't happen again."

Charlie nods back at Tina, his eyes burning into hers. "Let's hope not," he says, "because I have a new role for you, actually. Are you free to discuss it tomorrow morning?"

"Yes," she says.

"Shall we say eleven o'clock at the Pin?"

She nods.

"Oh," he says as an afterthought he nods at me, "Bring your friend."

He turns away from her and addresses the group as a whole, "Apologies for the interruption, please continue with your debauchery."

With that, there is a parting of the Red Sea and he leaves with Terry in tow.

Tina does a little 360-shuffle-dance ending with punching the air above her head.

"You seem happy," I say, unable to hide the fact that I am not.

"I got my job back," she says, "at The Corner Pin."

I don't feel much like dancing so I duck back into the kitchen.

Clair follows me.

"Hey," I say.

"Hey," she smiles.

She looks nervous, like something's on her mind.

"That was weird," I say. "Who was that guy?"

"Charlie?" Clair says, "Yeah, it's weird that he's giving Tina her job back after all he's done."

"Why? What's he done?"

"He sacked her for no reason and then he blacklisted Barbara's market stall."

"I don't understand," I say, "What do you mean, 'blacklisted'?"

Clair comes closer so she can talk quieter. "He told everyone they can't buy stuff from Barbara's stall. He even had one of his goons standing there making sure no one even spoke to her."

"Can he do that?" I ask. I'm stunned to hear that people would accept this kind of intimidation.

Clair shrugs. " He did it. Barbara didn't know what to do, after a few days, she just walked off and left the stall unattended. All the stuff got nicked and Tina still has to pay for it somehow."

"All because one man said people shouldn't buy anything her stall?" I ask, not sure I've understood this or maybe it's some kind of urban myth.

Clair nods. "Its best not to get on the wrong side of Charlie."

"What was his problem with Boogie?"

Clair nods but purses her lips together. "Charlie was there when his brother died. He was his manager."

"What?"

Clair looks up. "Steve Callaghan," she says. "The boxer."

I know the name from the local forums and Facebook groups. He was Bedworth's favourite son, a rising boxing star with a big heart. He was unbeaten and fought for the National Title but suffered fatal blows in the ring and died.

"That was Boogie's brother?" I whisper.

Clair nods again. "Boogie was there, that night, too."

"Oh my God! That's awful."

"He was only about fifteen at the time," she tells me, "they say he was never the same after that. And-" Clair paused and double-checked nobody was in ear-shot, before continuing, "-Boogie blamed Charlie for his brothers dying."

CHAPTER 21

Charlie has gone, but the party is over.

Boogie has a face like a slapped arse and no one is giving him eye-contact as he prowls the living room like a wounded lion.

The first bad sign is when he threatens Walter for some perceived diss about the condition of the premises, although Boogie is calling it 'taking the piss', which is a wide umbrella term for a range of issues, depending on context.

Walter denies the charge and stands his ground.

Boogie, stockier but shorter than Walter, makes a determined advance across the room but stops short of any physical conflict. He also stops short of passing a racist comment, but only just, with the question, "Who do you lot think you are?"

"Who's 'you lot'?" Walter asks back.

Boogie looks at the assembled faces staring at him and reads the room. "All of you," he says. "You come here, enjoy the party, then start saying what a shit-hole my house is."

"Nobody would do that Boog," someone says. It's Tina. She steps forward from the group. "We love it here," she says, "and we love you mate. Anyone that don't wouldn't be invited."

Boogie's eyes never leave Walter. If Tina's declaration has moved him at all, then he is yet to show it.

After a tense moment, he turns to Tina, nods, and then retreats to the kitchen saying, "Party's over."

I want to reach out to Boogie, he's hurting, but I can't find the courage and something tells me it would be the wrong thing to do.

I also get the sense that this turn of events is not uncommon as, without saying a word, everyone collects their coats and we file outside.

There are about twelve of us and I'm getting to know most people by name and getting an idea of what they are like.

Clair and Walter are the coolest couple on the planet and have never given any indication of being anything else. And yet they have no ego or make any demands, they don't dominate conversations and they dance with the same degree of lunacy as everyone else (albeit Walter does take care not to 'harm his threads' as he put it on more than one occasion).

Sharpy and Johnny have what I would call a 'punk aesthetic', but not to their faces as they'd assume it's an insult. They are the wild boys who will do literally anything if the shock value was deemed high enough. I've heard the stories of daring stunts on motorcycles and railway lines I hoped weren't true, but having spent some time with them I'm pretty sure that they are. They're dynamic, violent, loud, aggressive and at the forefront of everything.

Sarita is never far from her bestie Lisa and the two of them never stop smiling. They just seem pleased to be there and count everything else as a bonus. They cleaned up the beer cans and emptied the ashtrays although no one asked or thanked them for it, and they either sat out the boisterous bouncy pogo-ing songs or retired to the kitchen. They wore matching fish-tail Parkers with the fur-lined hood up and walked with their arms folded beneath their boobs. They looked like twin two-tone angels.

Another would-be suedehead type, Mark or Martin, I'm not exactly sure what his name is, seems nice enough although I didn't talk to him directly. I did hear him say that he works delivering coal, a task performed by lugging huge sacks on your back from a lorry down the side of a house to the coal shed in the back, which explains his muscley physique. I would say he is more ripped than most gym-monkeys I know and has never seen a bench press in his life.

Mark/Martin has latched onto Pricey, who seems fine with it but is keeping her options open. She is thin, wiry even, has long brown hair and is the one of us who wouldn't look out of place back home in 2020, where all girls have long hair without exception.

There's a shy geeky guy, with glasses naturally (Proclaimers-style), who might be Alex, but I know he's sometimes referred to as Brains. I can only assume this is both a Thunderbirds and an intelligence reference. He intrigues me, and he's not unattractive once he's engaged with you, but he's cripplingly short of self-confidence. When we spoke at the party he asked me two questions: did I like Syd Barrett and did I like magic mushrooms? I think he likes both, but I answered honestly and said, No, as I hadn't tried either.

He laughed and looked handsome doing so.

The other person in our group is a boy who is mostly unidentifiable, wearing jeans and a plain t-shirt and I swear he hasn't danced or spoken a single word all night. And nobody has spoken to him either, but then nobody seems to mind.

Maybe he's a ghost and only I can see him.

We gather on the pavement outside Boogie's house and head towards town. The Working Men's Club is dark, its patrons having either left or are drinking behind closed curtains with the lights down. I'm guessing it's just gone midnight.

We're in high spirits, and yes we are noisy. We recreate the Madness bummer-walk and der-der-derrrr the song in unison. And yes there are houses where no doubt we are preventing someone from sleeping.

The upshot is by the time that we have crossed the Rye Piece Ringway and reached the top end of the Civic Hall car park, a car swings around the corner and we're hit by the full beams of two headlights.

Someone shouts, "Jesus Christ mate!"

Someone else shouts, "Hey!"

Then someone shouts, "Pigs!" and then everyone runs.

Except me. I stand there shielding my eyes from the glare so I can see who gets out of the car.

The car doors open and I'm grabbed by the arm.

"C'mon run!" the person who's grabbed my arm says.

I run, but not because I want to, I have no choice as I'm being frog-marched. I find my stride and break into a sprint, wrestling my arms free from them. Now they're running beside me I can see it's Clair and Alex.

The police are shouting for us to stand still.

Alex tells me to run faster.

I see Tina up ahead, at the mouth of the alley between the Civic Hall and the library, another rat run that most of us have instinctively darted for.

Tina is imploring me to keep running and that, combined with the voice of a policeman some way behind me saying, "You little bleeders! Wait til we catch up with ya!"

I go up a gear and sprint away from Banjacks who has steps aside to let me through. Tina grabs my arms as I pass her and we run together through the alley, all the time she's saying, "Follow us, don't lose us!"

And I start laughing.

This is fun.

Although I also realise I don't really know what the consequences will be, and they might not be fun. What if I got arrested? Who would I say I was? How long could they keep me?

Don't get caught, was the best advice I could give myself.

At the end of the alley we dash across the road, veering to the left and I see Clair, Walter and Brains (sorry I know that's not your name) all crawling under the road-barrier to the graveyard. Everyone around me is heading in that direction too, the girls are being helped under the gate, the slow runners and being shepherded along, looked after.

Then, what I assume to be the same police car, appears again, this time with its blue lights flooding the street and high beams dazzling us. Tina and me are the last ones to the gate and we both get under in no time at all.

I see Sharpie break away from the group.

Walter, Mark/Martin and Twin Tub are there to help us to our feet and I look back in time to see the police car screeching to a halt. Sharpie appears in the glow of the headlights, raises his hand and theatrically drags it across the door skin. We can hear the screech of a metal on metal as he keys it from one end to the other.

In disbelief, I watch Twin Tub get under the barrier and then we're running again. The graveyard is pitch black. There are no lights, not even moonlight. All I can see is what remains of the glare of the headlights I stared into, but I know which way the path runs, and I follow my friend's footsteps and it's only when we slow down to a jog I bump into two people, both of which are suppressing laughter into sniggers.

I look around to get my bearings. I can make out the silhouettes of trees and houses. We are at the bottom end of the graveyard, there are no exits down here, just fences to the back gardens of Park Road.

Someone shushes those laughing and I look back to where we came from to see torch beams reaching out into the darkness.

"Get down," someone whispers. And we do.

We are way too far away for the beams to reach us, so as long as the cops don't venture into the graveyard then we are safe, for now.

Before too long the police go back to their car and survey the damage to the car door.

I'm sure, and I'm not alone, that I can hear them talking on the radio, and someone talking back. They don't sound very happy. Having your own car vandalised by a kid you were chasing would probably do that to you.

Someone else hears it too and says, "We need to go. They'll be more cops here soon."

A voice I recognise as Walter says, "Follow me."

He takes us away from the footpath, which even I know is not a wise exit, but he stays close to the perimeter and inspects sections of an area where the fence is only shoulder high.

God only knows how many graves we're trampling on, but they're kind of unavoidable. We all switch our glances from Walter inspecting the fence to the entrances to the graveyard for "PC Plods back up" as Brains puts it.

Then Walter announces, "Here we go," and opens a section of the fence which isn't secured at one end. It swings open, wide and inviting, leading into a garden. There's no lights on in the house. I can see a side gate to the street.

"Everyone go to mine," Tina says, "or you'll get picked up."

"OK," seems to be the general consensus.

"So let's go," Walter says, holding the fence open for us as we filter through.

I want to tell him I hope his clothes are ripped, but he seems more concerned with our plight than his "threads" right now.

We gather at the side of the house, peering out left and right, but there are no cars and no pedestrians, so as far as we can see, the coast is clear.

That doesn't stop us legging it full pelt across Park Road and piling into the stairwell in a mass of giggles and back-slapping.

We made it.

9:30am
Saturday
8th February
2020

CHAPTER 22

Laura took a breath and held it in her chest for a three-count. Whenever she saw Jimmy her heart would melt and somehow wring dry like a blood-soaked sponge. Now was no different. He may be in his nineties, but he is still her Jimmy.

To say Jimmy had been on a journey was a multi-award-winning understatement. Less than a year after his release from prison after he was homeless and living on the streets for six years. By the time Laura had tracked him down he'd been in and out of refuges for seven years and for the last eight years he had been in Leylands Retirement Home. Only the proprietor knew of his history. It had taken Laura months to persuade her to meet Jimmy, and it had taken Jimmy five minutes to convince her he was an upstanding, and very likeable, citizen.

He was free to tell whoever he wanted whatever he wanted, Laura hadn't asked and Jimmy hadn't said. She had seen, on her weekly visits, that he was a popular and much-loved member of the community and that was good enough for her.

She released her breath, exhaling slowly, then stepped through the double doors that lead to the common room.

Jimmy sat centre-stage, holding court with his homies.

No doubt he'd told them his girlfriend was visiting again today.

Well, Laura thought to herself, here I am.

He saw her crossing the room and smiled.

"Hiya, handsome," she beamed.

"Well hello, young lady," he grinned.

His house-mates gushed in admiration of them.

Laura was no stranger to the residents and if any of them were curious as to their actual relationship then they hadn't asked.

"I've come to steal him away from you," she told the assorted crowd. "If he'll come with me that is."

"I bet he could be persuaded," one of the said. "Besides, we'll be here when you're finished with him."

"I'll try to be quick," Laura smiled.

"Oh, you take your time."

Jimmy got to his feet with the help of his walking stick.

"Lead the way, my love," he said to Laura.

It was a lovely warm evening and they took the opportunity to sit outside on the veranda.

Once seated Jimmy got straight to the point. "Do I need to ask if you've changed your mind?"

"You can ask," Laura tells him.

"Stubborn as ever," he says to himself, then asks, "So Hannah's gone through?"

Laura nods. "It's the safest place for her right now."

"If we kept things as they are she'd be safe anywhere," Jimmy said, the exasperation in his voice causing him to go short of breath.

Laura reached for his hand and held it as his breathing went from short to a more steady cycle.

"We've been through this James," Laura said, "after tonight things won't be as they are. In a few hours, back there, he'll realise what really happened. And we both know what he's like."

"But we don't even know what will happen. We don't know if it will work."

"At least we'll have tried."

Jimmy looked down at this lap and shook his head.

"So you're still going back too?"

"I am," she says, "and I'll put him in his place, once and for all."

"Once and for all?" Jimmy asks. "We both know there ain't no such thing."

"We can make it so," Laura tells him, "I'm going to free you, my love, whether you want me to or not."

"Laura," Jimmy says and look at her. "I've had my life and-"

"It was taken from you," Laura interrupts, "and I did nothing. No, we agreed on this before, we're not changing our plans now."

Tears formed in his eyes and he sniffled as he shook his head. "Laura listen, you don't have to do this. You don't! I swear on my daughter's life, you gave me love, I thank God for that, but I've had my life. I'm ninety-seven years old, and I wouldn't change a thing."

"No, Jimmy," Laura tells him. "What happened to you was wrong, and we *will* change a thing."

10:45am
Sunday
29th June
1980

CHAPTER 23

Last night was mental.

I've never ran from the police before. I've never even spoken to a policeman before.

And I don't know what we did for the police to be concerned, I have no idea.

Johnny's explanation is we were guilty of GBH, Going Back Home. He also has ACAB tattooed on his knuckles; All Coppers Are Bastards, so he might be slightly biased. Maybe I'm naive, maybe my rose-tinted-80s-glasses have filtered out tales I've read about heavy-handed police as exaggerated urban legends.

And now Sharpie has given them something to be heavy-handed about. What he did to the police car won't be forgotten.

Everyone stayed the night. After an hour of chatting and smoking, we bedded down for the night. Clair and Lisa shared my bed and I woke them both up at least twice. Every time I started drifting off to sleep someone, in my head, would scream 'Run!' and I'd wake up kicking, if not screaming.

I heard murmured voices and the front door opened and closed about four times, but I decided to stay in bed and feign sleep.

I can't help feeling like a total fan-girl as me and Tina make our way across town to meet with Charlie. I'm not particularly looking forward to going back to The Corner Pin after my introduction to the place last night. The staring faces and the threatening atmosphere are still with me, but with the sides of my head shaved and Tina by my side I feel ready for anything these pathetic losers can throw at me.

We've dressed down for the occasion, well, compared to the plumage we adorned ourselves with last night. It's denim jackets, t-shirts, jeans and monkey boots, hair down but still goaded into place with hair-bands.

The precinct is empty as it's a Sunday and none of the shops are open. If I needed to buy a pint of milk, I might be lucky enough to find a newsagent somewhere, but in an hour so there'll be nowhere open. I guess people just had to plan for it. It certainly doesn't feel like the end of the world, more like a fair trade in the work/life balance equation that 2020 Britain has tipped totally to the work side.

"I've never known anyone dance as much as you," Tina tells me.

I smile. If only she knew!

The dance party last night was one of the greatest nights of my life, something I couldn't even put on a bucket list, but I lived it and I loved it. For Tina, however, it was just a regular Saturday night, a good laugh, but no big deal.

"You weren't too shabby yourself," I say. I can tell that I'm smiling too much and the spring in my step is bouncing to a jaunty ska beat, but I can't help it.

"Don't you have parties where you're from?" Tina grins.

"Not like that," I say. "Singles night at Boogies is where it's at, for sure."

"You say the weirdest things."

"Boogie didn't seem happy when Charlie appeared."

"Well," Tina says, "there's good reason for that?"

"Oh," I say, trying to phrase it as a question without seeming to pry.

Tina doesn't respond.

I try to sound casual when I say, "I heard that Charlie was his brother's manager or something."

"He was. They say Steve Callaghan was the person who would stand up to Charlie," Tina explains.

I nod without talking.

Tina goes on, "It was all before my time but, when his brother died, Boogie went right off the rails. At the wake Boogie started shouting that Charlie had killed his brother. He said Steve was unconscious but alive after the fight, then the doctor made everyone leave except Charlie, and then he died."

"Jesus, that would've screwed anyone up."

"It would, but everyone who was there says that Steve was out on his feet, but stuck on the ropes and the other fighter kept punching him," she says. "The referee guy didn't stop him until the bell went, which was what they did in those days, apparently."

That is sickening.

"Brain damage," Tina concluded.

"That's horrific," I mutter.

Tina nods. "So when Boogie starts saying Charlie killed his brother, everyone was sympathetic, but he was told, it was an terrible accident, but it *was* an accident."

As we cross the Civic Hall car park, a figure appears in the doorway of The Corner Pin.

As we approach, I recognise him and my heart sinks a little. Terry.

"So, what exactly is this job?" I ask Tina.

"Bar work," Tina says, "kind of."

"Kind of?" I ask.

"For the games room," Tina explains.

For the games room? I suddenly like this even less than before.

The Corner Pin and is on the same street as Boogie's place. From the outside, I could tell it was a dive. Roof tiles were missing for one thing and the wooden window frames were weather-beaten to the point of battery.

"You do know you're wasting your time, don't ya," Terry says before we even get to the doorstep of The Corner Pin.

He's stood in the doorway, strategically positioned to almost block our exit, but not quite.

"Lucky we've got plenty of time to waste then ain't it," Tina tells him as she pushes past him.

I can't help but notice though that his dirty looks are directed at me, not her. For some reason, he has a problem with me, or more probably my new relationship with Tina, some weird mind of jealousy that doesn't even understand himself no doubt.

After Tina has passed him he resumes his position of blocking the door, like a Weeble Bouncer. I don't have the confidence to shove him aside so I edge past him as he stands stock still and looks off into the distance (well, the Rye Piece Ringway).

The Sunday lunchtime clientèle looks eerily similar to the Friday night crowd.

"Hey up ladies!" says one overweight drinker from his seat at the bar. His jowls shake as he laughs alone.

I don't give him eye-contact as I pass, but in my peripheral vision, I can see his head turn to follow me.

Why are all the men in this pub dickheads?

Tina shows no trepidation on entering the place and I remind myself this is a triumphant return to her former stomping-ground.

I follow as close to her as I can and my instincts prove that if anything, I have over-estimated the place itself. I knew it would be run-down, even by 1980 standards, but it's closer to its inevitable dereliction than I had imagined. Seven generations of wallpaper layers are trying to drag themselves from the walls and the spit and sawdust hasn't been replaced since the war. And there's always the smell of cigarette smoke, but here it's like a permanent state of the atmosphere.

I hold my breath, but a few of the younger-old men nod to Tina in recognition. She seems to know where Charlie is and we head to the far end of the bar.

I spot him waiting by a door. Tina approaches and he opens it without acknowledging her.

Beyond the door I can see steps going down to a cellar.

She follows Charlie down the steps, but my path is blocked by a customer.

I try to side-step around him, but he shifts his stance just enough to prevent me from passing.

He sips his beer and says, "Who cut your hair, love? The Council?"

Instinctively, I turn to him and am greeted by leery laughter from the assorted crowd.

The comedian, who looks like a homeless person, is leering at me without even trying to disguise it. His grin displays the gaps in his teeth, it looks like a crossword on faded yellow paper. His skin is pale and his eyes are circled red. He's probably in his thirties, but it's hard to say. He also smells, even from a few feet away his scent is offensive.

We're very standing very and I give him eye contact but he returns it.

On closer inspection, he has too much muscle-mass to be homeless. He looks scummy enough to be a degenerate pervert, but there's something else about him that's more sinister than twisted. Beside his left eye he has two tattooed tears. Prison tats. He's served two sentences.

I am instantly super-conscious of how I'm dressed, my hair, and how much of my body shape is visible, but I'm determined to keep my composure.

Everyone is looking at me. I can't show any weakness.

All I really want to do though is get out of this shit-hole of a pub.

"What did you say?" I ask him.

He sneers with a tooth-missing grin, happy to repeat his gag for my benefit and that of this audience of cronies, "I said, 'Who cut your hair, love? The Council?'" He wipes the sides of his head to illustrate his joke, then adds, "I can see how that would come in handy."

His audience growls their approval of this poet-laureate of bar-room humour, but he doesn't break the fourth wall and stays in character. He puts his drink on the table and, in the process, forces me to take a step backward.

This is now going from wise-cracking to sexual intimidation.

For a moment I feel I should look down, avert my eyes, and be ashamed of myself, but then I come to my senses, no screw that. I keep staring him in the eye trying to gauge whether he would actually assault a female in front of witnesses in broad-daylight. I'm acutely aware I don't have a social reference to gauge the likelihood of this happening.

So I continue to stare and watch for signs.

He doesn't move but his veins seem to pulse in his neck.

I wait for the slightest flicker of doubt on his face, then I say, "Handy for what?"

He doesn't seem to want to spell it out for me and I try to relax my stance and defuse the situation.

His eyes leave me by an almost imperceptible degree. I think maybe I can actually relax but then there are some audience titters and he tenses up again.

"You don't want to do this," I say.

"Is that right?" he says, taking another step toward me, "cos it looks like someone has to teach you a lesson in manners, little lady."

I figure I had maybe four seconds to get enough distance between me and him so that he couldn't do any damage, but I underestimated him. Before I turn away, he raises a hand and takes another two steps towards me.

I spin back in time to see the palm of a strong arm slam into his chest hard enough to knock him off his feet. He staggers back and the bar breaks his fall.

The owner of the hand steps forward and stands over him. Charlie.

"What do you think you're doing?" he says to the stunned pervert.

"Nobody talks to me like that!" he snarls, his comment aimed directly at me.

Charlie takes a handful of his shirt and pulls him from the bar. "In my pub, she can talk to you any way she wants, understand?"

He hasn't looked at me, and I'm not sure why he's defending me.

"And if you ever start on a girl in here again, then I'll take the rest of your teeth out. Got it?"

The perv nods but has no more to say. He's convinced.

"Now drink up and get out!"

The basement is being renovated, although that might be considering flattering as the 'room' isn't much more than a hole in the ground with four brick walls. Three of the walls are begin roughly plastered and the third is being partitioned with a false wall. The floor has been recently concreted by the look of it and the ceiling is a network of electrical wiring and spot lights. Although there is some investment going on here, it feels to me like a cheap job and every corner is being cut.

I'm guessing that the work-force are on a short break, probably enjoying the hospitality upstairs.

I'm uncomfortable. This is the site of the alleged 'knocking shop' that lead to The Corner Pin being closed down and now that I am here, the actual practicalities of such a thing being its repulsiveness into sharp focus.

Its not a big room. How many girls were down here at a any given time?

Even though those events haven't happened yet, it gives me the creeps.

I have to push these thoughts from my mind.

I catch Tina's eye and give her a relaxed smile.

The three of us are sat at a large oval table which is covered in a white sheet.

Tina is beaming, she doesn't seem able to believe that Charlie would grant her an audience, like he's the Pope or Bono or something.

After the verbal altercation I've been invited in and offered a seat.

Before this turn of events, I'd thought that like most small town big-men, Charlie's reputation was built largely on bravado and urban myth, but seeing, and benefiting, first hand from his man-management, I cant deny that he is a domineering figure. I'm sure that he can be a charmer too when he wants to be, although I see that as a classic narcissist trait. He looks to me to be a stone-cold classic narcissist, all of which makes him dangerous to be around.

The first thing he says, he says to me. "I'd like to apologise for the behaviour you were subjected to."

"Why would you apologise?" I ask, "It wasn't you who said it."

He smiles, "I feel responsible, that's all."

I shrug, "Well, at the end of the day, you can't control everyone, can you?"

It's a good line, one I'm proud of, I can see that Charlie is dying to contradict me and demonstrate that he can and does control many people. And I'm sure he does, but the point is he can't control me. I can also see that he is making a mental note to prove his point at a later date, but this is not the time or the place.

"Besides," I say, "It was nothing, I've been abused by way worse perverts than that. He was a disappointment."

"Thanks, anyway," Tina chips in.

Charlie doesn't even glance at Tina, his eyes are fixed on me, but he doesn't speak.

"Oh," I say and scratch the shaved side of my head, "I hope you didn't expect me to just kiss your arse because you told a degenerate waste of space to wind his neck in."

I glance at Tina, she looks horrified.

Charlie looks both amused and only slightly insulted by my petulance.

But I know it's all an act and I adopt an even more bored posture and matching expression.

We both recognise kindred spirits and as Tina tightens her grip on the arms of her chair, he starts to smile.

"Are you finished?" he asks me. "That was a very impressive performance by the way. Bravo."

"Thank you," I say.

And we call a truce.

CHAPTER 24

Tina sits forward in her chair and puts her hands on the table.

"Thanks for seeing me," she tells Charlie.

He nods and smiles at Tina. "I have faith in you," he says, "Don't make me regret that."

"I won't," she tells him.

"You'll do Friday nights, starting next week," he says. "You might be needed to cover the bar some week-nights."

Tina nods. And smiles again. "I'm free any night-"

"Good," he says. "I'm having a few friends over for a card game, I thought you could help out, you know, serve drinks to the players, that kind of thing."

Tina smiles and nods then takes her hands from the table and puts them in her lap..

Charlie turns to me. "I'm told you're new in town."

I don't answer.

"You just got here the other day, is that right?"

I nod, bored.

"So where are you from?"

"Why does that matter?" I say.

He leans back in his chair as we engage in a staring match.

"I like to know who I'm dealing with," he says.

"You're not dealing with me," I tell him.

"Not yet," he says, "but I think you've got potential."

He smiles and looks down at the table.

"So, where are you from?"

"Lowestoft."

"Oh I know it well, whereabouts?"

"Pakefield."

"You don't have a Norfolk accent."

"We moved around a lot."

"How'd you get here?"

"On the train?"

"Where'd you change trains?"

"I didn't."

"But there's no direct train from -"

"Why do you care?"

"I'll tell you why! Because I don't mind bullshitters, but I don't like liars. And I want to know, which one are you?"

"I'm sorry, but you've lost me completely," I tell him.

"Terry told me your name is Laura."

"No," I say, "my name is Hannah."

"So," he says, "your name is Hannah, not Laura, and you came here on a train?"

"That's right," I tell him.

Tina is looking from me to him and getting more agitated with each turn of her head.

"Instead of swapping life-stories, why don't we talk business?" I say.

Charlie says, "I thought we'd done that."

He reaches for his cigarettes, flips open the lid and offers one to Tina. She slides one out of the packet and places it between her lips. He offers me one and I'm disgusted at myself that I feel the some pressure to take one.

"No thanks," I say.

"You given 'em up?" he asks, not disguising his grin.

"No, I'm saving my voice for the church choir," I tell him.

"You're too late," he says, deadpan, "the church just closed."

"Aww! I missed it?"

That line gets him grinning and he raises a smile that threatens to topple into a chuckle.

Charlie looks at his watch, which looks expensive but might not be, then he nods for me to go on.

Tina is also looking at me. I give her a glance and see how worried she is. I give her a smile that says, Don't worry, I got this.

"The market stall," I tell him, "We're re-opening it."

For a moment Charlie is taken aback, then he frowns, theatrically. "And you're telling me this because...?"

"Why do you think?"

"I have no idea," he says slowly.

I sense that Tina is staring at me so intently though the temptation to turn to her is almost overwhelming, but I resist.

"You're a man of means," I say to Charlie, "and we need a wholesaler."

"I'm flattered," he says without any humour, "but that's not my line of work."

I nod. "Oh, I thought...nevermind," I say, "but we'd like to do it with your blessing."

"My blessing?" he repeats, seemingly misunderstanding.

I nod again, assuming that he understands perfectly well.

Tina is writhing in her seat, "I-"

"I mean, it's not a deal-breaker," I say, "we're going to do it anyway, but, as I say, you're a man of means and we respect that."

Charlie turns to Tina and speaks calmly. "And you're part of this?"

Tina doesn't speak, but she nods her head.

Charlie ignores her protest and says, "I trust that your market stall work won't interfere with your role here?"

"No absolutely not!" Tina spurts out.

Then to me he says, "And you've only just got here, how do I know you're not going to disappear just as quick?"

"Like I say," I tell him, "We've got plans. I'm not going anywhere."

Not true, of course, but he doesn't need to know that.

"Very well, you have my blessing," he says. He smiles at us both and gets to his feet. "I must say, ladies, I am impressed with your style, and I like your attitude. May I thank you both for your time and please, enjoy the rest of the day."

As we walk out of the pub, Tina looks both happy and bewildered.

Terry doesn't look happy when he sees our grinning faces. He doesn't say anything, there's nothing for him to say, but as Tina passes, she takes a drag on her cigarette and blows smoke in his face.

I don't say anything, I don't give him eye contact. I follow Tina out of the door.

CHAPTER 25

For some reason, we are heading home across the park toward the swimming baths and we have held in our jubilation until we are out of ear-shot of The Corner Pin and its wonderful clientèle.

"Oh, my God! That was amazing!" Tina is gushing as she hugs me so tight I can hardly breathe.

We stop at the birdcage and watch the peacocks walk in slow circles.

When she lets me go I can smile without fearing for my life.

"I can't believe you did that!" she shouts.

People turn and look at us, curious as to what our celebration is about, but I find a cold stare deters most, if not all, of them.

"There's always an angle," I remind Tina. "But finding it was the easy part, now we have work to do."

"I mean," she says, "I can't believe I got my waitressing job back, that was amazing, but when you started saying about the market stall, I was thinking 'Oh my God! What are you doing?'

I don't tell Tina that the reason I brought up the market thing was the 'waitressing' job. I couldn't get the pub's reputation out of my head and knowing that it will be shut-down for its basement 'knocking shop' set off all my alarm bells.

I need to change the subject. "So this job," I ask, "what do you have to do?"

"Well," Tina explains, "mostly I do nothing. The men play cards and when someone wants a drink, I get it for them."

"And that's it?" I press.

She nods, "That's it."

"It's just waiting tables?" I ask.

Tina looks at me, for the first time, annoyed. She lowers her voice and says, "What's that supposed to mean?"

"I'm just thinking, it's an illegal card game in the cellar of a pub."

"How is it illegal?" Tina asks.

"Because he doesn't have a gambling license."

Tina dismisses my concern. "People play cards in pubs all the time," she sighs, "it doesn't mean it's illegal."

I decide not to push the point any further and we resume our walk home.

"Why did you get fired last time?" I ask.

Tina considers before even answering, then says, "He accused me of keeping a tip. We had to give him all the tips and he divided them up, but he said I kept a twenty-pound note from this guy."

I am careful to avoid even suggesting anything other than, "So, he made it all up."

"Yes. There wasn't even a tip."

"Seems a bit unfair."

"Tell me about it," she says.

"He doesn't seem the fairest employer does he?" I say.

"Why *did* you tell him about the market stall?" Tina asks.

"I'm sorry about that," I say, "I saw the opportunity and went for it, but I should've asked you first. I got carried away."

"If we can get the stall running again, it would be great," Tina begins to say and her eyes widen in wonder, "but we *cannot* mess with him."

"We'll make it work, Tina," I say, "I promise."

Tina says, with no humour, "I bet he hasn't been spoken to like that in a long time."

"Really? What do you mean?"

"I mean like he's *Charlie* and no one round here says 'Boo' to him, not to his face anyway."

"Oh," I say. He sounds more like a Mafia boss than the landlord of a seedy Bedworth pub.

"He doesn't just own the pub," Tina explains, "He's got a lot of businesses. Lots of people rely on him for work. He started the Sports Club, the football team, which he called Real Bedworth, he took over the Boxing Club, people look up to him. He's helped people, you know."

I don't know, but I'm going to ask. I don't like how Tina is defending someone who effectively shut off her income.

We walk in silence for a while.

As we near the flat Terry re-appears, calling Tina to wait.

"What does he want?" I ask Tina.

"You don't have to hang around," Tina says. "I'll see what he wants."

I don't need to be asked twice.

I say 'Hi' to Terry and head up to the flat.

Barbara has the radio on in the lounge room and is flicking through a magazine.

She and Tina both share the striking cheek bones and button nose. Judging by the framed photos scattered around the flat, she might have been even more good-looking than her daughter at her age. They could be the same person separated by time. The mini-skirts and flowers prints blouses date the era to be the mid-60s. She must've had Tina at a very young age and, as I've not seen any men in her photos, possibly outside of marriage, which couldn't have been easy in those days.

I can only imagine what she's been through in her life, and I'm certainly not going to pry, but somehow Barbara has maintained high spirits amid her understandable mood-swings.

I take a seat on the settee with her and immediately I'm subjected to a barrage of questions. She wants to know everything about me, which presents a few problems, but is irresistibly fun.

"Do you watch Crossroads?"

or

"Do you think a woman should walk in a pub on her own?"

and

"Do you like music?"

"I do," I say, "I love music. Do you?"

She nods. "Doesn't everyone? I suppose you're into them Bay City Rollers like our Tina?"

"Not really," I smile, "is Tina a big Rollers fan?"

"Yeah," she roars, "She's got all the records, sings all the words and her rooms covered in posters."

"Oh my God," I giggle, "she never mentioned this before."

I knew Tina's room was no longer adorned with pictures of Les, Woody and the boys, but it was hilarious to think that they once were.

It seems my favourite Goth-girl was once a tartan teeny-bopper like everyone else.

"Barbara," I ask, "does she still have those Bay City Rollers records?"

"Yeah, of course," she says. "Do you fancy a listen?"

"Ooh yes!" I smile, "I'd love to."

Barbara slips off the settee and sits cross-legged in front of the record player. After thumbing through the shelf of albums she retrieves 'Dedication'. The album cover is the band stood in front a lake, or more likely a loch. It's not the most inspiring art work I have ever see, but I guess it sold enough copies. She puts the record on the spindle, pushes a small lever and the LP falls onto the deck and the arm of the stylus awakens and lifts itself up. The record spins and the arm drops the needle onto it.

As she sits back on the settee, we are subjected to some cheesy 70s teeny-bop and I can't wait to see Tina's face when she walks in.

"I didn't know Tina was a Rollers fan," I tell Barbara, hoping to unearth some more embarrassing dirt on her.

"Yes, she loves these, plays them all the time. It drives me mad," she says. "Where is she any way?"

"She's outside talking to Terry," I tell her.

"Terry?" she asks.

I nod and Barbara looks concerned.

"I think it's about getting her job back at The Corner Pin," I say. I don't want Barbara thinking there's anything between Tina and Terry.

Barbara looks startled. "She's not going back to work for Charlie is she?"

I nod again. "I think so," I say, then add, "I'm not sure."

Barbara vigorously shakes her head. "God, I hope not," she says, "he's proper evil."

"Is he?" I ask. I've said too much and need to steer the conversation away from Charlie, but I hear myself saying, "Do you know him?"

"I've known him for years," she says. "He black-listed my market stall!"

"Yes, I heard about that," I say. This is what Clair has told me and if it were true, then it means Charlie is capable of serious intimidation, but I still wasn't sure it wasn't some kind of urban myth. "We're going to reopen it," I assure her, but her mind is already elsewhere.

"He's a nasty piece of work," she says, "mark my words."

Barbara seems annoyed that I don't seem convinced by her accusations.

She lights a cigarettes and jabs it at the space between us to punctuate the points she is making.

"He's always been up to no good, and no one will stand up to him, but let me tell you something about him," she says. "You know about the cop who got killed, right?"

"Err...no," I say, but-

"You must've heard about it."

"No," I say again, but I do know, maybe it's instinctive, maybe it's a case of my mind assuming the worst, because this is the absolute worst scenario imaginable at this point.

Barbara lowers her voice and moves closer . "He got-"

"Shot."

"Yes! You do know."

"Yes, kind of," I say.

"He got shot by Charlie's brother," she says. "Years ago it was. In broad daylight. He confessed, but never said why he did it."

No, I thought, it was Jimmy who shot the policeman. Unless…

…she's talking about Jimmy.

Unless Jimmy is Charlie's brother. Could that be possible?

I'm silent for a while, I don't know how long, my mind is spinning me round and round like a parachute in a tailspin. I don't want Barbara to look at me, but I know that if I don't say something then she will.

"Really?" I hear myself say.

Yes, I tell myself, 'Really'.

I can see my mother's face, I can see the spots of blood sprayed across her face, the streaks where her fingers had wiped it from her eyes, and I can hear her saying to me, "Hannah, we need to go! Now!"

Barbara takes a deep drag on her cigarette and stares at me for a moment. When she speaks smoke drifts between her teeth.

"There was a woman too," she says, "and she seen it all, Charlie's brother has never told who she is," Tina went on, "even after all these years. So she's still out there. Somewhere."

'Or maybe not', I want to say.

Barbara stops talking and I'm aware that she's staring at me but I'm staring at the floor at my feet.

"What was his name?" she ponders. "I'm usually good with names…"

Don't worry about it, I already know who his name.

"Johnny?" she asks.

I think I'm going to be sick.

Physically sick.

Barbara is saying that Charlie is Jimmy's brother.

And why has Charlie got involved with Tina?

"He's still in prison, I expect."

And why would Charlie give Tina a job just weeks before I arrive.

And there's no such thing as a coincidence.

"No, not Johnny," she corrects herself. "Jimmy. That was his name. Jimmy Randle. "

CHAPTER 26

I try to listen to the music to distract my mind, but I know that I need to focus on what Barbara has told me.

Could she be wrong about this?

What will she say to Tina?

What have I started?

Charlie must know about my mother and Jimmy. What else does he know.

Barbara stubs out her cigarette and chuckles, "I don't know what she sees in these."

I look up, not understanding, drowning in my thoughts.

She's looking at the record player. She's back on the Bay City Rollers. All of her anger and rage is gone.

My confusion is spinning out of control into a tornado.

I get up to leave the room, I need to be alone to figure out what is happening.

But then I hear a key in the door.

It opens and closes.

I sit back down.

Tina's voice is a blend of humour and embarrassment, "What *are* you listening to?"

"They're your favourite band," Barbara grins, "not ours."

What is happening here? Barbara seems to have forgotten about Tina working for Charlie or she's pretending not to know, but no one can act this well.

I turn from Barbara to Tina.

"Is this your idea?" she says, gesturing to the record player.

I shake my head.

"Oh my God," she says to me. "You do not look well. Are you OK?"

"I'm fine," I tell Tina. "I just need to think-"
"Think about what?"
"I need to lie down," I say, "excuse me."
I go to my room.
"Let me know if you need anything," Tina tells me.
"Thanks," I say, "I will."

I try to make sense of what I now know and what I knew before. It's torture but I need to confirm my suspicions, because they are not suspicions, they are known facts to me.

The man who my mother has loved for years and years (and, full disclosure, is probably my dad, although that's got nothing to do with this), confessed to a murder committed by his brother and witnessed by my mother.

And I remember it.

I heard the shots.

I was in Stubbs, as always waiting for mum to return. She was only going for an hour or so at this time, and I was told not to leave the toy shop, stay in the shop and don't leave under any circumstances. So there I was, staring at a huge collection of Airfix models and wishing I was skilled and patient enough to magically turn these grey plastic frames into a real-life miniature aeroplane from the olden days. Then I hear a bang. A sharp explosion. A blast that ricocheted all around me. Then another.

And someone says, "What was that?"

Someone else says, "Those were gunshots!"

Then there is silence.

Now I'm lost.

I know I should probably be taking some kind of action, but I don't know what that is.

I look around for direction from someone.

The shopkeeper is telling his daughters to go through to the back office.

"Hurry, quietly," he says, "I'll be with you soon."

I move away from the Airfix models so I can see the front door of the shop.

"Miss! Miss!"

I hear the words, and it sounds like someone is playing Battleships and the coordinates don't match with their ships. Then I think maybe they're calling out the results of the gunshots. Do people do that?

"Miss! Come with me."

I realise it's the shopkeeper and he's talking to me and I shake my head.

He is walking toward me in a crouched funny way.

"Come with me, into the back room, you'll be safe there, just in case," he says and puts out his hand.

I back away and put my own hands behind me. "No!" I tell him, "I have to 'stay in the shop'."

"What? No. You'll be safer-"

The door bursts open and my mother dashes across the floor of the shop.

"What have you done?" the shopkeeper says. "We heard gunshots!"

I'm outraged that he's asking my mother what she has done as if she is responsible for anything, but then I see her face.

My mother ignores the shopkeeper, and he tries to stop her from approaching me but she moves too quickly.

Her eyes are fixed on mine now.

No words are necessary, but I feel panic rising in my chest.

There is blood on my mother's face.

Maybe she has been shot! Maybe it's only her superhuman strength and determination that has brought her to me.

After all, we are not supposed to be here and it's important that we never get caught.

My mother scoops me up in her arms and dashes to the Staff Only room.

My mother's hands also have blood on them.

I don't understand any of this. I don't know if my mother will live or die and whether we'll get home or I'll be left here without her or anybody I know.

I start to wail.

We go through the door and I look back at the shopkeeper. He's going to be even madder now that we've disobeyed the Staff Only sign.

But he looks scared. He's backing away.

Other people enter the shop, signalled by the cheerful jingle of the bell above the door.

A man says, "Is that an exit?"

The shopkeeper says, "No. It's just a store room."

"No windows?"

"No."

Mum hasn't shut the door behind us. As I whisked away into the loo, I look back and I see the two men.

The shopkeeper is backing away, but the second man is moving forward, staring at us for signs of something, then taking more steps to the door as it slowly closes shut.

And I remember thinking about how tall he was.

My mother picks me up and carries me into the toilet cubicle.

She covers my eyes and screams, "Stay back! Stay back!" then I hear the door slam shut and my mother locking it and I'm crying as my mother hushes me and then everything is silent.

And then, we were gone.

CHAPTER 27

There's no such thing as a coincidence.

They simply do not happen.

Instead, there are reasons and causes for every effect.

It is not a coincidence that Charlie hired, fired and rehired Tina and black-listed Barbara's market stall.

He did it to get close to me. It's the only explanation.

I don't know how he knew I was going to arrive, but he knew.

I can't get Charlie out of my head. And maybe I shouldn't, now that he's in there.

I try to remember the things I said to him this morning when I was so confident and full of myself and mouthy.

My memory is not only vague but shaky, it's not working properly, and it's panicking.

I do remember I told him not to apologise for the perv's behaviour. I told him not to expect me to kiss his arse like everyone else. And he gave as good as he got, touché. I had thought it was a fair exchange between equally matched adversaries.

But now, I realise, it was a cat toying with a mouse.

And though I can't remember my exact words, I can remember him saying, 'I don't mind bullshitters, but I hate liars'.

He had known all along who I was, he knows where I came from, where I had really came from, he knows my mother and he's Jimmy's brother.

Which means he knows as much as I do, and, obviously, a lot more.

I had a decision to make.

And, although my mind is scared to admit it, the last thing I saw, as my mother carried me into the staff room that day, I looked back and saw a man pursuing us. A tall man. A tall thin man younger than Charlie is now. Was it him or am I imprinting him into my memory?

Of course, it was him.

I wonder how long he stood outside that door, kneeling down to look under the door and not seeing our feet and then kicking the door in and we're not there.

We disappeared. Into thin air.

And how furious must he have been?

And probably still is.

I'm supposed to go back tomorrow night. That means abandoning Tina and Barbara, abandoning Tina's market stall plan, abandoning the friends I had made. And abandoning Tina means leaving her to be preyed upon by Charlie to do his worst, and his worst could be very bad.

I could leave Tina the money that she needs to get away from under Charlie, and more besides, Tina could have it all.

But could I do it? Could I do to Tina what I did to Mia, possibly worse?

And why did my mother insist I can't go back until Monday night?

My mother had hidden so much important stuff from me, I had no idea why she would be so insistent on me coming back at a particular time: 8 o'clock, Monday night.

As I see it, I have only one option: To go back and speak to my mother, then return and do what I need to do to help Tina.

I needed information and there was only one place I could get it.

OK, so I kind of knew that my mother wasn't quite the helpless love-interest in that story, but the one big-thing I can't grasp is how badly she is portrayed and perceived by people. The murderer's accomplice. I'm sure that she has been portrayed as the one who put him up to it. That she is evil and coerced him into killing.

Maybe this shouldn't surprise me, the victors write the history books and all that, but they didn't write my history book, which was solely penned by my mother and my mother alone. And it was a very thin book with very little plot.

I was told that we are no longer going to Stubbs.

Why?

Because it wasn't safe any more.

Why did you have blood on you mummy?

Because there was an accident.

Did someone get hurt?

Nobody that matters.

OK.

I remember those three words - Nobody that matters.

Not to us. Not many people did. It's how we are.

The most important thing is that we keep the accident secret and trust each other.

Remember Hannah, secrets and trust, me and you.

I remember, I assure her, I'll never tell a living soul.

And where has that got me? I find out that the accident was a murder, the murderer was my mother's lover and my mother was a witness.

So much for trust.

So much for secrets.

What else don't I know? What else haven't I been told?

There are things I don't know and it infuriates me. My mother has been dishonest with me and that infuriates me even more.

Of course, I've thought about this image of her dashing into the shop spattered in blood and whisking me away. I've made up a million scenarios in my head where my mother is the innocent party in the wrong place at the wrong time or forced to witness something so horrific that all she could think about was protecting her only child.

Me.

I was her everything, or so she said.

But that wasn't strictly true either, as I now find out.
Secrets and trust. Both broken.
But that's not my biggest problem.

It's been too long now, so I can't be sure, and I think memories can be over-written, like a VHS tape, and it's hard to tell whether they are genuine or not, but I absolutely remember that the guy following us in the toy shop was a tall man. That I do remember. But I also now remember that he had strong features, a square jaw, dark eyes. I've probably over-written these details, superimposed them on the image in my mind, but even if I have, it could still be him. That man was Charlie.

The policeman had been shot. My mother was fleeing the scene, of course, he would follow her, prevent us from leaving, and follow her into the room without windows, trapped. Except he didn't prevent us from leaving.

I wonder what he thought.

I wonder what he knows.

It does seem that he knows everything. Then and now.

And it's kind of important for me to know that, because, here he is, conveniently, helping out the new kid who just happens to be me.

He was the one who asked, 'Where did you change trains?'

'I quite like bullshitters, but I hate liars,'

He knew all along. He saw through my cover-story straight away, maybe even before he even heard it.

Maybe he knew exactly when I was coming here and was expecting me.

Nothing would surprise me.

And I hate not knowing stuff.

Maybe I should cut and run, I tell myself. All bets are off right now as my mother has either misread this situation or she hasn't been as honest as she should. Either way, I'm on thin ice.

But I can't go back because I can't abandon Tina.

Secrets might be out of the window but trust is still something worth fighting for. The rest of Sunday I am very quiet and get some excessive usage out of my Brave Face. After Barbara had told me about Charlie and Jimmy being brothers, and me realising that my mother was there when the policeman got shot. And I was there, right next door. And I remember it.

My mother is aware of all this, to put it mildly, and to my mind, it would have been beneficial to have shared that information with me before asking me to come here. But then mother would also know that if I had known this, I would never have come.

Which is probably why she didn't tell.

And why she told me to keep a low profile.

To put it mildly, I was furious with my mother.

She had put me in harm's way, and 'keeping my head down' wasn't what I would call keeping me safe.

Tina sensed that something is wrong, but her gentle probes to prise it out of me only made me clam up even more.

We help Barbara with Sunday dinner, a full roast chicken with four veg, Yorkies and thick gravy.

It should be fun, us three girls in the kitchen talking girls' talk, and I pretend it is. But it isn't.

3:42pm
Monday
10th February
2020

CHAPTER 28

Laura steps into the Bear and Ragged Staff with an air of confidence that some might object to in a woman of her age, but none would be brave enough to challenge her. Not yet anyway, maybe after a few more drinks, but even then Laura's brand of female disarming charm and indirect intimidation will diffuse most situations.

She's wearing an outfit that could be a contender for the most nondescript ensemble of clothes ever to adorn a human body of any age: light brown cotton trousers, a grey brandless hoodie with the hood up, and plain all-black trainers. Her black sunglasses are the huge bug-eyed frames that hide her eyes. The bag she's carrying is not a handbag. It's a cyclist's shoulder pack that slings over her shoulder diagonally, but she is carrying it in her hand. It seems to have weight to it, but is far from bulging at the seams.

There are maybe thirty people in the pub.

There's plenty of room at the L-shaped bar.

Laura heads to the far end and takes a seat on the corner facing the door where she just came in.

She sits with the bag in her lap and pulls out her phone, which she occasionally scrolls.

Within a minute, nobody pays her any attention, except the barman, who saunters over and says, "What would you like?"

The job of barman carries some occupational hazards and this thirty-something professional seems to be a victim of most of them. He's overweight, pale-skinned, has a backbone that shouldn't curve over the way it does, and, the moment he talks, has a smoker's rasp to his voice that occasionally needs clearing. Which he does, frequently.

He also has thick glasses, ice-cube thick, that magnify his eyes.

"Could you make me a Bloody Mary?" Laura asks in a tone suitable for a request of the highest skill-set.

"Sure," the barman says, and shrugs, no big deal for a man of his calibre.

He delivers the drink, and Laura pays cash.

She sips her drink and scrolls through her phone.

In the next ten minutes, two men arrive at the bar, order a round of drinks and say 'Hi' to Laura.

"Hi," Laura chimes back, both times, with a bright but brief smile.

Unfortunately for the two men, assuming their intention was to engage in conversation, Laura's phone chirped into life within a second of her greeting. Her next smile says 'I have to take this' and she talks quietly to her caller as she turns away.

The second call lasts longer, and she signals the barman for a second Bloody Mary, which he delivers and she pays for without breaking her conversation on the phone.

When nobody's watching, the Bloody Mary gets tipped into a drip tray and she throws her bag over her shoulder.

Laura steps into the ladies' loo and scans the room. It's empty. The door to all four of the stalls is open.

She needs to be quick. She needs to get this done.

She hurries to the third stall and stops dead at the door.

There's a body on the toilet seat.

Laura's lungs demand rapid breaths and her heart is doing somersaults.

The person, an old man, hasn't moved. His head is bowed onto his chest and has lolled to one side. His hands are in his lap. He is very old. Extremely old.

But he is breathing.

Before Laura gets her thoughts in order, her first impression is one of sympathy; the old man has obviously wandered into the wrong bathroom, obviously the worse for wear, and flopped himself down on the seat.

At least he's fully clothed, she thought to herself.

But then, she remembered her own advice - 'There's no such thing as a coincidence'.

A man is sitting in the third stall of the ladies' bathroom at the very time she needs to use that stall.

That can not be a coincidence.

She recognises him even before he raises his head, opens his mouth to reveal rotten teeth, and says, "Hello Laura. Long time, no see."

Laura doesn't speak. She knows this man; she knows that once upon a time he was a dangerous individual who wished to do her harm. Now though, he was in his nineties. He was no longer dangerous; he was decrepit. Laura knows that she could counter any move on his part with time to spare.

"I found you," the old man says again. His tall frame looks gangling in the confined area. His slack lips form a smile. He looks at her with eyes almost white from cataracts. "I waited a long time," he slurs, "but I found you."

"Are you gonna move," she says to him, "or am I gonna move you?"

He chuckles at that, and his stifled laughs brings on a coughing fit. His head lolls back and balls of brown phlegm are flung from his mouth to loop through the air.

"I don't think I'm going anywhere," he tells her.

"Jesus Charlie," she says to him, "you look like crap."

He nods almost imperceptibly, conceding the point without argument.

"You should be taking it easy in a comfy chair somewhere," she says. "Not here."

The man is still smiling as he tries to untangle his arms from his lap, but was having difficulty doing so.

"Why don't I help you up?" she calls to the man.

"I'm not going anywhere," he says again.

"Charlie, you know I can't-"

He is holding a gun.

"Remember this?" he says.

She has seen that gun before.
She has heard that gun before.
She is very scared of that gun.
She falls back as she tries to scramble away.
The old man raises the gun. "I told you," he says.

Laura pushes herself away, like a crab, dreading the moment that she is looking down the length of the gun barrel with that hideous face behind it.

But the barrel passes her and keeps going until it's pointing upwards.

He nestles his hand on his chest, the gun barrel pointing up to his chin.

He turns his head from side to side, as if getting comfortable, then pushes his chin forward.

"I ain't going anywhere," he says again, "and nor are you."

And he pulls the trigger.

8:30pm
Monday
30th June
1980

CHAPTER 29

The letter I have left Tina is woefully inadequate. I had previously prided myself on writing, actually writing and not just the words and sentences, but hand-writing style too. I refer writing with a pen and paper over a keyboard. However, trying to explain my reasons, even without the added complication of how I got here, proved impossible.

I considered going without leaving a note, but I just couldn't.

All I could do was leave a rubbish letter and do everything I can to make good of the promise it contained. To come back, tomorrow or the next day, or soon, and explain everything.

I've also left £1000 in cash in the envelope.

Now, standing at the back door of the toy shop, I am seriously considering staying. I don't want to let Tina down and I don't want to confront my mother, the only person who I've trusted for the whole of my life.

But I know that I'm also responsible for my predicament and, as such, I need to act accordingly.

And that means breaking and entering into the shop.

I'm fairly sure that no one is in the shop itself or the office space above. It's Monday but it's late. Nobody is anywhere near the shop. Still, I don't want to make any noise. The back door has been repaired. I know this because it's back in its frame, but that's about the limit of my detective skills.

My task is simple: break the glass, open the door from the inside, get to the loo and go home.

I've bought some masking tape to apply to the glass to prevent it from shattering and a pair of gloves so I don't leave fingerprints. These two things are the sum total of my planning. However, as I stand before the window, about to commit the act, I realise how ridiculous that plan is. Any noise the breaking glass makes won't be heard by anyone and my fingerprints aren't on any records, now or in the future.

The square pane of glass is as big as a single record sleeve. There is no shortage of half-bricks in the yard and I have armed myself with one of them. The lines of tape are in place and do their job when I tap the glass with the corner of the brick. The glass cracks and gives way, but the resulting pieces stay stuck to the tape.

As I peel the tape back, most of the glass shards come with it and the only pieces left are wedged into the window frame. Working as quick as I can, I wiggle these pieces free and waste no time in reaching through the empty pane. I find the latch with my hand, but immediately I can tell it's new. My fingers frantically grope for any kind of knob, button, or sliding mechanism. The things I find, I turn, push or slide, and once convinced I have done the necessary, I withdraw my hand and grab the door handle.

I guess that the shopkeeper has installed more locks whilst the door-frame was repaired. Of course he did, why wouldn't he?

But why didn't I, instead of buying masking tape and gloves, come to and recon the shop? I would've seen the new work and changed my plans accordingly.

I'm about to run, but I am convinced that if I do, I'll get caught, or seen.

I can't stay here, but I can't leave.

Then I realise there is another way.

I can go through the window. If I can get it open.

Without using my tape, I smash another pane and unlatch the window.

Using my rusty, and never that good, gymnastic skills I manage to get through the window, but I can't manoeuvre my feet to lead the way and end up face-diving on to the floor.

But I'm in.

This is nearly done.

My key to the storage room still works, even with my shaking fingers operating it.

Once inside, I shut the door, welcome the darkness, and try to get my heart to slow down.

But something is in the way, literally, physically, I can feel something taking up the space I need to move into.

I don't know what it is but my heart rate is soaring and in less than a minute I can feel the very possibility of travelling drifting away from me. It's like my energy is depleting and I'm left sitting on the toy shop toilet seat with no option but to go back.

I get up off the seat.

I go back to the door.

I find the new deadbolts, one top and one bottom, and slide them across to free the door.

Before I leave, I close the broken window. I don't know why.

Then I close the door behind me and head back to Tina's.

I'm not really paying much attention, but I don't see anyone until I get to Park Road.

CHAPTER 30

My aim now is to get back the flat before Tina and retrieve that letter with her name on it.

I nearly made it. I got close, but no banana.

I'd dashed across Park Road and had my foot on the pavement outside the flats, then I heard Tina's voice.

"Hannah!" she called from the HyperMarket car park.

I turned and waved, forcing a smile before realising I really shouldn't.

"Wait there!" she shouted and disappeared in the direction of the stairs.

I was tempted to leg it up to the flat anyway and grab that letter from the top of the tele, but I couldn't come up with a good enough excuse.

And by the time the words 'desperate for a pee' popped into my head, Tina had emerged from the car park and was crossing the road.

"I've just spoken to Dodgy Dave about some badges he's got from Cunninghams," she'd beamed.

Cunninghams was a Bedworth factory outlet that made embroidered badges. They produced thousands of designs, including bands and football clubs, and such things were much sought after. I'd read online that it wasn't unheard of that thousands of these badges, would smuggled out of the factory and made available in the pubs and on street corners. This would be followed by a tightening of security, until the next time.

I didn't go into the issue of selling stolen property less than two hundred yards away from the premises they were stolen from, as I had other things on my mind. Like getting to that television before Tina and grabbing that envelope.

So all I say is, "Brilliant!"

"I was thinking of doing a huge banner with our name on it to hang it behind us so people would just come and look at it."

"I've been thinking about our meeting with Charlie," I say. "I don't trust him, do you?"

"What? Of course, I don't trust him," Tina shrugs.

"So I was thinking maybe we should set up on a different market, where Charlie won't bother us."

Tina shook her head, "There is nowhere else."

I wanted to argue, but really I wanted her to stop getting up to the flat.

With every step on the pavement and each of the stairs and out onto the veranda, I prayed for some kind of inspiration, waiting for the Big Idea that would save me, but none came.

The best thing I could come up with was to ask Tina for her key and then to wait outside while I went inside, but I couldn't think of a reasonable answer to her question of 'Why?'

So I just let things happen. I was powerless.

Tina talked the whole way, never once mentioning her waitressing job, always the market stall.

Outside the door, as she slid her key into the slot, she says, "Do you really think we could one day own a shop?"

"Sure," I say, then add, "It's a natural step."

Maybe, I thought, she'll go into the kitchen and I can go straight into the living room and grab the envelope that is leaning against the ornamental ship on top of the tele.

Tina has no interest in the kitchen. She stood for a moment in the hallway to take off her jacket., I took my chance and slipped past her, headed straight for the living room and crossed the carpet, but-

I nearly made it.

My fingertips were inches away when I heard Tina say, "What's that?"

And it was too late.

I couldn't hide it behind my back and say 'Nothing'.

It wasn't just a treacherous goodbye note, pathetically written and not acted upon by circumstance and not through choice.

It was more than that.

It was a fat envelope, stuffed with the only thing and that ever makes envelopes fat.

Cash.

Tina knew exactly what it was.

Still, I picked up the envelope and looked at the tele, waiting for my fate to be handed to me.

She holds out her hand and says, "It's got my name on it."

I handed it to her without saying a word.

She ripped the envelope open and took the letter out. As she opened it she let the twenty-pound notes fall to the floor, sliding like unmanned canoes falling over a waterfall and spreading on the floor at her feet.

She read the letter in silence and then put it back in the envelope.

"So you were just going to leave and not say anything?" she says to me.

I shake my head.

"What then?" she says and waves the letter at me. "That's what you've written here, isn't it?"

"I couldn't do it," I say.

"Clearly," she says, "but you wanted to."

"It's not that simple," I say, "there's things I need to sort out."

That explanation doesn't cut it and Tina's blank expression tells me as much.

I try to explain further by saying, "I was going to come back."

Tina nods, "Yes, sure you was."

"I was."

She looks down at the money, then looks up to me and says, "Can you pick this up? I don't want my mum to see it."

And she leaves the room.

CHAPTER 31

There's an atmosphere in the flat. I can't blame Tina for being mad at me, but there's not much I can do about it. I need to get out, not just to give her some space, but to get my head together too.

I can't stop seeing that look on her face when she let the money fall to the floor. That had to be more money than she's ever seen in her life. But she didn't take it, her principles wouldn't allow her to. Barbara may not have much going for her as a single mother who raised a child with no support from anyone, but her daughter has turned out infinitely more principled than I am. I would've taken the money and convinced myself I had some kind of right to it, either morally or I bloody well-deserved it.

I should be ashamed of myself, but I'm not.

Sorry, not sorry, as Mia would say.

I have this ability to brush shame aside, to justify the cause of shame as an unwanted by-product of my imperfect personality.

I've done it to Mia a million times and to Finn more than that. I've made excuses, lied, even dodged having to speak to them on many occasions, and always told myself it's because I have stuff to do, I don't have time, I need to be somewhere else.

I make a pledge to myself that when I get back, I'll be honest with Mia, make a proper apology and a proper effort to value her friendship. If she wants it. She might not after what I've done. Finn too.

I miss them.

But then there's the issue of getting back. That 'thing' that stopped me going back today, and it definitely felt like a physical 'thing', is hopefully only a temporary obstacle.

I do not allow myself to conjure the image of someone using the third stall toilet as I tried to return, but it's a possibility, even the most likely, but I did wait long enough and…

Maybe that's a more pleasing prospect than another alternative that maybe the obstacle is something more permanent, like a brick wall physically, and permanently, blocking my return.

I can't think of that because then I'd be stuck here. Like it or not. For years. Effectively forever.

If so, I may as well go and find my eighteen-year-old mother and scream at her for sending me here in the first place.

Tina's watching The Krypton Factor with her mum. I'm tempted to join them just to check out the show, but, as they say, there's a time and a place.

It might be just me, but there's a change in the atmosphere.

"I'm gonna get some fresh air," I say.

They both look around and smile and say, "Right oh!" in unison, and I leave it at that.

I cross the balcony and prop my arms on the railings. It's a good place to get my thoughts together, but who am I kidding? I know where I'm going.

The Saunders Hall hosts the Bedworth Boxing Club on Monday nights. I've read about this on people's Facebook groups where they reminisce about their Bedworth childhoods, and I think I've read them all. I also know because it was mentioned in Harry's Cafe the other day. Not that I'm interested in the boxing, or boxers, or trainers. And I'm not tempted to indulge in a boxercise session either, although it would raise some eyebrows.

The doors are open and I enter through a corridor.

The main hall has been transformed into a gym for the night, complete with an actual boxing ring, raised four feet off the ground, in the centre of the room. In the ring are two pairs of boxers and trainers. Instructions are shouted and followed, punches are thrown and bodies duck and weave.

Scattered around the ring are the types of apparatus that I've seen before in boxing movies, big bags to punch and dance around and little bags that you punch faster but at a standstill. The only exercise that doesn't involve punching is skipping, which I reckon I could do although I'd be a bit rusty.

It takes about thirty seconds before the whole operation comes to a halt. After all, there is a girl with the sides of her head shaved standing in the doorway, and you don't see that every day. I doubt if they have ever seen a girl in here before on boxing night. I expect to be told that 'Tuesday night is ballet night, love' or something equally original. Or maybe boxing is serious business and joking is not the done thing. Who knows?

There's a lad about my age who looks like Mike Tyson's little brother, who's punching the big bag and winning, from what I can see at least, and I choose him as my target.

I make a bee-line for him projecting body-language that says 'don't bother to start punching again, I have business with you first'.

He gets the message and waits as I cross the room. He holds the bag with both arms outstretched like he's preventing the bag from swinging a crafty punch while his attention is elsewhere.

"I'm looking for Charlie," I tell him.

"Mr Randle?" he asks.

"Whatever."

He's not amused by my lack of respect for this social benefactor, but life is full of disappointments.

"Office," he tells me and nods to the far end of the hall.

"Thank you," I say, then nod at the big bag and say, "Carry on!"

The office smelt of Vicks Vapour rub. There was a wire basket full of boxing gloves in, a war-issue filing cabinet, two chairs and an empty desk.

He sat on his chair and I sat on mine, the desk sat between us.

He was smiling, a permanent smile that didn't leave.

He was wearing a polo-neck golf shirt, a pair of check trousers like those from the movie Caddyshack, and tan brown brogues. I would have found this golf-chic comical, but nothing about him is funny any longer.

I had no intention of putting all of my cards on the table, not yet anyway, but I had to do something to protect Tina and Barbara.

It was the least I could do.

Charlie sits across the table from me. He's made us both a cup of tea, but I'm not thirsty. He's lit a cigarette to go with his brew.

Of course he has.

He takes a drag and looks me in the eye. "I'm going to go out on a limb here and say that you've realised that we have met before. Albeit briefly."

"So?" I ask, as there's no point in lying.

Charlie smiles. "Oh my God, I do like your bravado," he grins, "I've seen some nerve in my time Hannah, but you are the top of the pile. You just sit and say, 'So?' as if I don't know what you're doing, where you from and why you're here."

"I don't," I say.

"You don't know why you're here?" he repeats, "You want me to believe that?"

"Not bothered either way, to be honest," I say.

"But you do know who I am and you do know what happened and you've been given enough information to fill in any blanks, so unless you're a complete idiot, which I don't think you are, you can figure most of this out and have a reasonable idea about just why you are here. Am I right?"

He has a point, but I know a bluff when I see one. "If you know so much," I tell him, "why are you asking?"

Charlie nods, "That's a good question, and my answer is; I'm asking because there's something about you that intrigues me and something I admire, so I'd hate for you to get the wrong idea about what actually happened."

"Oh, so what did happen, actually?" I say. I tell every muscle in my face to freeze and not to react in any way to what he just said or what he is about to say, but unfortunately, a frozen expression is still an expression.

His smile widens, he knows he's got me and I don't have a clue how he knows. I should never have walked into this conflict without knowing at least as much as him, but it's too late for that now. That split milk is everywhere now and pretty soon it's going to stink.

I have nothing to say though so I say precisely that. Nothing.

"It was horrible, what happened," he says as if he's just throwing out useless information.

I get up to leave, my cheeks burning red, my eyes searching for anything to look at except for this man in front of me.

"I have to go," I tell him.

"What did you say your surname was Hannah?"

"Walker," I say, but it's a bad lie, too similar to Wallace.

He smiles. He never stops smiling.

I try to take the lead. "I did some due diligence," I tell him, "I found out about Tina's mum, how ill she is, and I've decided we can't get involved right now, not me or Tina-" I know it sounds pathetic, but they're the best words I have right now.

Charlie laughs at me. "You don't want to be involved?" he says, "Whatever gave you the idea that you had a choice?"

"I'm just saying that we can't do anything at this time, maybe when things change-"

"Listen, sweetheart, I decide when you're involved," Charlie says getting to his feet. "I decide when anyone is or is not involved, not you. And I have decided that you, and Tina, and Tina's gibbering head's-in-the-shed mum are very much involved, so get used to it. And I'll tell you why-"

He leaves me hanging there, he takes to staring out the window at nothing.

The wait is hurting me more than him so I end it by saying, "Why is that?"

"Because," he says and turns back to me, he leans over the table, studying me from too close for my liking, "I want you to stay here. Do you understand? I don't want you to go back from where you came from. And if you do, I promise you that anything that Tina and her mum have been complaining about so far will seem like a holiday camp compared to what happens next. Am I making myself clear?"

I've just about had enough of this headmaster's lecture, I need to find out what he knows and take it from there.

"How would you know where I'm from?" I tell him. I give him a quick stare and then look down and shake my head to clear the image from my mind.

"I know you ain't from Lowestoft," he says, more anger in his voice now than in his previous tone.

I say, "So where am I from?"

Charlie says "You're from the same place as Laura."

I try not to react to the mention of my mother.

"Now ask me how I know about Laura?" he says leaning so close I can smell the stale smoke on his breath.

"In fact," he says, "I'll give you this one for free, and I don't even need to see the look on your spotty little face, so you keep looking at the table like the stroppy little brat that you are, but the reason I know about Laura, and about you and where you're from, is that for a while we were all great mates; me, Jimmy and Laura. We did everything together."

I can't stop myself from reacting at the mention of Jimmy, I pull my hands from the table and bury them in my lap.

Game over, he knows everything.

He laughs at me again. "Jimmy said you'd be like this. 'Headstrong bitch, just like her mother' he said, to quote him directly."

"Whatever," I say, not very convincing.

"Well, yeah, whatever," he sighs, "Why would you give a shit about Jimmy? But it's not that easy for me, I feel responsible for what happened to him if I'm honest and that's why I tried to build bridges over the years with regular visits and so forth. We're quite close these days believe it or not. I'm a big believer in the power of redemption, it's a wonderful thing, Hannah, it really is."

I sit back and take a long breath, holding my head up, but avoid eye-contact.

"And so this is your task, Hannah," he says, drawing to a conclusion. He sits back in his chair and makes a precise tap of the cigarette to the wall of the glass ashtray. "I need you to tell Laura that Jimmy wants to see her and put his mind to rest about where she's been for the last fifteen years, OK?"

I nod, then say, "And what do I get?"

Charlie laughs. "What do you get?"

"Yes," I say, "I'll bring Laura to speak to Jimmy, and what do I get?"

He sits back in his chair. "What do you want?"

"I want Tina and Barbara to be left alone," I say.

"Is that all? Really?"

"You have to promise," I tell him.

"I promise," he smiles, "In fact, consider it an act of good faith."

"Good faith?" I say.

He nods, "Good faith, between us. Me and you."

I'm an introvert. Most people think that means I don't like to socialise and keep my thoughts to myself, but that's not really it.

The truer condition of an introvert is that at the end of a busy day, which would probably include lots of extrovert-behaviour, an extroverted person would seek to recharge their batteries by seeking the company and socialising with others. An introverted person, however, would choose to be alone, reading, watching TV, or working on a solo project.

And that's me. I can do extrovert when necessary, but given a choice, I prefer introversion and to be alone.

And that's what I need tonight. 'Me Time'. Time to think. Time to recharge. And I'm fairly sure that Tina needs it too.

When I got back from the boxing club, it was 9 o'clock. I stuck my head past the living room door and said I was going to have an early night.

Tina and Barbara both bid me goodnight.

I washed and lay on the bed, waiting, thinking, going over what I knew and what I should do.

But mostly I was waiting. Waiting for a distraction for the mess I have created. Waiting for 10 o'clock.

I'm sharing my pillow with Barbara's kitchen radio tuned to 275m AM Radio One and someone is reading the news, but fascinating as that is, it's not the reason I'm so excited I could stretch every limb to its absolute limit.

Me and tens of thousands of others, are here for The John Peel Show, two hours of inspired new music and sardonic commentary from the Godfather of indie music, good indie music. Sir John Peel. And I can absolutely guarantee that not one of the thousands listening in, wherever they may be, is as excited and grateful and humbled as me. The nation takes this nightly oasis of life-changing enlightenment for granted, but not me. This is my first show and may be my last, but already my soul is cleaned and my heart is stronger. This is another of the greatest moments in my entire life, which makes it three for this week. Peely opens with, "Well, I'm back and I'm proud…at least I'm better and looking rather lovely here in the subdued lighting of the studio."

I cannot believe that John Peel is talking to me, directly to me, live, on the radio.

He thanks Paul Gambaccini for 'looking after the show last week', apparently he was indisposed.

The first songs he plays are The Dead Kennedys, 'Short Songs' and 'Straight A's'. I wonder what the listeners will make of a song of twenty seconds in length, but the clue is in the title. Next up are Pauline Murray and the Invisible Girls, Only Ones and Hitmen, all of which would probably have been lost to history, in fact never found at all, if it weren't for Mr Peel.

I listen to the whole show.

It is sheer brilliance.

I can die happy.

11:30am
Wednesday
12th February
2020

CHAPTER 32

"I knew it was him when I saw it on the news," Jimmy said, looking solemnly into his lap. There was sadness, but no mourning.

Laura sat in the armchair beside his. She didn't speak. She tried to clear her throat but managed only a dry croak. They were alone in Jimmy's room, neither one of them wanted to be with other people, never mind socialising.

They had lost their daughter. They didn't know when she would be able to return.

Jimmy slowly raised his head and reached out with a trembling hand. "He stopped you going back?"

Laura nodded and took his hand. "Yes."

"You were there when he did it?"

She nodded again. "He knew. He was waiting for me."

Jimmy squeezed her hand, from anguish as much as affection or love.

The very thought of Charlie's suicide triggers a cascade of memories that she is unable to prevent.

She left the pub instantly. People in the bar seemed stunned, unsure of what they had just heard. Laura puts a hand to her mouth, as if about to sneeze, but the hand stays there covering the bottom half of her face. The top half was still covered by her oversized sunglasses. Once again she left the scene of Charlie's crime, spattered with blood caused by a bullet fired from his gun. Fired by him. She knew there'd be CCTV footage this time, but she hopes her face was covered enough. It is what it is.

She had raced to her car, driven to a farm lane and splattered both number plates with mud. She had then driven to a stand-alone mobile caravan near Offenham in the

Vale of Evesham. She burnt all her clothes in the fire pit and threw the ashes into the river Avon.

She stayed there for two days, checking the news.

The suicide of a 'ninety-year old retired gangster' re was no mention of a woman leaving the scene, but that might mean that the police are not releasing that piece of information.

Only then did she think, she thought it would be safe to leave the caravan.

Laura edged to the front of her seat, her eyes finding his and both of them tearing up."Hannah is still there," she said. "I don't know if she's OK or-"

"She'll be fine," Jimmy whispered. "She's a smart kid, and he knew nothing back then."

"He knew I was going back," Laura said, then firmly pushed her lips together.

Jimmy shook his head.

"I'm sorry," she said.

"What now?" Jimmy asked.

"Once the police leave and the pub reopens, I'll go back," Laura says.

"You have to be careful," Jimmy insists, "You can't get caught."

"But I can't not go," Laura tells him, "Hannah needs me."

Jimmy nodded.

Someone coughed and gasped for air in the corridor. Laura watched as two ambulance staff pushed a patient past on a gurney.

"Oh dear," Laura said. "That sounds serious."

"They've been arriving every day," Jimmy commented.

"Arriving?" Laura frowned. "Don't you mean leaving?"

"No, they're being brought here to make room in the hospital for people with that COVID-19, apparently."

"Oh, my God."

5:31pm
Tuesday
1st July
1980

CHAPTER 33

I'm not gonna lie, but I'm kinda disappointed that although 1980 fish and chips are served in newspaper, there is a sheet of grease-proof paper between the food and printed pages. I'm also still kinda thrilled and it's another item ticked off the bucket list.

Tina and me both have cod and chips and a can of Panda cola, each of us has enough food to feed an army for a week and it comes to £1.25. Also wood-chip sporks are neither offered nor requested. Sweet!

We grab a bench in the precinct and tuck in.

Tina has been fine with me all day, perfectly fine. Too perfect. Neither of us have mentioned my note or the money I had to pick up from the living room floor. But it needs to be talked about.

"We have a saying where I'm from," I say, looking into the remains of my battered cod. I didn't look up to gauge Tina's reaction, I went on, "It's 'Nobody mentions the elephant in the room'. I've no idea where it came from but everyone knows what it means."

"The thing that no one talks about," Tina says, "but everyone can see."

"Yes."

"The elephant in the room," she recited, as if to commit to memory.

"I'm sorry about yesterday," I say as we eat, "I was supposed to go, but in the end, I couldn't."

"It's OK," Tina says like it's no big deal when it's a very big deal.

"No, it's not," I say, "I'm sorry, but I promise you I was going to come back. Honestly."

Tina nudges her shoulder to mine and offers her own apologetic smile. "I'm sorry too," she says. "I shouldn't have reacted that way."

"It wasn't your fault-"

"It's OK," Tina says, cutting across me. "Let's just forget about it," she goes on, "I knew you'd come back, that's all that matters."

I nod. No words. I'm not going to mention the money. Not now. I *was* going to come back, and that is all that matters.

"I bet you have good chippys in Lowestoft being close to the sea?" Tina says.

I nod and blow out the steam from my hot fish a little longer than I need to. "You can't beat fresh fish," I say, "although this Bedworth Cod isn't bad either."

"I needed more salt," she sighs, although the shop lets customers add their own salt and vinegar and I distinctly remember Tina's chips looking like the Dead Sea if you drained all the water away.

"He doesn't believe you," Tina says looking into her chip wrapper on her lap. "Charlie."

"He doesn't believe what?"

"That you're from Lowestoft."

"I know," I sigh. What can I say? I can't lie to Tina, but I can't tell her the truth either. "He must have a suspicious nature."

"And you don't have an accent," Tina adds, "which I thought you would. I thought you'd speak like my aunt Edie."

I don't comment, I want to change the subject, but I know that it's too early.

It dawns on me that if Tina contacts our relatives in Lowestoft, that would not be good for me. They could do some digging and find that Laura Wallace is either missing or has in fact returned safe and sound. Neither of those scenarios would be good for me.

I need to keep a lid on things for at least another week, maybe two.

"We moved around a lot," I say, "I got bullied for my Norfolk accent enough times to get rid of it and never tried to bring it back."

Tina half-smiled, "I can't imagine you being bullied."

"I haven't always been this brutal shit-kicker you see before you!"

Her genuine laugh returns, "What's a shit-kicker."

"Someone who kicks shit," I say, and gesture to myself as an obvious example.

"You're insane," she smirks. "How did you get so…crazy."

"I don't know," I say, "It just happened one day."

She calms her smile and asks me again, "It just looks like since I spoke to Charlie you've been acting like something is wrong."

I don't answer, I look at my chips.

Tina goes on, "Are you jealous or something?"

"Jealous?" I say. It was an accusation I was not expecting. "Of you?"

"Well-"

I shake my head and look at her. "I'm not jealous of you," I tell her, "I mean, I am extremely jealous of your gorgeous good looks and personality! But I am not jealous of you working for Charlie."

She laughs, which is good.

I decide to go on, "But I don't like him, and I don't trust him. There's something about him that makes me think you might regret working for him."

She stops laughing and a frown appears. "I don't have to like him or trust him, but I need to earn money Hannah unless you've got any better ideas." For a moment I think she is going to mention the cash, but she doesn't, although it's there, between the lines' as they say.

"There must be another way to earn-"

"Like what?" she says. "I don't know what it's like where you're from but here there's nothing. And if I get given a chance, then I'm taking it whether you don't like the person I'm working for or not."

"I'm sorry, I shouldn't have said anything."

"And he's not like a monster," she goes on, "He's helped a lot of people around here over the years. People look up to him and respect him for that."

My heart sinks, I never envisioned this as being part of the plan, having to lie to someone that I've grown so close to so quickly.

This is what people like Charlie do, they have a way of poking into things and turning everyone against each other with their interfering and shit-stirring.

"I don't blame him for not believing me," I tell Tina. "I lied to him so he probably figured it out."

"You lied to him?"

"Yeah," I say, munching some fish. "When he asked me how I got here, I thought, 'Why does he want to know that?' so I said, 'On the train', which was a lie, but why should I tell him anything? People like him think they can just click their fingers and everyone has to kiss their arse, well not me."

Tina is staring at me.

I shrug.

Eventually, Tina nods her head and purses her lips. "He made things really shitty for mum and me," she says, her voice a whisper.

"I know," I say, "that won't happen again, I promise you that."

Tina nods her head again, but this time with far less conviction.

She seems to have thawed a little.

And with that, her enthusiasm for the market stall multiplied.

"I need it to work," she says as we headed home through the concrete corridors of the HyperMarket car park.

"We will make it work," I say.

"For my mum," she says, to herself more than to me.

"Tina," I say, "I swear we will make it work. We'll do whatever it takes to get it up and running and then nothing will stop us. We simply cannot fail by that point."

Tina nods.

"Just don't do anything stupid," Tina says to me, but there's a humour to her voice that was missing before.

"I won't," I answer, "and I promise to tell you, whatever I do."

We emerge opposite the flat, but Tina doesn't cross with me.

"I need to go see Terry," she says.

"OK," I shout but don't look back as a Ford Escort Mexico is baring down on me from one side and a white Transit van from the other and I have to get to the other side.

When I turn back, Tina is gone.

CHAPTER 34

"The fair's in town," Tina says as she walks into the flat.

Me and Barbara are watching Ask Aspel on TV.

"Oh, I do love the fair," Tina's mum says.

"Is it in the park?" I ask. The fair visits two or three times a year and is always been in the park.

"In the park?" Tina asks. "No, it's on the fairground."

"Oh," I say. This balance between engaging in conversations and saying the wrong thing is a thin line to tread.

"Do you remember when you won that goldfish Tina?" her mother asks.

"Yes, mum."

So what better way is there to spend a Tuesday night than at the fair?

And to my amazement, there is indeed a fairground, a football pitch size area of wasteland that's sole purpose is to host the fair two or three times a year. At some point in the 2000s, it will be re-assigned as a housing estate, as is every other piece of ground near town (except the Miners Welfare Park).

We wander across town, Tina, me and her mum, and immediately the streets are filling with the masses heading to our shared destination. Excited kids pull their parents along the pavement and older boys wrap an arm around their girlfriends in their best stuff.

It's a beautiful night, and beneath the clear blue sky, despite it being 7 o'clock and still broad daylight, the neon and fairy lights of the fair are enticing. Every colour of the imagination is equally represented, as is every sound and smell.

Tina hooks her arm on my elbow as we cross the road and make our way along the well-worn path from the pavement.

"Boogie's doing his mobile disco," she says and points to a flat-bed truck parked on the edge of the grounds.

"Really?" I ask and as I peer over I see my new friend at the decks between two stacks of speakers. Needless to say, The Specials are booming out, Rat Race. Behind him, a huge white sheet of hardboard is emblazoned with the words 'The Full-Tilt Boogie Mobile Sound System'.

"We'll have to say hello later," Tina tells me.

The prevalent aromas are fried onions and candy floss. Neither are pleasant and together they are borderline repulsive, which makes it hard to understand why my mouth is watering and my stomach demanding room-service.

I have serious Health and Safety concerns about both the food and the preparation method, but I also know that these concerns will be overpowered by my burger-desire. It's pointless to fight it, acceptance is the path of least resistance.

Everyone is here. Everyone that I've met anyway. All of the kids from the party at Boogies, Saturday morning in Harry's Bakery, all of Tina's neighbours and, no doubt, everyone she went to school with, everyone she ever worked with and 'anyone else who knows me'.

It's easier to say, everyone is at the fair.

And everyone says 'Hi' to Tina, which means everyone says 'Hi' to me.

Tina keeps her mum close, but not shackled to her. She seems fine wandering between the rides and games and the food stalls, staying within eye-sight, but not within easy reach.

Those no bumper cars, but there is a Waltzer, Up 'n' Over Cage, Punch Bag Machine, Helter Skelter, Ghost Train (which was awful), Tea Cups and more than one Merry-Go-Round (one with exquisitely painted horses). As if that wasn't enough fun for one night there was a Hook-a-

Duck, Rifle Shoot, a Darts game, bouncing a ping-pong ball into goldfish bowls thing and variations on those themes.

In addition to Burgers and candy Floss were hot dogs, chips, battered sausages, scallops, cans of Fanta or Vimto or Irn Bru, as well as tea or coffee in plastic cups.

We went on every ride and every stall and tried every beverage and item of food. We laughed and screamed and shouted at people that we knew and they did the same to us, but there was no time to talk, no room for idle gossip and no chance of spending any quiet time with a friend or acquaintance.

It was full-on fun, with a bit of argy-bargy. You know what boys are like. In that competitive arena their natural-apeman comes out and there's much chest-beating and swinging from trees and loud aggressive wailing, all to determine that precise lineage from alpha male down to barely male in order of capable savagery. I imagine that to onlookers this naked-ape re-enactment would be more entertaining than all of the rides combined.

Eventually, I had to accept that my stamina was no match for theirs and I decide to take a breather. Call it a generation gap if you like or whatever, but I slipped away and sat on the wall behind a toffee apple vendor. That sickly syrup was a delightful smell, but I knew better than to partake.

I didn't notice the guy until he somehow appeared in front of me and actually made me jump.

"Hey," he says, smiling.

I didn't answer his greeting. He wasn't one of Tina's enormous circle of friends I had been introduced to or had pointed out to me over the last few days.

"I'm Ricky," he says.

This time I do look at him, but still no comment.

The first thing I notice is he's older than us by a few years and he isn't a mod or a greebo or a rude boy or anything. He's a normal person, in a plain t-shirt, pin-striped faded jeans and Pumas Ticino.

His dark hair is regulation length for an office junior or shop assistant and his eyebrows are thick and dense they look black. He is a good-looking guy, even though his forehead is a wide, curved expanse of pale pink skin, but his nose and chin are kind of pointy, and not enough to detract from his overall aesthetic which is pleasing.

When he smiles his 'looks' are accentuated and that kind of stays in the memory for a while after he's stopped smiling.

He is smiling as he says to me, "Cat got your tongue?"

"What cat?" I say, paying particular attention to the coconut-shy to his right, my left.

He purses his smile a little and says, "Yeah, it's a turn of phrase."

"I know," I say and give him a three-count before looking up at him and asking, "Can I help you?"

He ponders the question, then says, "No."

I involuntarily raise an eyebrow and immediately regret it. I'll never make a poker player with 'tells' like that. "Well, unless you're going to propose marriage, you're taking up the space of someone who might, so-" I motion for him to move aside.

He smiles, again, and turns to scan the lack of crowd behind him. "When the queue starts to form I'll step aside."

"Thanks, Ricky," I say.

"Oh, you remembered my name!" he beams.

"Should I know you?" I ask.

"No," he says and sits beside me on the wall. We both people-watch for a few moments, and then he adds, "I'm Jimmy's nephew."

I freeze. This I was not expecting.

I take a slow breath, then say, "Oh really! You're Jimmy's relative! And who's Jimmy?"

"Do you want to speak to him?" he says, ignoring my lines.

I go back into silent mode. Do I acknowledge this person's assertion that I do in fact know who Jimmy is, although I haven't seen him in a long time (whichever way you look at it).

I look straight at him and say, "Not really, I want a lot of things, but that's not one of 'em."

"I can't say I blame you," he says, "under the circumstances."

"You don't know anything about my circumstances," I tell him.

He nods to concede the point, then says, "But then again, circumstances change, and people change too."

"Very philosophical."

"Anyway," he says, "I don't want to take up your time, I just wanted to introduce myself and let you know that if there's anything I do to help at any time, I'd be pleased to do all I can."

Who does this guy think he is?

"Yeah," I tell him, "that's great, thanks. It was a pleasure to meet you. Have a great night."

"It's probably best if you don't tell anyone that we spoke yeah?"

"Don't worry, once you're gone I'll forget you instantly," I tell him.

"See the crossroads at the entrance to the fair?" he says "If you go straight across, our is the last house on the right."

"I'm pleased for ya," I sigh.

"If you wanna ask anything, you know where to find us."

"What would I ask him? What's it like to be a killer?"

"All I'm saying is we can make it so you can ask him whatever you like. He's allowed phone calls, so you wouldn't have to visit-"

I do actually laugh at this suggestion.

Ricky senses our chat is coming to a conclusion and asks, "So what do I tell him?"

I shake my head, "I'm not interested in talking to a murderer."

"Maybe you won't be, " he says.

"I look at him and for a second I'm convinced he's not lying, but back, in reality, this guy only knows what he's been told same as me.

He gets to his feet and puts his hands in his jeans pocket. "If you change your mind," he says and nods to the crossroads. "I'm sorry for bothering you," he adds and walks away.

I want to tell him it's no bother, but it is. An invitation to talk to a murderer is always a bother in my opinion.

11:22pm
Wednesday
2nd July
1980

CHAPTER 35

I spent most of the morning going through 'market stuff' with Tina. I've tasked her with writing a list of clothes that will be most in demand.

I don't know if Tina is happier that the market stall is starting up again, or if Barbara is getting involved in the outside world again.

Plus, Tina herself is buzzing with the thrill of 'doing business' and, hopefully, it's beginning to look better than her 'waitressing' job for Charlie.

Me and Tina nip into town to talk business and take a break. We stop at Harry's for a tea and it was cool that it was just us and we just talked about stuff. Pretty soon though, all of our conversations came back to the market stall: What else could we sell? How could we advertise? How could we expand operations?

So it was a disappointment when we came out of Harry's cafe and she said she wanted to go to The Corner Pin.

I didn't ask why, instead, I cried off, saying I was going to go back to the flat and chill. Except I stopped myself from using the word 'chill' and went with 'relax'.

We parted in the precinct.

Barbara was smoking in the kitchen when I got back. She looks up and smiles, "Afternoon, love."

"Hi Barbara," I say, "How are you?"

"Have you been on the stall?" she asks.

"No," I say, "we should be starting up soon though-"

Barbara does get confused about things. Or seems to, it's hard to say. At first, I thought she was in some way pranking me, or somehow amusing herself by pretending she was a teenager again. Like now.

"I can't do next Saturday by the way," she says, "I've got a date with Roy."

"What do you mean 'next Saturday'?" I ask. I thought we were talking about the market, now she's saying she has a date with someone called Roy. "Who's Roy?"

"My shift on the market," she says with a minor eye-roll, "You said you'd cover for me, don't pretend you forgot."

"Oh, yes, I remember." I nod. This does not feel like a joke any more. I take a seat at the table.

Barbara has obviously confused me with someone else, but she also seems confused about the market stall.

But this doesn't seem like a joke. She's serious, at least in her own mind.

I sit opposite her at the table.

I'm not an expert in mental health issues, I just have some experience with my mother, but she was an individual case and one I was very close to.

"Ciggie?" she asks and offers me her packet.

"No thanks," I say.

"When did you give up?" she asks, "Bloody goody two shoes now are ya?"

"How long have you known me, Barbara?" I ask.

Barbara pulls a face further implying that I'm losing it, but she plays along anyway. "Since you started on the stall," she says, "what's that? About three years."

I nod that I agree as Barbara takes a drag on her cigarette.

"Why do you ask?" she says.

"I was just thinking," I say.

"Well you know what thinking does," she tells me and smiles.

Alzheimer's, I think to myself.

It would explain why Barbara doesn't go out much.

I think back to our previous conversations, all the times she seemed confused or was winding me up. On the face of it, she seemed perfectly healthy. And perfectly happy.

Do people even know what Alzheimer's is in 1980?

I'd done my share of research and I knew all about music, movies, books, comics, TV shows, and all kinds of pop culture, and as part of that my research spilt over into news stories, politics, social issues, that kind of thing, but the provisions for mental health within the NHS did not appear on my radar.

And I have seen some things that indicate that there is no provision for it whatsoever unless a person is acting violently towards others.

Charlie blacklisted Barbara, apparently.

And now I know why: Charlie knows who I am, and he's inserted himself into my life by getting to Tina and Barbara.

I need to find out more, and the only way to do that is to talk to Barbara.

It's a massive gamble, I'd be risking my friendship with Tina again, but I'm running out of options.

"Hey," I say, leaning across the table, "I was talking to Charlie yesterday."

She nods, but doesn't say anything.

So she knows him. She remembers him.

"He's nice isn't he," I say, "but I'm not sure I trust him."

Barbara nods and eyes me closely through tendrils of cigarette smoke. "You can't ever trust him," she waves me to lean in closer. I lean across the table, my hands clasped in front of me. Barbara whispers, "There are some who say he got away with murder."

"Murder?" I say and in doing so, and without much thought, I had willingly and knowingly abused this kind woman's serious, and undiagnosed, mental health condition. And the reason I did, and if I'm honest I'd do it again, because I knew exactly what she was going to say, not by joining the dots or working with some subliminal clues that I had solved with my own genius, but by pure intuition, if such a thing were possible.

Barbara gave me a serious look and I held her gaze with subservient concern.

"I know someone who was there, outside the room, when it happened," she says, assuming, correctly so, that I know exactly the thing that 'happened'. "And she heard Jimmy say that he would take the blame for it."

How did I know this? I have no idea, but from the moment we moved across the table I knew, word for word, exactly what Barbara was going to say.

And I wanted to say, 'Who was it? Who was there?' but again I didn't need to.

I knew that too.

"It was him," Barbara says, "Charlie shot the policeman and made his brother confess."

CHAPTER 36

Me and Barbara are still at the kitchen table when Tina gets back.

"What you doin' in here? Is the tele broke or what?" she asks, looking at us like we're drinking tea with an alien or something.

"We're just chatting," Barbara tells her daughter, "life doesn't always revolve around the goggle-box."

"It's been fun," I say.

Tina takes off her coat, throws it on the hanger, pulls up a chair and says, "Oh yeah, well don't let me stop you gossiping, carry on."

I smile at Barbara who was telling me about how she tried to see the Beatles at the Nuneaton Co-op Hall 'two years ago' but she couldn't get in. She did see The Rolling Stones there, although, 'they were shit' in her esteemed opinion.

My heart-rate increases as I sit in smiling silence. I'm waiting to see if Barbara will pick up where she left off and if Tina will, whether she wants to or not, see that her mother is not well mentally. I'm not even sure that Tina knows that her mother has Alzheimer's, but obviously she must have experienced her episodes for herself, more than once. Unless it's considered acceptable not knowing what year it is.

Barbara, however, has tired of chatting. "Cup of tea, Tina?" she says and gets up from the chair.

"Love one thanks, mum," Tina says.

"I'll make it," I say, "now I've mastered the kettle there should be no stopping me."

"Go on then," Barbara says, retaking her seat. "I won't fight you over it."

"Cheers Hannah," Tina says. "Milk and one, please."

"Milk and one what?" Barbara asks her.

"Milk and one sugar," she tells her. "What did you think it was?"

"Why didn't you say 'sugar' then?" Barbara scolds her daughter.

Mother and daughter do seem very happy together, despite recent hardships and problems, but if this is denial then it's painful to watch. I know I can't interfere, at least, not in front of Barbara. On the other hand, if this is not ignorance then Tina has a right to know. That knowledge won't come without resentment and accusations for the messenger and I can't do that to either of them.

I also don't know much about how mental health patients are treated medically, if they are treated at all, or how they are treated socially, which I fear would involve dismissal leading to ridicule and worse.

I put the kettle on the hob and grab the 'Land of the Giants' matchbox. I strike a match and apply it to the hob whilst turning on the gas and, if I do say it myself, the kettle is now 'on' and done so with some considerable skill. I empty the teapot, swill it out and add three tea bags.

Tina catches my eye.

"I spoke to him today," she nods.

I get that she means Charlie and this is between us and not her mother. So I nod back. I understand.

"He says that if we get things running as they were, or better. Then everything will be fine, we won't be black-listed any more."

"That's good of him," I say, regretting it straight away, but my mind conjures images of him staring down from the business end of a gun and I can't shake it. I can feel this run-away train gaining momentum as it rolls faster and faster to a disaster I can't stop, no matter how hard I try.

I actually think to myself, 'if I could turn back the clock-'

Which is kind of ironic.

"We don't have to like it," she tells me. "We just have to do what we said we're going to do."

"What are you two going on about?" Barbara asks.

"Nothing, mum," Tina tells her, "just girls' stuff."

"I was thinking we should sell school uniforms," I say. "When does the term start? August is it?"

"I thought it was September?" Tina says, then adds, "Maybe not. I didn't pay much attention when I was there. And even less now I've left."

"Either way," I say, "We've got a few weeks to get some stock in."

"Yes," Tina says, "And it's a good idea. Even the trampy kids need school clothes."

Barbara tells us she's decided not to go to Coventry market today, which we are pleased to hear, and she goes on to regale us with tales from the famous indoor round market in our neighbouring city.

I listen intently as I finish the tea, but Barbara tells her stories in a timeless fashion where they could've occurred last week or forty years ago.

Is it possible she could've subconsciously developed a skill of conversing without giving any specifics about the time or the era?

When I pass Barbara her tea, she has a lit cigarette in her hand and when some ash falls into the cup, she says 'Oops' and retrieves it between pinched fingertips.

"Thanks love," she says, "Lovely cup of tea, that is."

"You haven't tasted it yet," I smile.

"I can tell by looking at it," she assures me.

The three of us sip our tea in silence for a few moments.

I am more than a bit miffed that Tina has spoken to Charlie without telling me, especially as she said she was going to see Terry. Was that a lie or did things just pan out the way they did?

I knew that I shouldn't talk to Charlie without her, not the other way around, and it is her stall after all.

Plus, I don't know how much longer I'll be here.

8:53am
Thursday
3rd July
1980

CHAPTER 37

The next morning, I make Tina some breakfast, boiled eggs and toast. She seems pleased when she wanders into the kitchen, wiping her eyes and smiling through a yawn.

Barbara is still asleep. Yesterday she didn't emerge from her room until gone ten. It's eight-thirty now. So I hoped we had time to talk.

"I need to talk to someone about Charlie and the only person I can talk to is you," I tell Tina, "And I'm sorry about that, but that's how it is."

"No," Tina says, "You do not have to talk about him. You don't even understand what's happening."

"I know that someone died," I say.

"So what!" Tina shouts.

I hope Tina's raised voice doesn't wake Barbara.

Once inside the door, she glances out the window and then stares back at me. "Someone died, someone killed him," she hisses at me, "the person that did it is in jail, and none of it matters any more."

I shake my head, "How-"

"No, Hannah," Tina says, "It doesn't matter what happened then. All that matters is what happens now. All that matters to me is that I can look after my mum because she can't look after herself. And that means I have to work with Charlie."

I don't say anything, even though I've got plenty to say.

"So thanks for helping out, thanks for making me believe in myself again," Tina says, releasing her grip on my jacket but keeping her eyes fixed on mine. "But this ain't Scooby Doo, we ain't gotta stick our noses into a murder that happened years ago. So forget it, Hannah. Either forget it or leave."

"Tina," I say, "Don't you think it's a coincidence that Charlie gives you your job back just days after I arrived?"

"What?"

"He's doing it to get to me," I say. "He knows me-"

"He doesn't know you!" she snaps. "How could he?"

I can't make myself say the words, and I can't think of a way to continue my lie. So I say nothing.

"Do you know what he did to my mum?" Tina says, "He made our life a misery, we had no money and people wouldn't even talk to us. We were cut off, completely cut off. And I can't allow that to happen again. So I'm going to work for Charlie and nothing is going to get in my way. Not even you."

"Some people," I say, "believe that he killed a policeman. Doesn't that mean anything."

Tina breaks our eye contact and looks away. I can see that she is fighting the impulse to lose it completely.

"Who told you?" she says, looking out of the window.

CHAPTER 38

"Who told you?" Tina demands again. "They need to know that's gonna bring them some trouble."

"I can't tell you that, Tina," I say.

"Tell me!" she demands.

I sigh, a long breath that feels like life leaving my body.

I say, "Please, don't do this."

"Tell me," she says again.

I can't allow her to think that I'm protecting anybody more important to me than her, but I know it's going to be extremely painful to rip the band-aid off.

"OK, look, I'll tell you what happened," I say. "But don't-"

"Just tell me!" Tina says again, her frustration approaching boiling point.

"When I was drinking tea with your mum," I begin.

Tina's eyes lock onto mine as they narrow into slits of hatred and fear. "No!" she says.

"Tina, she's ill. She needs help. She got confused about who I was and she went back to when she was younger."

"How could you do that to her?" Tina almost spits each word into my face.

"I didn't do anything to her-"

"You must've led her on. She would *never* talk about that," she insists. "She wouldn't just come out and say it, not after everything that happened to her."

"Tina, at that time, she didn't even remember what's happened to her," I say, "she went back to that time, in her head."

"Do you know what he'll do if he finds out that my mum said anything? It'll be a million times worse than before. You can't even imagine how bad it will be for us."

"Tina, listen to me," I plead, "your mother is mentally ill-"

"Mentally ill?" she growls at me, "What does that even mean? She gets confused, that's all. Do you think Charlie is going to forgive her because she's ill? Do you think that makes it OK? You made her tell you! You tricked her. You took advantage of her because she's-"

"She doesn't need your help! What she doesn't need is you telling people she accused Charlie of murder. And you don't seem to understand that."

"So why don't we do something to stop him?" I say.

Tina closes her eyes and pushes her plate away.

"Why are you doing this to me?" she says, "I helped you, I let you into our home. Now you're trying to destroy us?"

Again, I don't have an answer.

"I'm sorry," I say, "Really, I am. We were talking and she said it. I couldn't 'unhear' it. And I swear on my mother's life I have not and would not tell a living soul about any of this."

"I hope you mean that," Tina says to me.

"I do," I say.

I take a step back.

As she turns to the stairs and says, "We're mates, Hannah, but you need to know, if you do say anything, so help me God, you will regret it."

I let her go. I don't follow. Something tells me I'm not welcome right now.

9:30am
Thursday
13th February
2020

CHAPTER 39

Jimmy looked pale as if his tears has washed the remaining pigment from his face. Laura's heart broke again and her guilt raised its head for the hundredth time that day. His breath was short and he had started coughing when he tried to speak.

They were in his room, it was cold, but it didn't seem to matter.

It reminded Laura of their room above The Corner Pin, back in '68. Jimmy in a white vest stretched cross his chest, his chiseled shoulders and biceps bursting with strength.

They'd sat at a kitchen table and he'd explained how the cop, Unsworth, was blackmailing Charlie.

Jimmy had taken a deep breath, then said, "Laura, *we* have the money."

She had turned him down flat. Then she asked him, again, to leave here and come back, with her.

"Charlie's going crazy, he's close to cracking," he'd said, "if *we* don't do something, I don't know he'll do."

"We'd be giving blood money to a crooked cop," she told him.

"It's not blood money," Jimmy said.

"It will be," she said. "Trust me."

Jimmy exhaled and conceded, "You're right, we can't do it."

"If Charlie goes down, will he really take you with him?" she asked.

Jimmy nodded.

"Why don't we just leave?" Laura pleaded with him. "Nobody would ever-"

"I can't just leave him," he said. "He's still my brother."

They had talked into the night and came to an agreement. Laura would get the money, Jimmy would give it to Charlie, then they'd walk away and he, Laura and Hannah would leave for good.

That had been the plan at least.

The outcome of that day, had been quite different. Laura had got away with Hannah, Jimmy went to prison.

Now they were together again, but separated by forty years.

Laura wiped phlegm from his lips and waited for him to catch his breath.

Jimmy raised a hand and placed it on her arm as he said, "So you're going back?"

Laura nods and composes herself, determined that her own tears wouldn't show.

"I'm going to bring Hannah back," she says. "I won't come back without her."

Jimmy nods, his shoulders moving in unison with his head as if his neck were immobile.

"What about him?" he says, and a coughing fit threatens to overwhelm him again, but he recovers this time.

Laura shakes her head. "That will have to be for another time," she tells him, "I'm sorry Jimmy. You know I wanted to do this to give you the life you deserved, but you were right, I should never have involved Hannah in any of it."

Jimmy nods again and then ponders the scenario.

"You just bring her back," he says.

"I will."

"Promise me," he whispers.

Laura nods. "I promise."

Jimmy smiles but says nothing. He lifts his hand from hers and his body seems to deflate as he sank into his chair. His eyes close to a narrow slit.

"I love you," Laura tells him, but she knows he hasn't heard her.

Jimmy is sleeping.

Laura gets to her feet and lets the tears flow.

"We are the decisions we made," she told her sleeping lover. It was something that he had to told her many times since they had met. It was inherited wisdom, he told her, picked up from some 1930s matinee movie.

And it was never more true than in Jimmy's case.

Then again, she wondered if the future were nothing but fate, and decisions were a illusion. As a theory it made it easier to come to team with with the series of decisions that lead to the separation.

Whenever she relived the events of that day, it's the decisions they made that haunted her the most.

The while thing was vividly etched in her memory.

She climbed the stairs of the Bedworth Liberal Club having left Hannah in the toy shop next door. 'I'll only be a few minutes', she had promised her daughter.

"To fetch uncle Jimmy?" Hannah had asked.

Laura didn't where Hannah had got 'uncle Jimmy' from. She'd never actually told her daughter that Jimmy was her father. She promised herself that as soon as this was over and all three of them were all safely away from here, they would tell her everything.

Jimmy was waiting at the top of the stairs.

She gave him the envelope and said, "Be quick. Let's go."

He took it, then hesitated.

"Jimmy!" she said.

"Just a few minutes," he says, "I need to make sure it's OK."

"Jimmy, we agreed this, you give him the money and we leave. Now"

"Just a few minutes," Jimmy said again. "I promise."

The door flew open. Charlie, dressed in a dark blue suit with a tie skewed to one side, beamed a demonic smile to Laura. "You won't regret this," he told her, talking too loud and shifting his feet.

She hated him so much. And not for the first time, Laura was astonished that two brothers could be so totally different in every conceivable way.

"Make sure I don't," Laura said to the both of them.

As she left, she passed Unsworth on the stairs.

She waited in the stairwell, praying that it would be over in 'just a few minutes' and that Jimmy would appear on the stairs.

Instead, she heard voices, raised voices.

She ran back up the stairs.

She burst through the door.

And she heard the two shots.

Unsworth was dead.

She looked at Charlie, who, for some reason, was pointing the gun at her.

Jimmy was the first to speak, "Charlie, put it down now."

Charlie didn't answer. He was staring at Laura.

"Charlie," Jimmy said again, "put it down."

"She saw it Jimmy," Charlie said.

Laura stopped breathing.

"Give me the gun," Jimmy said, taking a step closer to his brother.

"She saw it," Charlie said again.

"She didn't see anything," Jimmy said. "Give me the gun and we'll say I did it."

"But she saw it!" Charlie shouted.

"We don't have much time!" Jimmy shouted back. "Give me the gun, we'll say I did it, and Laura will leave here and never come back."

Charlie looked at his brother and let the pistol drop to his side.

Jimmy took the gun from his brother and said to Laura, "There's a tape in his hand." He gestured to Unsworth's body.

"No!" Charlie growled.

Jimmy pressed the gun to his brothers ribs. "Laura, get the tape."

She got the tape and she ran.

Jimmy did not follow.

'The cruelty of life and justice' was a phrase that he had used to describe his explanation of the life he had led. A life sentence served in jail for a crime he didn't commit, an old age of alienation from society, only finding peace at the age where peace was devalued by debilitation. Yet still, he adored it and revelled in it.

'I mixed with the wrong people', he had also said, typically taking the blame for the crimes of others.

Laura had finally tracked him down ten years ago. He looked ravaged, helpless, she had thought, and he did so for weeks before his body could recover from the suffering it had endured.

'And then I met you,' he had said, referring to the very first time they had met, at The Corner Pin pub, 'and you saved my life.'

Laura had shaken her head and, knowing the opposite was true, and said, "No I didn't, but one day I will."

At the door, she pauses and looks back at the old man that she had loved for God knows how many years. She grabs a tissue from her bag to wipe her eyes so that her last look at this man isn't teary.

She took a breath and tells him again, "I didn't save your life, but one day I will."

"Excuse me!" Laura heard the voice as she stepped out of Jimmy's room and pretended that she didn't hear it.

She just wanted to leave.

"Excuse me," the voice repeated, a lot closer this time.

Laura knew that the person was closing in on her and she was not going to make it to the end of the corridor.

She turns to see a nurse who waves. She is slim without being athletic, she looks out of place in this ghastly place, even in her unflattering nurses uniform and Covid-issue face mask. She moves very quickly and as she approaches Laura revises her initial age estimate from being in her thirties to her forties or even fifties.

"Sorry to bother you," the nurse says, "can I have a quick word?"

Laura reaches into her bag and pulls out her own mask. "I only took it off for a minute," Laura says and replaces her mask. "It won't happen again."

"Oh," the nurse says, "no, it's not about that."

"Then-" Laura starts to say.

"It's about Jimmy," the nurse says, "if you have time?"

2:22pm
Friday
4th July
1980

CHAPTER 40

There's only one place I can go. Well, two, if you count the toy shop, and that is a definite option. But I choose, for better or worse, to go to Ricky's.

I walk through the park and cut across to the canal. From there I stumble through the undergrowth on the opposite side to the tow-path, hoping that Ricky's rear garden has a back gate or at least a scalable wall.

As it turns out, it has neither. In fact, there's nothing to mark the property boundary except the defeated remains of a picket fence. From there I look at the 'last house on the right'.

There's a light on the ground floor. The kitchen, I imagine.

Hopefully, it's Ricky and, hopefully, he doesn't mind unannounced visitors arriving at the tradesman's entrance.

I knock, and he opens the door.

He doesn't look surprised to see me, but my appearance does seem to shock him. I must look more bedraggled and exhausted than I thought.

Without a welcoming wave of the arm he steps aside. I climb the two steps and enter the house.

The ambience of the kitchen is twinned with that of the garden and exterior. It, too, is eroded, but by the forces of man, not by nature. The pre-war cupboards, tables and chairs are stubborn in their resistance, but their time on earth is running short.

Ricky makes me a cup of tea. Nothing else is offered, and he doesn't seem overjoyed to see me, but he's not disappointed either.

"So what do you want to know?" he asks me across the kitchen table.

"The truth," I say, "if anybody knows what that is."

Ricky nods. "Well, I can tell you what I was told, why I believe it, and what I want to do about it. You'll have to decide if it's the truth or not though."

I nod back to him. Deal. But I can't muster too much enthusiasm. The truth has been lost, never to be found again. Post-truth is alive and kicking and has been here all along. But as Ricky says, I have to choose which truth I believe and then decide whether I believe it enough to do something about it.

"OK," he says, "so the first thing is that Jimmy didn't shoot Unsworth, the police officer. Charlie did."

"I heard that already," I say.

"I guessed that's why you're here," he says.

I nod. I don't see the point of denial any more.

"You've probably also been told that this police officer was a nasty piece of work," he goes on, "and he was. And you've probably heard that he had something on Charlie, and that's why he shot him?"

I say nothing, and I try not to change my expression, but the act of doing so is an expression in itself. And if there was such a thing as the truth ringing like a bell, then I could hear distant ringing at the back of my mind and getting louder.

"Unsworth was a alcoholic and a crooked cop, he was in debt and he blamed Charlie. And that was a big problem for Charlie, because Unsworth could fit him up and put him away for a long-time. So he started tipping Unsworth to bet on Steve Callaghan's fights. And he went unbeaten, right up until the UK Title fight. Callaghan was a massive favourite, but Charlie told Unsworth to bet everything he's got on him losing.

"Unsworth says there's no way Callaghan will go down in his big fight, but Charlie assures him he will, and he won't get up again to tell the tale either."

I sip my tea and wonder whether any of this is true.

"And we know what happens. Unsworth collected on his big bet, calls Charlie to celebrate and, according to him,

Charlie openly brags about drugging Callaghan before the fight and paying off the doctor."

"What?"

"That's what Unsworth says, and-"

"So, Boogie was right?"

Ricky nods. "But Unsworth gets greedy and blackmails Charlie," he goes on, "who, in turn, decides to kill him."

"And we know the rest," I mutter.

"Jimmy tried to stop him," Ricky explains, his expression and demeanour unchanged, "and he was too slow to stop the first bullet, and when Charlie turned the gun on your mum, he offered to take the blame for murdering a police officer, if Charlie would spare Laura."

I nod my head, but it's an involuntary twitch I can't control.

Ricky sits back in his chair and looks at me.

"Go on," I say.

He shakes his head and says, "Your turn."

"I don't know anything," I tell him.

He laughs. Loud.

"I don't," I protest. "How could I?"

Ricky's laughter has left a loud and proud grin on his face that doesn't suit him. It makes him look arrogant and condescending.

He puts his forearms on the table and leans forward, just a little. "How could you?" he asks. "I don't know, Hannah, like I don't know how your mum was there, and how she even knew Jimmy. So how you could know anything is a mystery to me, but you do know right?"

"So, if Jimmy had the gun," I say, "why did my mother run?"

"I don't know," he says, "Jimmy says he doesn't know either and she's kept him waiting about thirteen years."

I shrug. "None of my business."

"I have a theory," he says and takes a sip of tea. "Jimmy did have the gun, but nothing else, and he needed something else, so he told Laura to take whatever it was that the policeman wanted to trade."

"Like what?" I ask.

"I don't know what it was," he says. "But I'd bet that she got it and I'd bet she still has it."

"I need to speak to Jimmy," I tell him.

He shakes his head.

I sip my tea. It's still boiling hot and burns my tongue.

I say again, "I need t-"

"He won't speak to you," Ricky says.

"Why?" I demand.

"I'm sure he has his reasons." Ricky sighs, "but I didn't ask."

"So how am I supposed to-"

Ricky grabs a newspaper and tears the corner from it.

He writes a phone number on it.

"This is my number," he says to me. "Call me in a few days, I'll ask if he'll reconsider."

CHAPTER 41

"Listen," Charlie says, "Over the years me and Jimmy have cultivated our friendship and deepened our relationship. I respect the guy, what can I say? And I think he respects me, despite our previous differences."

"Differences?" I ask, "That's one way of putting it."

We are alone in The Corner Pin bar.

"Anyway," he shrugs, "me and Jimmy came to the agreement that it would be best for us to put our cards on the table and be honest with each other. Which is what we did."

"Really?" I'm not buying any of this, but I still want to hear it.

"So I started making these regular trips to Longleat Prison, an intimidating place, have you been there?"

I shake my head and give him an eye-roll.

"And the thing Jimmy most wanted to talk about was Laura, which, I guess is understandable, but, you know, I was like 'Come on Jimmy, move on with your life'."

"Move on in prison, you mean?" I ask for clarification.

"Yeah."

I nod, "OK. Good advice."

"But you know what some guys are like; they get obsessed with one woman and it takes over their lives."

"I think they call it 'love'," I say, "but I'm not 100% on that."

Charlie sneers at the mention of the word and we both actually laugh. I'm getting a sense of bizarreness about this whole thing and remind myself I need to focus, ease up on the jokes and sarcasm.

"Anyway this Laura, when the shooting starts, she just disappears into thin air, gone. And Jimmy is convinced," he emphasises the word twice, "he is absolutely convinced that she will come back. And as the years go by and she doesn't get in touch, it eats him up."

"Very moving story," I say.

"Interesting though isn't it, this Laura tells Jimmy he's the love of her life, then the first sign of trouble, she leaves him?"

"The first sign of trouble being murder?" I say.

"Which is unfortunate," Charlie concedes. "And it's the same difference at the end of the day, but why didn't she take him with her?"

"I guess we'll never know," I say. "Maybe with you going round shooting people she preferred the company of others?"

"Listen," Charlie says, "I didn't shoot anyone, Jimmy did, but it was an evening of madness and things got out of hand. I wish I could change it, but I can't, we just have to deal with it."

I can't quite believe this but I do know this act is for my benefit.

"But I did promise Jimmy that I would do whatever I could to get him the opportunity to ask Laura 'Why?' and I think he deserves that, despite everything. He's been waiting for thirteen years now Hannah, don't you think he deserves it?"

"I don't care what Jimmy deserves, I don't care about Jimmy and what Jimmy and my mum did or didn't do. Zero shits given by me," I say, staring him down cold. "All I care about is what happens here and now, my situation, that's all."

"Really?" he says.

"Yes, really," I say, "and the only reason I'm here is that you might be able to help me and I might be able to help you."

"If this is what Ricky Fuller has been telling you-"

"Who?" I snap.

"Ricky," he says, "I can only imagine the bullshit he's been feeding you."

I shake my head, but I don't have the energy to deny it.

"His ambition and his banter don't match his abilities. I must confess, I am mildly curious to know what rubbish he told you, he does have a fine line in patter does old Ricky. Loves to tell people what they *want* to hear, but not what they *need* to know."

"He didn't tell me anything," I say.

"Did he tell you he's a cop?"

"A cop?" I say, "No, he can't-"

Charlie smiled, pitying my naivety.

"Whatever," I say.

"Yes quite," he sighs, "You were saying something about how you could help me."

I gather my thoughts and move on. "I want you to tell Tina that the reason I lied to her was that my father is a murdering scum-bag and I was ashamed and scared that people wouldn't accept me."

"You shouldn't talk about your father like that," he sighs, "If Jimmy could hear you-"

"Why are you so concerned with what Jimmy wants?"

"I'm not," he sighs, "I'm attached, emotionally, that's all."

As if.

I say, "And so you want me to have a word in Tina's shell-like and put a word in for you, and reel off some sob story about you begin ashamed of your awful father?"

"That's right."

"And what do I get in return?"

"I'll bring Laura to talk to Jimmy," I say.

"You can do that?" he says.

I nod. "I might need to employ some deception," I say, "but I won't be the first daughter to lie to her mother, will I?"

"Are we in agreement then?" I ask him. "I'll bring you Laura and you bring me back into the fold with Tina?"

"And you bring Laura to speak to Jimmy," he nods.

"Then we have a deal," I say. "It's a bit like that Mutually Assured Destruction thing isn't it, except we don't have nukes."

CHAPTER 42

"I went to see Charlie today," I tell Tina, I just come out with it. We're outside the flat.

"I heard," she says.

"You heard?" How did she hear? Who from? What did she hear?

I thought I had a deal with Charlie that was going to say positive stuff, but Tina does not look like the recipient of anything positive right now.

Tina nods.

"What did you hear?"

"I didn't *hear* anything," she tells me, "just that you went to see him."

There's something more to come, and I know what it is, but still, I have to wait.

So I wait.

A car goes by. A Mk I Ford Escort. We both watch it. The driver is an old man, at least sixty.

Then Tina say, "And we agreed that we were a team."

"We are a team," I say.

Tina gives me a pronounced sneer.

"I just want to help," I say, "I did help."

"You shouldn't go behind my back," Tina says to me. "This is important to me, and to my mum."

"I know it is."

"And you're not even going to be around that long, are you?"

I didn't know what to say. But I knew I had to say something.

So I say, "The man who shot the policeman, and the woman who was with him; I know them."

Tina Looks at me, unimpressed.

I pause here only to determine whether I actually believe what I'm about to say. I don't get to a decision, but I say it anyway, "I've always known."

"You're full of surprises," she says and looks away. She considers something for a while, then says, "So that's why you're here. Everything else was lies and I'm still supposed to trust you."

"You can trust me, Tina," I say.

"How can I trust you? You're leaving soon. And I'm not going anywhere."

"So whatever you think your problems are, you can leave them behind," she says, "but I can't, I'm here, for good, and I don't get the stall back, I lose my house too."

"It won't come to that Tina, I promise."

"You promise?" she says. "Oh, that's OK then."

CHAPTER 43

I've walked halfway to Bulkington and I'm outside a pub called The Prince of Wales, opposite Nicholas Chamberlaine School. I wanted to be away from town, away from prying eyes and I have found what I am looking for.

A red telephone box.

It took me a moment but I've managed to find which of the four sides of the box is the door. Somehow I also managed to haul it open and get inside. For some reason, the door weighed a ton and fought me all the way. I'm expecting the same wrestling match when the time comes for me to leave.

Inside it's filthy. The smell of cigarette smoke overpowers the smell of God knows what else, which might be a good thing. I hope that the puddle beneath my feet is rainwater, but I can't see how rainwater would get in. I decide not to think about it.

I don't know whether I need to put the money in the phone first or dial the number first and although there were some instructions beneath a clear perspex cover, the whole thing is burnt to a char and unreadable.

I place the scrap of newspaper that Ricky gave me on top of the huge grey box that holds the telephone itself and lift the receiver. I can't believe how heavy it is and it feels weird that a handset has a chord, which itself is heavy with a wound steel sleeve. The whole handset must be heavier than my 54" television. When I put it to my ear I hear a crude buzzing tone.

There's a slot for money, and it looks to be about the same size as a ten pence piece. I place my coin in that slot, but something inside the slot is stopping me from inserting it. Maybe it's broken.

The phone has a winding-dial. I've seen enough old movies to know how these work; you put your finger in the hole of the number you want and turn it all the way around to the metal tag at the bottom right of the dial (the metal tag stays still as you dial). The dial itself then turns back to where it started and you dial the next number. The handset makes a whirring noise as I dial and the dial winds back. This winding back can take a while, a few seconds, and it's easy to forget what number you just dialled. Twice I got lost and dialled the wrong number, or at least I think was the wrong number but there's no display to monitor where you are. When that happens I have to replace the handset and get the buzz-tone again. No wonder there were so many 'wrong numbers'.

On the third attempt, I am pretty confident I have dialled the right number and indeed it starts to ring, although the equivalent I hear in the handset is a buzz-buzz noise, instead of a ring-ring.

The buzzing stops and a voice says 'Hel-, but is cut off by a fast repeating beep-beep-beep which makes it impossible to hear the person at the other. I figure out that this is my signal to top 'insert coin'.

I push the ten-pence coin down and this time the mechanism gives way and the coin disappears into the grey box.

The voice I then hear is clear and recognisable. "Hello."

"Thanks for telling me you're a cop."

"You didn't ask," he says. Then goes on with, "What's going on?"

"You should've told me," I say, "the police aren't that popular around here and I can see why."

"It's not my job to be popular," he says, "it's my job to put bad people in prison."

"Is that right?"

"Yes, that's right," he says. Now that his cover is blown, he's lost his persuasiveness and is all business. "Is your mother going to bring what she's got or not?"

"Maybe," I say.

"Either she is or she isn't," he says.

"Yes, that's very perceptive of you," I tell him, "and you'll know when it's time for you to know." This is my best bluff, but I know that it's weak and, probably, unconvincing.

"Listen, Hannah," he says, "I understand you're nervous about this, I would be too, but something is going on."

"Like what?" I say.

"Like Charlie is up to something," I say, "I don't think he knows about us, but he's making moves."

"What kind of moves?"

"You know I can't tell you that," he says. "We both have secrets that are best kept to ourselves for the time being, but all I can say is that if you do plan to help with this, then let me know when and let me know where and I'll see to it that you come out of this in one piece."

"That's good to know," I tell him.

"Is it?" he says, "You don't sound very impressed if I'm honest?"

"Whatever happens will happen soon," I tell him. "I'll let you know."

"If you don't trust me, Hannah, I need to know."

"I don't trust anyone," I say, "Does that answer your question?"

Someone walks past the phone-box and I physically jump.

"Are you OK?" Ricky asks. He must've heard my voice jump with the rest of my body.

"I'm fine," I say.

"Look, if you can't trust me-"

"Tomorrow night, I'll get this done, I'll call you on this number at seven."

I hang up.

CHAPTER 44

I get out of the phone-box and the violent over-weight door makes a sharp lunge at me that I manage to dodge by only a matter of inches. I'm not surprised these phoneboxes were vandalised. I hate them already.

Ricky is playing on my mind as I make my way home, well, back to Tina's place.

I know that there are only a few people on the planet I can trust and only three reasons I can trust them; blood, friendship and mutual objectives. And although blood has its issues and complications, it is the most stable of the three. Friendship is not necessarily a constant human condition, as everyone knows, and mutual objectives are absolutely fluid over both the long and the short term.

Ricky may technically fall into the 'blood' category, as we are both related to Jimmy, but in my book, it doesn't count; it's too distant and I wouldn't care if he was my long-lost brother.

He is certainly not and never will be a friend.

But we do have a mutual objective; we both want Charlie to see some justice. And if I am actively going to pursue that want then that makes Ricky an ally. It doesn't necessarily mean I can trust him, but trust has degrees and at some point, I'm going to have to trust someone for at least a couple of those degrees.

Either consciously or otherwise, and I was so deep in thought that I can't remember, I've gone the long way around to get to Tina's, probably to avoid the dark alleys and unlit footpaths that make up the direct route.

I'm at the bottom of King Street, on the opposite side of town to Tina's flat. I can see Boogie's house and the Corner Pin pub to my left. Ahead of me is the empty precinct and to my right the downward slope of the Rye Piece Ringway.

There's a man behind me. I glanced at him when I went to cross the road and he suddenly took an interest in the motorbikes in the window of Alf England's showroom. I'm sure he was doing something similar when I scrambled out of the phone box. It's not cold, but he's got a Parker jacket on with the hood up.

I decide against the empty precinct and consider going to Boogies and knocking on his door. I could say that I'm freaked out by a guy I think is following me. He might scare the guy off, or he might not remember me, or he might not be in.

If either of the last two were the result, then I'd have walked into a dead-end of darkness and effectively got myself cornered.

I didn't feel lucky enough to take the risk, so I turned right and crossed the road to the other side of the Rye Piece Ringway.

At the bottom of the slope, some two hundred yards away, is a footpath through to a street that leads back to town. I decided once I got there, I'd take that left and then take off as fast as I can. By the time he got to the corner, I would have got a good twenty-second sprint ahead of him and good luck to anyone trying to make that distance up. Especially when I had adrenalin coursing in my veins and I was pretty sure that was going to happen real soon.

I walk at a fast pace, just short of power-walking. I wonder if I'm being paranoid, but a casual glance behind me proves I'm not; he's there and gaining. I estimate that he's matching me for pace, but has a longer stride. In that single second I see him, I know this, but I still can't see his face which is shrouded in darkness by the fur-lined hood. His hands are tucked into his jacket pockets, which is unnatural to me. Why wouldn't his hands be in his jeans pocket? It's not cold, so why would his hands be in his pockets at all?

I'm not even halfway to the footpath which is more than one hundred yards ahead. That will be the most part of a minute. By that time the guy will be just a few steps behind me. If he pursued me then, with no head-start, I might struggle to stay ahead of him.

I fake looking at my watch and start to jog as if I've just realised I'm late. I can't look behind me, but there's no one about and no reason that he wouldn't break into a jog of his own, or a sprint. He could catch me before I'm halfway there.

If I have to confront him, I might buy some time, I might find out what he wants and take it from there, or it might just constitute a surrender. If he has a weapon, I'm defenceless. Even if he doesn't, he'll overpower me.

As I run, the ground at my feet is illuminated with the vast reach of a car's headlights.

I look behind me. He's there, he's running too and he's gaining on me. His hands are out of his pockets now and I can the glint of steel in the headlights.

I keep up my sprint for as long as I dare, twenty, maybe thirty yards at most, and the headlights are getting brighter. When I can bear it no longer I stop and spin round and walk backwards with my arms raised, palms waving for the car to stop.

The car speeds up.

The man puts his hand back in his pocket and resorts back to his fast pace walk with huge strides. He's twenty feet away from me now, my backwards paces are diminishing in length, and all my energy is going into my arms and hands begging the car to stop.

But it's going too fast, not even slowing to take a look, it's going to fly past this guy and fly past me and then I'll have to do whatever I can, but I feel the paralysis of fear locking my muscles into knots that I can't untie.

His hand is out of his pocket again.

He's holding a knife.

CHAPTER 45

I put my arms up to stop the car, but it shows no signs of stopping.

If I need to defend, myself I will.

I'm not going to talk. There'll be no negotiation or reasoning.

If I need to, I will strike first.

The man closes in on me.

The car roars into an accelerated surge forward and swerves toward the pavement. The front tyres hit the kerb and the car leaps across the pavement, thrust forward by the rear wheels.

It lands just a few feet in front of the man and skids to a stop between me and him.

It's Ricky.

He's out of the car and charging at the man and before I can shout, 'He's got a knife', they are toe to toe.

The attacker thrusts the knife waist-high at Ricky's torso, but in one smooth motion, Ricky grabs the arms at the wrist and turns sideways on. The man's arm is wrenched back at the elbow and Ricks slams the back of his head into the attacker's nose. Although He drops, out cold from the reverse head-butt.

Ricky somehow folds the man's arms together and rolls him onto his belly. He puts his foot on the man's back and picks up the knife.

"Come here," he says to me, gesturing with the hand that holds the knife.

I don't move. Things are happening too fast.

"Hannah, quickly come here," he pleads.

I do as he says. He has just saved me from... I don't know exactly. Would he have just threatened me with the knife? Would he have actually used it? I can't stop myself from creating a mental image of the knife piercing my skin.

I try to shake the image from my head as I approach Ricky.

"Thank you," I say. I sound weird, remembering my manners when I could have been viciously beaten, or dead or dying.

"Do you recognise him?" Ricky smiles. I expect him to be raging on adrenalin, but he's not even breathing hard. He looks concerned, but in no way stressed.

I consider his question, which seems like an impossible conundrum to even understand and then I manage to construct the logic of the sentence, and I shake my head. "No," I say. "I don't know him."

Ricky yanks back the hood.

"Recognise him now?"

His nose is gushing blood and doesn't look right, his eyes are closed and his mouth is hung open.

And yes, I recognise him.

Terry.

"Looks like Terry wanted to earn a promotion," he says.

"You know Terry?" I ask.

He nods. "He's one of Charlie's 'gang', what we in police business call a 'Henchman'. You met him the other day when he walked Tina home, which wasn't a coincidence by the way."

There's no such thing as a coincidence.

"Are you saying that Charlie sent him to stab me?" I say, "Or to threaten me?"

"Not to threaten you," he says, "not here."

Ricky holds up the knife; it's about eight inches long, the handle has a thick black grip, one side of the blade has a curved razor-edge, and the other has serrated teeth.

"You OK?" he says.

"I'm-" I start to say, but I'm not sure what I am.

Ricky put his hands on my upper arms. "Hannah, you need to leave and let me take care of this. Go back to Tina's and wait there."

I stare at him for a second, then say, "You want me to leave?"

He nods.

"You want me to leave?" I say again.

I hear myself suck air into my lungs.

"You need to go, Hannah," he says and hands me the knife, "and take this."

"Why do I need that?"

"Just in case," he says.

"Just in case what?" I ask, but I don't want to know the answer.

"Hannah," Ricky says, "we don't have any time. I need to call this in first so that the good cops turn up, not the bad cops. If anyone asks, then the driver ran away, that way," he says and points down the slope. "But no ones going to ask you because you're going to leave now and go back to Tina's. OK?"

"OK," I say.

I don't know whether to take the knife.

Ricky says, "Officially this will be reported as a mugging I intervened on, but the knife doesn't fit the story. You need to take it. Please. And go now."

I take the knife.

I leave.

CHAPTER 46

I leave Ricky and the car and Terry.

It's only after I run clear of the footpath, and jog into town that it hits me. Once I have time to think, I have a panic attack. I don't know what to do. I stop, I head for the police station, then stop. I literally run in three different directions for a few paces, then stop, then another.

To Stubbs.

Tina's flat.

Back to Ricky.

To Stubbs again.

I have a clear understanding of the trouble I'm in but I don't know what to do or where to go.

Can I trust Ricky? Is he really going to say Terry was mugged? He's a policeman! And why did he give me the knife? Is he going to frame me? Should I get rid of the knife?

The answer to everything I ask myself is, 'I don't know'.

I have to go somewhere, I can't stay here, so I decide to go to the person I trust the most.

I turn the corner at the HyperMarket and instantly see that something is wrong. There are a crowd of people on the balcony outside Tina's flat. I can see Barbara being comforted by the neighbours.

I break into a sprint. My legs are screaming from exhaustion but I run faster than ever and I try to block out thoughts that what was intended to happen to me has happened to Tina.

I should never have come here.

I should never have put these people in danger.

I get to the balcony and dash to the door.

The second Barbara sees me her face turns to thunder. "Here she is!" she shouts and points her finger. "It's all her fault!"

"What's happened?"

"It's all your fault!" she screams again and lashes out at me, her fingertips clawing at my face.

I dodge to one side and get pushed back by a person in the crowd.

My balance doesn't desert me and I make it to the open door.

Inside, everything is trashed, furniture is smashed, the TV screen is shattered, photos frame lay in pieces and the walls bear the scars.

I turn back to Barbara. "Where is Tina?"

"If you hadn't come here none of this-"

Then a voice from behind me. "I'm here."

I turn to see Tina coming out of the kitchen.

"Don't bother trying to explain," she says to me, "You haven't been honest since you got here so I don't expect you to start now."

"Tina, who did this?"

"Who else knew you had that money?"

"Who did this?"

Tina stops and stares into my eyes, just inches away. "Terry barges in and starts shouting at my mum 'Where is it?' and she has no clue what he is talking about. Then he says 'Where is Hannah's stuff' and trashes the place."

"What?" I say.

"He must've known you had that money. Who did you tell?"

"Nobody knew," I say, "it can't be-"

"He must've known," Tina screams at me. "When he couldn't find it he smashed everything-"

"What happened to your mum?" I ask, "Is she OK?"

Tina doesn't answer. She pushes past me and through the crowd shouting, "This is all your fault. You lied to me over and over again."

"Tina, where are you going?"

"Where do you think I'm going?" she spits the words into my face, "I'm going to sort Terry out and I don't want to see you here when I get back. Do you understand? I don't want to see you ever again!"

"Tina, this wasn't just about the money," I say. "Terry tried to attack me."

CHAPTER 47

"When did he attack you?" Tina snaps at me. "What are you talking about?"

"A few minutes ago," I tell her, there's a crowd around me now, lots of people I don't know. More seem to be joining them with every second. "He was chasing me, he had a-"

I don't say it. It's just going to complicate things.

"You're wrong," Tina shouts.

"I swear to God Tina," I say, "I'm not lying. I was in town, he chased me, and-"

A woman I don't know steps forward and pushes my shoulder. "You can't trust her," she says, "she talks to coppers."

"I didn't know he was a copper," I snap back. "And he saved me, he stopped Terry-"

"Who's a copper?" Tina demands, "Who've you been talking to?"

"Ricky Fuller," the woman says, and she delivers it with the tone of the final nail in a coffin.

"Ricky Fuller?" Tina asks me, her disgust rising up in her expression.

"I didn't know who he was," I say, but I can tell this isn't going to cut it.

"You've been busy," Tina says. She's not hearing a word I've said.

"He was talking to Jimmy for me," I say, "that's all."

Tina frowns as her neighbours all gasp in unison.

She shakes her head, "Jimmy would never talk to Ricky Fuller. Jimmy hates Ricky Fuller!"

"What? No, he's-"

"Are you that naive?" Tina says, "Do you believe everything you're told?"

"I didn't know," I say again.

I start backing away.

"Is that what this has been all along Hannah?" Tina asks me, "Revenge for Jimmy?"

I turn and walk.

"Who do you think you are?"

"Grass!" the woman says.

"Filth!" says another.

I don't stay around to find out what happens next.

I turn and run.

There are a few raised objections, but I hear Tina's voice over them all. "Let her go!" she tells them, "She's not worth it."

CHAPTER 48

"Get in."

I recognise the car.

I also recognise the liar driving it.

He's wound the window down and is driving beside me at walking pace.

"Hannah, " he says, "we need to talk."

"I'm finished talking," I say, "I'm just... walking." The rhyme makes me sound pathetic and I can feel my resolve evaporating into thin air.

"So where you walking to?" he asks.

"I don't know, I'm just walking."

"Hannah," he says. "Come on. Get in."

"Everyone knows I talk to cops," I say without looking in his direction.

"What do they know?" he says, "What parts of his do they understand?"

"They understand that you can never trust a policeman," I tell him. "Only I didn't know you was a cop because you never mentioned it."

"What difference would it make?"

I stop walking.

"If I'd known who you were from the start, I could've made my own decision," I say staring at the pavement, "If you'd have been honest with me, I might not have been so accommodating for one thing." I was trying to sound sophisticated, but realise immediately I've scored an own-goal.

"That's why I didn't tell you," he says, accepting the gift of a tap-in.

I let out a theatrical sigh.

He stops the car and I make my way around to the passenger side.

"And Jimmy?" I ask, "Are you related to him? Or was that just more bullshit? Was you just telling me what I wanted to hear?"

"He's my uncle," Ricky says, "My mother's brother, as you've pointed out, we're way past the bullshit stage."

Ricky pulls away. I open the glove box and rummage in the contents for no reason other than to wind him up.

It doesn't work.

"So what else do you know?" he says.

"Nothing," I say. He's not getting any more of a response than that.

"He wants the evidence," he says. We stop at a red light. I look up to see people going about their lives, walking to the shops, chatting in the street. I want to swap places.

"What evidence?" I ask, with zero interest.

"Everyone knows that he killed the policemen," he says, "We know, he knows, Jimmy knows."

"That's not everyone," I say.

"Everyone who matters," he snaps back.

At last, my petulance is getting the desired result.

"So why isn't he in jail?" I ask.

"Two reasons," Ricky says. He pulls away from the traffic light. "One reason is that Jimmy confessed, and the other reason is a lack of evidence."

"So if there's no evidence and Jimmy confessed-"

"I didn't say there was no evidence," he tells me, "I said there was a lack of evidence. That's not the same thing."

"I'm glad we cleared that up."

"Hannah, I don't know how you fit into all this, but you are. And getting out of it ain't gonna be easy."

I don't answer, except with a small sigh.

"But what I do know is that there's someone in the middle of all this who connects everything to everything else. She is the reason Jimmy did a deal with Charlie that saw him put away for life. She is the reason that there was a witness to the murder because she is the witness. And she is the reason that there is a lack of evidence because she has that evidence."

I don't want to hear this. I don't want any part of this any more.

Ricky steers the car down a side road, then a narrow alley leading to rows of garages.

"And then *you* show up," he says, "and, unbelievably, you not only look like this woman, and I mean exactly like her, but also, you have the same name."

He stops the car and pauses to let the information sink in.

I have nothing to say. I'm trapped in this car and trapped in this conversation, with nowhere to go.

"And even more incredible than all of that," he says, "Charlie was expecting you! He knew your name, he knew where you'd be and he knew when you'd be there."

"How do you know that?" I ask. I know the answer. I don't know why I'm asking. I'm not fooling anyone, and I never was.

"I don't know how he knows," Ricky says, "I was going to ask you. But then what would be the point in that?"

Part of me wants to tell him.

But how can I?

"But at the end of the day, it doesn't matter," Ricky says. "All that matters to me is that Charlie goes down for what he did. That's the only thing I care about."

I look at him, hoping that is true.

He goes on, "And there's one thing that can do that and that's the evidence I think the woman who shares your name has got. I bet she's got it tucked away, safe and sound somewhere. And I thought you might know where it is, but now I think maybe you don't."

"I don't," I tell him. Our eyes are locked together.

"But I bet you can find it," he says, "And I guarantee you that if you do find it, and do the right thing, then he will go down and Jimmy will go free."

"And we'll all live happily ever after in Fantasyland by the sea," I smile, "Or maybe not."

Surprisingly, he smiles back at me. "Yeah," he says, "Maybe."

I feel sick just looking at his smug grin.

"By the way," I say, "in case we don't get to chat again, Jimmy lived with his mother until she died. He and his brother were her sole heirs. They inherited everything, which wasn't much, but it was all theirs. They didn't share it with a sister, because there wasn't a sister."

For once, Ricky is silent.

"So you're not related to Jimmy," I say, "You're not even a very good liar. But like you say: What does it matter now?"

"OK," he says.

"I just thought I'd let you know."

"I have my reasons for wanting to see Charlie behind bars" he says. "Personal as well as professional."

"Oh yeah?"

"Yeah."

"Proper deep and mystical underneath the ugly exterior ain'tcha?"

"Listen," Ricky says, "I've been doing some digging."

"You're too late!" I snap at him.

"Hannah! Listen!" he says. He gets my eye contact and says, "I've spoken to a retired cop, he was around in the old days and nothing much went past him. He told me something, it might be important."

I don't even want to listen to this useless drivel, but I can't even begin to formulate a plan of my own.

"Charlie owed Unsworth," Ricky says, "at least that's how Unsworth saw it. And Charlie made sure he got lucky by making sure that Callaghan lost the fight."

"So what?" I shout. "Why does this matter now? Nobodies going to believe whatever we tell them-"

"We don't need to tell them," Ricky says, "They can hear it."

I frown. I don't get it.

"Unsworth had a tape of it," Ricky says, "he recorded Charlie confessing to killing Callaghan and he blackmailed him. Charlie probably thought, 'Why pay for it when I can just...kill him?'"

For a second it made sense. But only for a second. "So why did Jimmy take the rap for it?" I say.

"Well," he says, "the only think that it can be is that Jimmy and Charlie did a trade. Jimmy would've given anything for your mother, including serving the rest of his life in jail."

I shake my head. "So what did he trade his life for?"

"The tape!" Ricky says. "Your mother took the tape and Jimmy took the rap for the murder."

I don't speak. I daredn't. I'm scared of what I'll say.

CHAPTER 49

I get to the Corner Pin and am met at the door by a henchman who I haven't seen before but is obviously expecting me. With my head shaven on the sides, I guess I'm easy to identify.

"Round the back," he says, with all the charm of white dog dirt. He jerks his thumb to indicate the direction I am to follow.

Without giving him the satisfaction of eye contact, I take the lead.

We make our way across the dry mudded area that passes for the car park to the only door at the back of the pub.

The tradesman's entrance.

The henchman opens the door and ushers me inside.

I'm further directed down a narrow staircase to a black door. We're in another part of the basement.

He knocks on the door and a voice I recognise says, "Enter."

He even opens the door for me, but he gets no thanks.

I enter into a small room, not much bigger than my box bedroom at Tina's. It's sparse, but for a desk and three chairs, there is nothing else in the room except a coat stand. No picture on the grey walls, but there is a small window.

It doesn't take me long to realise that from where we are in the pub, if my barrings are correct, then that window is at the back of the mirror in the card room.

Charlie stands before it. Watching.

After a few moments, he turns to me and smiles, "Come and see."

He looks pleased with himself like he's sharing a secret that I too will enjoy.

I stand beside him and look.

I am looking at the card table. There are three players.

Tina is standing in the corner of the room.

Charlie smiles, his smugness in its prime. "They can't see or hear us," he tells me.

I kind of gathered that myself, but I keep my mouth shut. Something tells me the time for sarcasm has passed and we are getting down to the business end of this thing.

"Are you watching?" he asks.

"Yes, I am," I say.

Charlie returns to the doorway and raises his hand to a white doorbell I hadn't noticed before. He presses it firmly, there is no sound and returns to stand beside me.

"Keep watching," he says.

The man with his back to us puts his cards down and gestures to Tina. He says something to her that I can't hear and she scurries over to him.

I turn to Charlie, "Why are you-"

"Just watch!" he snaps back at me.

The man waves at the empty glasses on his table and Tina reaches over to collect them. As she does the man turns to face us, looking up at the mirror, smiling. I recognise him instantly. Below the corner of his left eye he has two tattooed tears. He was here that first time I set foot in the place, he's the guy I thought was a down and out, the creepy guy with the short temper. It seems he's come up in the world playing cards in the back room.

There's no such thing as a coincidence.

I freeze, petrified, as I realise why he is there.

The whole environment and everything in it is being controlled by Charlie, even that first unpleasant meeting was probably a set-up with this pay-off in mind.

As Tina takes his empty glass from the table, he looks up her up and down.

He looks back at us and smiles at Tina as he gives her an order.

She smiles back and leaves the room.

"You have something that I want," Charlie tells me. "I thought it must be at Tina's place, and Terry assures me was very thorough when he searched the place, but he couldn't find it."

"He trashed their flat!" I growl at him.

"Its good that you're angry," Charlie tells me, "as long as you understand the seriousness of the situation."

And I *am* angry. I'm also scared. Very scared. Scared of what he can do.

"I don't know what you want," I tell him. "I swear, I don't."

"How do I know you're not lying?" he asked.

"I swear-"

"Hannah, listen," he says as he sits down at the desk. "I do understand, your loyalty is to your mother, of course, it is. And your loyalty is big and strong, and I'm guessing, so correct me if I'm wrong, but I'm guessing it's big and strong because your mother raised you that way."

I don't speak.

"So you can see my predicament," he goes, "your strong loyalty to what your mother told you is a big obstacle for me. I need to be as persuasive, to you, as your very own mother."

Charlie raises both palms from the table to express the futility of his objective, but I know that his plan is anything but futile.

"And then," he says, "I had an idea."

And I knew immediately what his idea was.

And I knew who it was.

Tina.

"I'll do anything," I say, "I'll give you anything you ask. But I don't know what you want."

"I think you do," he says. "So go get it."

I start to say, "I swear to God-" But his face is empty and I know he's not going to give me another second.

"That man in there," he says, "he's a bad man. A very bad man. I find what he does, what he's been convicted of doing, quite distasteful, but as you are no doubt imagining right now, it does have its uses."

I can't let that man do anything to Tina, but I don't know what to do to stop it. I don't know what he wants from me.

A flash-fantasy goes through my mind where I batter Charlie with the coat stand and cave his head in, but even then it destroys my soul that still Tina would die.

I should never have come here.

I should never have listened to my mother, this whole thing was madness from the start and now that madness is playing out.

"There's nothing I have that I wouldn't give to you," I tell him. I turn to face him and when he doesn't respond to me I stand before him, blocking his view of the window. "But I don't know what it is you want," I shout.

He doesn't flinch. "Well then work it out," he says. "Work it out in that pretty little head of yours."

"Why harm her?" I demand, "Why not harm me?"

"Because you have the thing I want," he says.

I don't answer. I can't stand to look at him, so I move away, face the wall and try to think.

"Go get it," Charlie says, "before I lose my patience."

"This is crazy," I beg, "You know what it is, I don't!"

He shakes his head.

"Tell me what it is!"

"No more games," he says, "No more pretending. No more talk. You bring it to me or *my* friend gets to play with *your* friend."

I leave.

CHAPTER 50

I'm in a complete daze as I step outside.

It seems impossible that the world outside of the Corner Pin is carrying on as normal.

People are walking, talking in groups, even laughing.

A stray dog trots past me, on its way to where it wants to go with no interest in what I or anything me or anyone else is doing.

Cars roll by. None of the drivers looks at me, seemingly not understanding what is happening before their very eyes.

"Get in the car," Terry orders.

"Where are we going?" I ask.

He has a limp, a graze on his face above his left eye and he's wearing shades and gloves.

"You tell me," he says.

I don't know where to go. I wish I did.

Maybe I can offer Charlie something confusing and pass it off as something meaningful just to buy some time. I could swear blind that it's the thing that I've been told by my mum to protect with my life.

I can't even think of anything to offer him though, my mind doesn't respond in any way at all.

I get in the car and stare at the glove box.

Terry says nothing as he shuts his door and starts the car. The engine mumbles into life and when the radio starts to seep out Union City Blue by Blondie, Terry switches it off.

"Not a fan?" I say to him. He's not scary, not to me, not any more.

"Where we going?" he says, ignoring my question.

"Can you drive?" I say.

Again, my question goes ignored.

I think about turning the radio back on and sitting here in the car park until Terry or Charlie called time.

I had no other choices and listening to Blondie was always an inspiring experience.

In fact, screw it, I thought to myself, I'm going to do it.

I turn to the radio and raise my hand, then stop.

My eyes fix on the radio fascia. Between the volume and the tuning dial was the frequency range with its red line that physically moved as you turned the dial. And below that was a type of letterbox flap with the profile of a cassette tape imprinted on it. Although I'd never operated a car's tape machine, I did know that you push the tape into the letterbox and it plays automatically.

You could buy records on tape, which came in a folding plastic box, or you could buy blank tapes and tape your mate's records on them, or the Top 40 chart show from Radio One, or anything else you wanted if you had a microphone.

You could literally record anything. You could record yourself singing. Or talking. Or being interviewed. By the police.

I find myself listening intently to the words in my head. It's as if I'm trying to pick out a conversation in a crowded room which is only just out of reach, but if I strain my ears, I can make out certain words and put them together to make sentences by filling in the gaps.

'The tape,' are the first words I make out.

They're important these words.

Terry is saying something but I'm not listening to him.

'Mum's record box.'

I'm then able to rearrange what I know and add the rest myself.

'The tape in mum's record box, *that's* what he wants. Unsworth's recording that Ricky told me about'.

I need to get that tape and trade it with Charlie for Tina's life.

But I'm trapped in the car.

"Do you know where it is, or not?" Terry says.

I hear him loud and clear now, but I don't need to listen to the rest of the angry noise in my head because I have what I need. I know what Charlie wants from me.

"No," I say, but it's obvious I'm lying. "Well, maybe," I add. "But only maybe."

"So?" he asks, turning to glare at me.

"So what?" I say, staring back at the glove box.

"So are we going to get it or what?" he says too loud, "I'm not bothered, but you might wanna get a shift on."

"Take me to the HyperMarket," I tell him, "Top floor of the car park."

Terry releases the hand-brake and clumsily guides the car onto the Rye Piece.

I glance at him to gauge his expression but it's unreadable.

I fear mine is not and spend the short journey looking out of the side window and hoping I have enough time.

CHAPTER 51

Terry is the worst driver I have seen, ever. He doesn't seem to be able to coordinate operating the steering wheel, never mind the clutch and accelerator pedals. I'm not sure if he knows there's a brake pedal, but he rarely gets the car over twenty miles an hour and when he does, we're kangarooing along in the wrong gear.

For the first time in years, I actually feel motion sickness, and I promise myself that if my body does regurgitate, then I will not hold back.

However, we get to the front of the HyperMarket with the contents of my stomach staying where they started.

"Drop me here," I tell Terry and reach for the door handle.

"No chance!" he says, "You said it's on the top floor."

"Yeah, so wait here and I'll go get it," I tell him.

"I'm not letting you out of my sight," he tells me.

He's interrupted by the blare of a car horn. Talking and driving have proven too much for his skill set and he has veered into the path of oncoming traffic. He clumsily wrestles the car back to our side of the road and gets a mouthful of abuse from the driver of the car we narrowly miss as it passes.

"It'll be quicker if I walk," I say, "and safer."

Terry shakes his head. "Do I look that stupid?"

I don't even answer that one.

Miraculously we get to the top floor without hitting a car or a wall, but it would have been quicker to walk up the four floors and back down again and back up again.

I get out of the car and make my way to the stairwell in the corner nearest to Tina's flat.

I glance back to see Terry who is out of the car and watching me intently.

I hope he's buying this and I hope it buys me enough time.

At the stairwell, I carefully clamber up to kneel on top of the wall and reach up to the shelf above my head.

I crane my neck and stretch my body as I reach up higher for something out of Terry's line of sight. Then I relax my body and shake my head. I take a second then carefully get to my feet whilst performing a precarious balancing act and reach up the hidden spot where my evidence is supposedly stashed.

I look back at Terry. He hasn't moved.

"I got it," I shout at him, and, from this distance, he seems to nod, I'm not sure.

I clamber down from the wall and make my way back to him. I put my hands in my pockets and head back to Terry, but I swerve away from the passenger side and head straight for him. I feel inside the lining of my jacket for my wad of cash and slide off the elastic band.

"Get back in the car," Terry says.

I take my hand out of my pocket and show him my huge pile of cash.

"Here," I say, "I don't know how much is here, but you take it."

Terry stares at the money. It's a massive amount. The wheels in Terry's head are racing out of control and about to blow.

"Put it away and get in the car!" he shouts.

I peel off a twenty-pound note and drop it at his feet.

Terry makes a grab for it, but, with perfect comic timing, the wind shifts it out of his reach.

He makes a second grab for it and succeeds this time, but I drop two more before he pins the first one to the floor.

Terry starts to play twenty pound note Whack-A-Mole and he can't stop snatching up the notes I drop as I back away.

Once I reckon I'm a safe distance from him I say his name, "Terry!"

He looks up.

"Are you ready?" I ask.

He doesn't answer. He doesn't understand what he's supposed to be ready for. All he knows is he's holding more money than he's ever held in his life and I'm holding literally a hundred times more in my hand.

"Are you ready for this?" I say and throw the wad of notes high above his head.

Another sweep of breeze arrives and the roll of notes explodes like a falling satellite burning up in the atmosphere. Paper flutters to the ground in a wide radius around Terry who can only stare.

I don't stay to admire the scene, much as I'd like to, but instead, I'm running.

I get to the stairwell, hop onto the wall and use my momentum to jump as far as possible and hope I make it.

It's a leap in the dark, literally, and I estimate it to be equal to jumping off the garage roof onto the grass in our garden like I did as a kid, maybe a bit more. But I wasn't a kid any more. And I'm not jumping onto grass.

I'm dropping for a second, bracing myself to land but the ground doesn't arrive and for the next few nano-seconds, I can feel my body accelerating and my brain calculating its adverse effect on my landing.

Then the ground hits me.

Hard.

My ankles flex to absorb as much impact as I can but it's not enough. My knees slam into the concrete and pain shoots through me before the rest of my body lands with a thud.

It takes another second or two for my body to respond to my instructions to get up and move. Intense pain in my arms joins that from my legs and I'm waiting for a similar status report from my head that I'm sure hasn't escaped unscathed.

I pray for adrenalin as I get to my feet and stagger in the direction of the sloping road that is the spiral exit ramp.

I manage to put one foot in front of the other and repeat the operation enough times to gain some momentum despite the amping up of the pain which each step.

"No!" I hear Terry scream from behind me.

Before I can stop myself, I'm looking back. He's leaning over the wall at the spot where I jumped from. He looks at me and then down at the ground, assessing his own chances of following me directly.

I don't wait to see what decision he makes. All I can do is vacate the exit ramp as fast as I can.

My right foot seems to be seizing up and slowing me down. My 'run' is becoming a lolloping step and a half-step cycle that refuses to gain any momentum.

As I have been wrestled to the ground, I reckon that Terry didn't fancy the jump, or if he did, he sustained even worse injuries than I did.

That means he went back to the car and this was confirmed when I hear the engine fire up, scream into action and the screech of wheels chewing up the tarmac at a rapid rate of knots.

I'm three floors up. I've completed maybe one full circle.

I'm too high to jump and not far enough in front to outrun a car.

It's time to test out those Parkour skills that I refined trying to keep up with Finn.

I feel that release of adrenalin into my muscles, my heart and lungs. I convince my cautious brain that protecting my injured ankle is a false economy that will result in us losing the race and it agrees.

I start to run, ignore the pain, and if the ankle gives out (I cannot allow myself to use the word 'break') then so be it.

I'm certain that I've increased my odds by a considerable margin and I use this knowledge to push on, but I see faint lights appear on the wall in my peripheral vision. The roar of the engine now overpowers the noises of my own body racing at full speed and I get the sense that the car, smelling blood, is also benefiting from a burst of adrenalin.

I put my head down and sprint.

Then I hear another sound, that of metal scraping on concrete. I guess that the increase in acceleration has resulted in a loss of control and the lights beside me fade a little as the car slows and corrects itself.

The HyperMarket building is passing me on the left which means I have completed another cycle and I'm now two floors up.

Halfway down.

But the car has covered a lot more ground than me in that time and there's no way I can make it to the bottom in one piece.

I keep running but make my way across to the outside of the ramp. The car lights are now all around me and I'm chasing my long shadow down the ramp. Neither the car nor me are showing any signs of slowing which means the impact is seconds away.

Which means it's now or never.

I make a leap for the side wall, my intention is to get as much of my torso onto its flat top as I can. This I do and I can hear the scraping of metal against the wall again from just meters behind me. Instead of correcting itself this time, the car maintains its course leaving not even a millimetre of space between it and the wall.

I use whatever momentum I have to swing my legs up behind me and as I do the car appears in my view for the first time. I even get to see Terry's face as he flies past me. Our eyes meet and I see his hatred aimed directly at me which I take as a sign that I've evaded the car unharmed.

Well, almost unharmed.

My agonising muscles and bones might beg to differ, but they are once again called into action.

I get to my feet and put my arms out for balance as I run.

The car has stopped. Terry is getting out.

I'm running, trying to navigate the curvature of the wall, its narrow plank-like width for my feet to land on and at the same time gauge where the pedestrian ramp is ahead of me.

By the time Terry is out of the car and throwing himself at the wall I'm already past him. I take another ten steps, then jump.

My feet have done taken the brunt of my landings previously and I know it would be too much to ask them to take another. This time my intention is to land on the opposite wall with my stomach, flip myself over as it hit it and hopefully land on the floor of the pedestrian walkway somehow alive.

I don't know how exactly, but somehow I must've managed to do just that and I find myself on my side, safely out of view from Terry and apparently with no additional injuries.

I hear the car screech to a halt and the drivers door open.

"Bitch!" I hear Terry rage.

I don't stand up. I can see that I'm halfway to the exit to the street and halfway to the entrance back into the labyrinth of the HyperMarket walkways.

If I don't show myself, Terry won't know which way I've gone.

I crawl back to the HyperMarket as fast as my screaming knees will allow me.

When I look back from the end, Terry is nowhere to be seen.

Limping but with a defiant grin, I make my way to Boogies.

CHAPTER 52

I get to Boogie's house and I'm overwhelmed by the happy memories of the last time I arrived here, surrounded by great people, in the highest spirits, wild with anticipation of the fun that lay ahead.

This time is the polar opposite. I have put my friend in danger, it is down to me to help her, and I have one chance to get it right.

I am also exhausted and my mind is on the brink of panic. Knowing this doesn't help. Illogical fear and logical fear have joined forces.

I feel useless and rotten on the inside.

There is an undeniable truth here that this is all my fault.

And because of that, I have a mountain to climb tonight, but that is just the start of the battle.

Even if I can get Tina safely away from Charlie tonight, then what?

I knock on Boogie's door and tell myself 'one thing at a time'.

A blurry-eyed Boogie opens the door and scratches his head.

"Hi," I say.

"Hannah," he says, "you look terrible, what's going on?"

"Can I come in?" I say.

Boogie swings the door open and ushers me in.

He doesn't seem annoyed at the intrusion, in fact, he seems genuinely pleased to see me, if a little confused. He doesn't mention the time even though I have obviously woke him up, even though he's dressed in his ever-present jeans and t-shirt.

I give him the low-down, as best I can without going into crazy territory of course. and when I get to where Tina is working and what I saw through the mirror, he almost loses it.

I must've done a good job of convincing him that there was only one way of resolving this as he soon focused back on what I'm saying.

I end my story with a question.

"So I need my record box," I tell him.

"What record box?" Boogie asks.

"At the party," I say, "I brought a box of singles. It's blue and old."

I do the two-handed universal hand signals to indicate the approximate width, depth and height of a box.

"It's by the record player," Boogie ponders but doesn't make a move. We remain standing in the hall.

"Mind if I go take a look?" I ask.

Boogie puts two and two together and his face is struck by enlightenment at the genius of my suggestion. He stands back and silently waves me through to the living room.

It's not there. The record player and sound system are surrounded by 45s, pretty much as we left them on Saturday night.

"Shit!" I hiss, "It's not here."

I kneel and shuffle a few of the piles of records around just in case, but there's no way the box could be obscured.

"What are you looking for?" Boogie asks.

I'm not sure if he's trying to be funny, and maybe, (hopefully) he's anticipated I will come knocking his door looking for my record box in order to watch me squirm.

Stranger things have happened, but not many.

I look up at Boogie and he is scouring the floor with an intensity so pure I can see instantly that he's not pranking me.

"An old blue record box?" I explain.

Boogie's eyes seem sharper now. I can see his mind pondering behind them. I hold my breath.

"How big is it?" he asks.

"Yay big," I say, repeating my two-handed approximation of a 7" cube.

Boogie stops looking to concentrate on thought.

So as not to disturb this intense process, I whisper, "It's blue."

And it does the trick. Boogie clicks his fingers and heads to the kitchen.

He returns carrying it in both hands like an offering to the gods.

"This record box?" he asks.

"Yes!" I beam.

One day, I promise myself, I will ask him why it was in the kitchen, but instead, I take the box from his hands and place it on the floor before me.

I take a deep breath, let it go and push in the worn chrome clasp. It slides up, out of its slip and I lift the lid.

The box is empty.

Except for a single Memorex C90 cassette with '10/10/78' written on it.

I reach and take it out.

Boogie is watching me intently.

"Boogie," I say, "I have a plan, but I need your help?"

CHAPTER 53

It's a short walk from Boogie's house to the Corner Pin. I have my hand in my jacket pockets the whole way and I hold the tape in my hand with a firm grip.

I don't run, but I walk as fast as I can.

There's nobody around. Except I'm sure there are people waiting in hiding for me, somewhere in the shadows. I didn't look, I kept my eyes front and told myself that if it happened, it happened.

Then I heard the voice. "Hannah, don't look at me," the voice says, "keep walking."

The voice is coming from the waste ground to my right, a space that contains nothing but dark shadows. I do as the voice says, I don't look, not because I was obeying its instructions, I had already decided to plough ahead no matter what.

Besides, I know who it is and I wouldn't choose to see him.

Ricky.

"Just leave the door unlocked," he says.

I walk on a few steps then I do look, but there's no one there.

Just shadows.

I keep walking.

I'm back in the secret room at the Corner Pin.

Charlie is standing before me staring into the one-way mirror.

I can't see Tina, I don't know if she's OK or not.

"Hannah let's not waste time," Charlie says, "You know better than that."

I don't have much choice but to trust him, I'm out of ideas and we're not playing games any more.

I step forward and place the tape on the table. My hand is shaking. I don't want to place it in his hand, I don't want to get any closer than I absolutely have to and he looks up, disappointed.

"Now-"

"Hannah!" he shouts, "Please! Be patient."

He's frowning at me, seemingly mildly annoyed with an unruly child.

He opens his drawer and takes out a brand-new Sony Walkman. It has been, no doubt, bought especially for this occasion and he is determined to savour it. He's waited a long time for this after all.

I pray that Tina is OK. I pray that he is good to his word, but time, my time, Tina's time, is running out.

Charlie flips open the Walkman lid and picks up the tape. He inspects it, then the aperture beneath the lid of the slick powder blue unit in his hand and offers the first to the latter. When the tape slides into the machine and snaps the lid shut, he looks quite pleased with himself for accomplishing the complex feat.

"It's a personal, portable tape player. Incredible, isn't it? " he tells me without looking up. "What will they think of next?"

I don't speak because that's what he wants me to do, to engage in conversation and delay this agony further.

He picks up the headset and places the colour-matched powder-blue headphones over each ear. Sitting back in his chair, his moment now arrived, he works a self-satisfied smile onto his face and presses play.

Charlie smiles, almost. His lips purse together and his eyes beam satisfaction.

He listens intently to the words we can't hear, no doubt reminiscing about getting away with murder.

From the corner of my eye, I see movement in the doorway. Someone is stepping into the room. The first thing I see is the barrel of a pistol. Then two people, I can't look around, I have to stand still.

Ricky has the gun in one hand and is holding Tina by the elbow with the other.

My heart freezes again. I need to get Tina away from here before these two shoot it out, but that's not going to happen now.

Ricky doesn't look at me as he crosses the room. He keeps his gun, held waist high, trained on Charlie's gut. I stand in front of Tina and stare at Ricky. He lets go of her arm and puts his finger to his lips as if I need reminding to keep quiet. I put my arms around Tina and she holds me for a second. She's trembling. I don't know what she's been through, I just pray that it's almost over.

I glance back to Charlie and he is still standing there as he was, head down listening to the Walkman.

I can't breathe. The only positive thing my brain can come up with is that I'll have the pleasure of seeing Charlie shot if it comes to it. And it will be a pleasure, I have no doubt of that. Looking at the deathly grin on Ricky's face, it looks like it will come to it very soon.

He's less than ten feet from Charlie. And closing.

I don't look at him, I try to keep still, but Charlie is still listening to the Walkman, entranced by what it is telling him.

Ricky gets to within three feet of him, then two, then one.

He sticks the gun in Charlie's ribs.

Charlie doesn't flinch.

"Stick 'em up!" Ricky says in his ear.

Charlie raises his hands, but only to remove his headphones.

CHAPTER 54

"You took your time," Charlie says and the two men laugh.

Ricky steps back and tucks his gun into the waist of his trousers.

"You did well," Charlie tells him.

"Are you happy?" Ricky asks him, nodding at the Walkman.

"I wouldn't say 'happy'," Charlie says, "but I got what I needed."

Tina has a grip on my arm that is getting tighter. "What's happening?" she says to me.

"Tina!" Charlie glares at her, "the grown-ups are speaking. You speak only when spoken to."

She physically shrinks back and I try to increase my own size to make up for it.

"When did she figure it out?" Charlie asks Ricky.

"She didn't really," he says and looks at me and laughs. "In the end I had to more or less spell it out and tell her it was a tape that we were looking for. I had begun to think she'd never figure it out."

"You're not going to recommend her as a potential criminal investigator then?"

"I think not," Ricky laughs.

"But to be fair, she doesn't know what we know, like we knew that Jimmy was coming back last Friday. We made up that story of him robbing the pub. Knowing what we know now has been very helpful."

"Yeah but she didn't even figure out why Terry ransacked the flat," Ricky counters.

"That is true," Charlie says, "and now we know why he didn't find this."

Ricky nods.

"And did she make a copy?" Charlie asks.

Ricky shakes his head. "I had to let her off the leash for a short time while Terry was babysitting," he says, "but no, she didn't have time to make a copy."

"OK, that's good."

"How is Terry by the way?" Ricky asks.

"Not too good, sadly," Charlie tells him without a change of expression.

"So shall we conclude our business?" Ricky says to Charlie.

Charlie opens a second drawer in the desk and pulls out a brown paper bag. I know instantly that it contains the money I had thrown in the air above Terry's head, although it looks a lot less now, I guess some of it got carried away by the wind.

"How much did you sell me out for?" I ask him. He hasn't acknowledged me yet. And still, he doesn't.

Instead, he repeats my question to Charlie, "Yeah, how much did I sell her out for?"

Charlie shrugs, "I have no idea."

I step forward as he grabs the bag. Immediately Ricky pulls his gun from his waist and for the first time, I have a firearm pointed at me.

He takes a step forward to match my own.

"Back off," he snaps.

"This was your plan all along?" I say to him, spitting each word out.

"You should've figured out by now," he tells me, "ACAB. All coppers are bastards."

"Never a truer word was spoken," Charlie says. He has raised his own gun to the back of Ricky's head.

Realisation appears on Ricky's face, then Charlie pulls the trigger.

CHAPTER 55

Ricky's body hit the floor with the full force of gravity and no resistance from his body.

I saw the life leave his body the instant Charlie's pistol released its deafening blast.

I'm screaming. I can hear myself, but it doesn't sound or feel like me.

Tina, trembling beside me, mumbles, "What's happening?"

Ricky's face is looking up at me, already the life is extinguished.

I can see his hands, one holding a gun, the other holding the bag of money.

I thought there'd be blood, but there's not. Just death.

"Alright, that's enough," Charlie says to the both of us.

I do as he tells me. I stop screaming, but I can't stop gasping for breath or my heart hammering in my chest.

Close my eyes and try to regulate my breathing. I manage to form an O with my lips and exhale, but when I inhale my chest leaps up and I have to throw my head back.

"Are you finished?" Charlie asks.

"You shot him!" is all I can say. I point this out because Charlie doesn't seem to realise what he's done. And I don't want to say that he killed him, or he's dead, or he murdered him, all of those descriptions cause my heart to race again so I avoid and say again, "You shot him."

Charlie nods and says, "You seem surprised."

He looks to me like he's actually enjoying this. To him, it's not a necessary evil or a means to an end.

And his gun is pointing at me.

I would give anything at that moment for him to point that thing anywhere else. I am acutely aware that any second could be my last and it's stopping me thinking of anything else.

Charlie says, "Get your girlfriend and bring her in here."

"What?" I say. I genuinely don't understand the instruction. My eyes never leave the gun in his hands which he keeps trained on my gut.

"Bring Tina over here and sit her in this chair," he says slowly.

I kneel beside Tina who seems to be rousing from her induced sleep.

"C'mon," Charlie says, "Let's go."

He keeps gesturing with the gun for me to move and my fear is not subsiding, but am getting control of my breathing.

Tina lets out a low moan and I try to offer some soothing words as I help her to her feet.

She can walk, barely and only with my support. Her head lolls from side to side and only it falls back does she strain to lean forward and correct it.

Ricky's body is lying in front of us and I hope Tina doesn't see it as she starts to gradually open her eyes.

"Put her in the seat," Charlie orders.

"You have the tape," I say. "You win. What else do you want?"

"Unfortunately," Charlie tells me, "Someone has to take the fall for Ricky's stupidity. And that someone has to be Tina. You, however, still have a choice."

"Do I?" I say. "I don't think I do."

Tina is looking at me but I'm not sure whether my presence is registering with her.

"How long have you known this girl?" Charlie asks. "A week? Not even that long."

I don't answer. How long I've known her is meaningless.

"Her fate is sealed, there's nothing we can do about it," he says.

"Just let her go," I say, "she'll never talk. She'll move away-"

"Hannah," he says, "What's done is done. She has to go. But you don't, I'm, offering you-"

"The answer is 'No'," I tell him. "Whatever you're offering."

"You should at least hear me out," he says.

"Do I have a choice?" I say.

"You always have a choice Hannah," he says, "I made sure of that. I saw something in you, you're different from the rest. I don't know what it is, but I want to find out and that means you get privileges not extended to the rank and file."

Tina starts to move away from my side, I risk a glance at her, eyes are more aware. If she was in shock, she'll soon be back to full awareness. I squeeze her hand in mine.

"What's happening," she says, her words are slurry, it's a question more for herself than anyone else.

"As I was saying," Charlie says, his voice booming through the room, "Hannah, it's time for you to leave."

I shake my head.

"Don't worry," he says, "we'll meet again. I know where to find you don't I? Sooner or later?"

He points at the door to the stairs. He wants me to leave. He actually thinks I will leave my friend.

I look at the door, Ricky has left it half open. I can make out the steps from their shadows. There's no light coming from above, just pitch-black darkness.

Charlie says slowly, "I don't have all night."

I go to the door. It's about six or seven steps, each one is punctuated by my footsteps on the filthy flooring.

"Hannah?" Tina says.

I don't answer.

I open the door and peer up the stairs. It's silent. Not a sound and total darkness.

"I'll find you, Hannah," Charlie says.

I turn back and stare at him.

I have no doubt that he will shoot Tina without a second thought.

I also have no doubt that he'll fix the scene so it looks like Tina and Ricky shot each other.

But I didn't think he would shoot me. I believed that he was genuinely curious about where I came from, my relationship with Laura, and, although it sickened me to my stomach, I believed that he liked me.

But whether I believed it or not, it made no difference.

I turn to him and smile. "Before I go," I tell him, " there's something I want."

And he laughs. Amused. His smile is almost affectionate as he says, "You see, that's what I like about you Hannah, you just don't know when you're beat. You've got character. Balls. I do admire that, even when it gets you in trouble."

I walk back across the room. Our eyes never breaking from our staring contest.

"I want that," I say.

"What?"

"The Walkman," I say.

I almost get to the table and am about to make a grab for it when he snatches it up.

The gun is pointed at me again.

There's no panic this time, I even manage to laugh at his jumpiness and say, "I don't want the tape, just the Walkman."

He seems confused.

I stare at the Walkman in his hand with a deep longing.

I tell him, "You were right about me."

"Which part?" he says.

"I'm not from Lowestoft," I say, "I'm from here, but I'm from the future. I came back to find out what happened to Jimmy."

Charlie says nothing, but I can see he's considering this.

"And, believe it or not," I say, "I know what happens now. I know that I walk out of here and that you get away with murder, again, and there's nothing me or you or anyone can do about it. Just like there's nothing anyone can do about Jimmy spending his life in jail for the killing that you did."

He's almost smiling as he takes this in.

"It's fate," I say, "it already happened as far as I'm concerned, so although it makes me sad, there's no point in me fighting it, but, while I'm here, I might as well take that Walkman. Where I'm from a mint Marque I Walkman will sell for a fortune. And I don't want this to be a wasted trip."

He laughs but doesn't seem to know whether to acknowledge that he believes me.

But I know he wants to.

"Look," I say and take the Walkman from this hand. Amazingly, he lets it go. I hit the eject button and as the tape springs out, I grab it and hand it to him. "See the housing is machined from aluminium? Next year the whole thing will be made from plastic. And this," I point to the orange button on the top, "the 'Hot Line' button," I roll my eyes, "this was included so you could press it if someone spoke to you and their voice would come through the inbuilt microphone and to the headphones." I pointed to both the mic and headphones in turn and added, "I'm going to need them too." And took them from his head.

He looked both impressed and annoyed.

"The 'Hot Line' button and the microphone were also deleted from the next model as research showed that nobody cared if they couldn't hear what people were saying, they just wanted to listen to music. The same goes for the dual headphone sockets on the top, see?"

I don't wait for his answer. I turn and make my way to the door, giving Tina a raise of my eyebrows.

"By the way," I say as I spin back around, "do you have the blue carry-case that came with it? And the charger?"

And I throw the Walkman side-arm, as hard as I can at the fluorescent light above Charlie's head.

It hits. The light explodes and glass shatters all over Charlie followed by the lights frame.

I'm already dashing for the door, Tina's arm in my hand. There's a blinding flash and the sound of shattering glass, then pitch black.

I don't look back. The flash helps us see the doorway. I push Tina through first and manage to snag the door handle as I hit the stairs and I hear the door slam behind us.

The gun goes off again.

I don't know where the bullet lands. All I know is that me and Tina are still charging up the stairs so neither of us are hit.

There are two more booms from the gun. I know he's shooting blind but it's petrifying.

We reach the top of the stairs and Tina hits the door with both hands, it flies open and we charge through it.

CHAPTER 56

Tina reaches for my hand as we sprint across the road and I grab it. It may slow us down but I want t feel that connection, no matter what.

Instinctively we head up King Street. When I get to the Post Office I look back just as Charlie emerges from the fire exit. He sees us and breaks into a sprint.

Tina is already slowing due to the incline and it is obvious that we are not going to get to the top. I don't know if Charlie will shoot us in the back, but I don't want to find out.

We almost pass the alleyway to Stubbs toy shop when I see the opportunity.

"Down here," I yell to Tina. We veer into the alley after a 90-degree high-speed turn.

We sprint to the end, well before Charlie gets to the alley and Tina goes to run across the car park.

"No," I whisper, "this way."

I take her hand again and dash to the back gate of the toy shop.

It's unlocked and we slip inside just in time to hear Charlie's footsteps stomping down the alley.

They stop just feet from us and scrape the ground as he surveys his options.

"Bitches!" he grunts, and then we hear his footsteps move across the car park.

I can imagine him having to choose which way to go. Left or right. Up or down.

'We're behind you!'

Except we're not safe yet.

He could still figure it out.

We can't stay here, but we can't go wandering the streets either.

Tina still looks terrified. I grab her in a tight hug and whisper, "Thank God you're OK."

"You saved me," she sobs.

It feels so good to feel her cheek next to mine and I close my eyes to savour a second of that feeling.

When I open them, I see the back door to the and although it's dark and my eyes are blurry from tears, it looks, only slightly, ajar.

I can't believe it. I screw my eyes shut, open them, rub them, but still, it looks to be open.

"Look," I whisper to Tina, and point to the door.

She looks but cowers away.

"Come on," I say, "we can hide inside."

As I near the door, I can see that it is indeed open albeit by less than an inch, but that's enough.

This is the door that has a new frame, the glass window I broke on Monday night has been fixed too, which makes it all the more strange why the door is not only unlocked but open. However, that will have to be a mystery for later.

I open the door and step inside.

It's dark. Tina stands at the doorway peering in.

"It's OK," I tell her. "Come in, we can close the door and hide in here."

Once she's inside, I hear the voice.

"Hannah!" it says, "Thank God!"

Tina screams, a ghastly long howl of pure fear.

I can't breathe, but only for a second.

I grab Tina and tell her that it's fine, there's nothing to be scared of, it's my mother.

She appears from the shadows, arms out to greet me.

My heart melts and I want to hug her to death but I can't let go of Tina.

In seconds, the three of us holding each other and sobbing together.

Then we hear the gate creak open.

Mother's head shoots up first and immediately ushers us to the back room.

"Go to the place," she whispers, "wait there for me. If I don't come, you two just go. Do you understand?"

I shake my head.

"Hannah, you have to do this," she says, "Trust me!"

I shake my head again.

"Do it for Tina!" she commands me.

I stop shaking my head and nod.

Me and Tina crawl on all fours to the storeroom door and I open it.

From behind the door, I listen.

I hear the door open. A slow creak. Then two heavy footsteps.

I gasp when I hear my mother's voice, "You took your time."

Charlie grunts, then says, "So this is where the magic happens?"

"Yeah," she says, then sings, "Sur-prise!"

Charlie sighs. "Where are the girls Laura?"

"They're gone," she says, "I made sure they're safe. There's nobody here but us chickens."

Without making a sound, I raise my frame and get to my feet. Through the perspex glass window in the door, I can see the two of them, vague shapes in the blackness, stood six feet apart.

Charlie, his voice rough and angered, says, "Don't make this any harder than it already is."

My mouth goes dry as my mother swings her arm up and points a pistol at Charlie.

"They're not here and soon I'll be following them," she says. "The only question is whether you live to tell the tale, or I leave your brains splattered over that door behind you."

There's a moment's silence. Nobody moves. Then Charlie says, "Hmm, well let me consider those options."

My mother's arm flags, the gun in her hand dips and then rises again, almost imperceptibly, but not quite. I notice it. And so does Charlie.

"Or maybe there's another option," he says, "maybe you ain't calling all the shots."

He takes one step closer to her.

"Maybe," he says slowly, "the other option is that you're bluffing."

"You know I don't bluff," she says, "don't you remember? Bluffs are as pointless as threats, actions always speak louder. We agreed on once that didn't we?"

Charlie nods. "We did," he says and takes another step toward her, "but times change."

She doesn't waver this time, but she doesn't make any advances of her own.

"And I'm thinking 'needs must'," he says, "so maybe there's a first time for everything and maybe that ain't even a real gun."

Neither of them moves. There is silence, but only for a second, the Charlie starts to laugh.

"You did, didn't you?" he grins. "You actually did." I can see his eyebrows rise up his forehead as his shoulders bounce with laughter.

"Stand back Charlie," my mother says, "you know I'll do it. I'll enjoy it too. And it's the least you deserve."

"Do what Laura?" he says, "Shoot me with a toy gun?"

Laura says nothing.

"You did, didn't you? You went and got a toy gun from the shelf. I mean, it's dark enough in here, right, dark enough to fool anyone. What is it? A Colt 45? Or a James Bond special? Or a water pistol."

With each accusation, he takes a step forward and at the end, he is an arm's length apart and the gun in my mother's hand is pressed against his chest.

"I see where Hannah gets her balls from," he tells my mother. "We're gonna go a long way me and her."

There's a rumble in the distance. A diesel engine fights its way up King Street and comes to a stop.

"I need to go," Charlie says to my mother, "but I need to take the girls with me, so if you'll just point me in the right direction, then you can go on your way."

"I told you," she says, "they're gone."

Charlie reaches for her gun and takes it from her. Without looking at it he throws the plastic toy onto the floor and takes out his own gun.

"In that case," he says, "you can take me to them. Let's go."

My mother doesn't move. He pushes her back. She staggers.

I open the door and step out of the storeroom.

"Hannah! NO!" my mother shouts.

"Mum, it's OK," I tell her.

"NO!" she screams, "He'll kill you!"

Charlie points the gun at me again.

"I don't think he will," I say.

"Don't do it," my mother mumbles, "I beg you."

Charlie's face turns into a scowl.

"He won't do it, mum, because he needs me."

"Why do I need you?" he snarls.

"Because Ricky was wrong," I say, "I made a copy."

CHAPTER 57

"Hannah, we're going to leave, just the two of us," Charlie sighs. "I'd love to play happy families and bring everyone along, but, because of the mess you've made, that's not practical."

I don't respond in any way. My only weapon now is to ignore him.

"You did good, you know," he goes on, "I admire your tenacity, your loyalty, your guts. I thought you'd break, you surprised me, but everyone breaks in the end Hannah. And I will break you for good, I promise you. It's nothing to be ashamed of, it's just the way it is."

At that point, he did smile.

I stare at him. My final defiant act was to not show any emotion.

"I'm not anywhere with you," I tell him, "so do your worst, or so whatever, I'm over it."

And then I heard his voice again. And so did he. It was large and booming, amplified and it filled the room. "I told you Callaghan was going down and never getting up again," it said. "Phallium in his water will do that."

Charlie had lost his smile. He looked confused. The voice was undoubtedly his, but it was amplified and remote, like the voice of God in a movie. He craned his neck to identify its source. It seemed to come from the heavens.

It shook the room as the voice got louder, "It's tasteless, odourless and undetectable. And no one survives phallium poisoning. Not even a champion boxer."

Charlie stood up and headed to the door, seeking the source like a disciple ready to kneel before his creator.

From what I hoped would be a safe distance, I follow him.

As we moved to the front of the shop, the voice boomed even louder. From the window, we could see the flat-bed truck loaded with the Marshall stack amplifiers. We could see the words, 'The Full-Tilt Boogie Mobile Sound System'. I thought I could see the speakers throbbing with each syllable, but that could be just my imagination, even as I watched I couldn't be sure.

"What is this?" Charlie says, staring at the truck.

"This is you," I say.

"No!" he says. He came back to life, breaking out of his trance and charging at the door. "NO!" he yelled and could his panicked scream above the booming monotone of his amplified confession.

"So you got your money and kept your hands clean, I did all the dirty work, now we're quits."

I followed Charlie outside the door. He still held the gun as he clambered up onto the flat-bed and surveyed the scene. There was a line of amplifiers, maybe ten or more, each with wires sprouting from their fronts and backs; there was a generator, barely audible except in the short silences of the tape. Power cables were bolted into its terminals leading to a transformer which in turn spewed out lines of thinner cables in every direction.

"In fact, the way I see it, you owe me."

As I watched Charlie trying to find a solution to the puzzle before him, I noticed people were coming out of houses, lights were coming on behind windows.

Charlie started pulling cables out of the amplifiers. The difference was hardly noticeable. The voice still boomed out.

He tried to disable the transformer but those wires were sealed tight and he didn't seem to possess the strength to disconnect them.

He looked up, saw the eyes that were now upon him and turned frantically back to the sound system.

Then he saw the tape deck. Saw the small wheels turning inside. He raised his gun and fired a shot at it from five feet away. People screamed and fled. The tape player jerked back a few inches but the wheels kept rolling.

Charlie charges at it. He smacked his fist down at the control buttons on the front of the tape player. The music stopped and in the same second his head snapped back, his body curled his spine into its maximum apex and he discharged the pistol he still held in his other hand.

The bullet entered his shoe, leaving a small smoke trail as his body did a jerky dance for a complete second then he falls to the floor.

All that broke the silence was the rumble of the generator which sounded no louder than the contented purr of a cat.

The cab door opens and Boogie climbs out, smiling.

I hug him. He hugs me back. It's something I've wanted to do ever since I met him. And it feels every bit as good as I hoped it would.

"Thank you," I say.

"The pleasure is all mine," he tells me.

Only after Boogie turns the generator off do I climb onto the wagon and approach the lifeless Charlie. I prod him with the toe of my trainer. He looks alive. His eyes are open, they seemed conscious, but his body isn't moving.

When I knelt beside him, his eyes followed me and for the first time, I see fear there.

"Hey," I say, "You've had a shock. Well, maybe two shocks."

He wants to reply, his jaw moves slightly but his lips emit only a raspy breath and no words.

I look down at his foot, there was blood seeping through the bullet hole of his shoe and I couldn't resist adding, "Oh, and you've shot yourself in the foot. Also twice."

Then the street was fills with blue flashing lights.

Sunday
16th April
2023

Prologue

Me and mum are the only ones who know what happened. Or who remembered what happened, I should say, as no one else has those memories.

I think that's because we didn't 'live' through the 'new' years from 1980. We jumped forward, just like we jumped back. Literally skipping everything that happened in between then and now.

And I think time is like a Memorex tape. It can be rewound and taped over.

Speaking of Memorex tapes, Charlie was arrested that night, and the tape was used in evidence. He was found guilty of murder, amongst other things.

The police allowed me and mum to go to the hospital with Tina and sat with her for the rest of the night. We were joined by Barbara at 3am and by morning Tina was discharged with a clean bill of health. We went back to the flat, said our goodbyes, and went back to the toy shop and came back home.

In the cellar, I'd slipped the money into the secret pocket in my Harrington and before I left the flat, I tucked it under Tina's pillow. I didn't leave a note.

I knew she'd understand.

Back home, me and mum went into lockdown. We were the first ones, well before the rest of the country. We stayed in the flat and didn't go out or speak to anyone except Mia, who came over every day in between visits to the hospital. I'm pleased to say Mia accepted my apology, and even more pleased to say her dad made a full recovery and got home within the second week. They are both doing fine.

After that we were in lockdown for real and me and mum talked and talked.

I told her everything that happened over the last week and she told me everything that happened over the last eighty-years since Jimmy had tried to take cover from the Coventry blitz and stumbled into a forty-year hole in time.

And we talked about how stupid we had been.

And we talked about how brilliant we had been.

And we didn't agree on everything, but we never argued. Not once.

And we agreed not to look.

We didn't look for people or what had happened or anything. We were too scared, so we didn't look.

Not for three weeks.

Well, we already knew about Tina.

The nurse who had asked mum for a word at Jimmy's Retirement Home, that was her, of course. She was passing on a message from someone she met back in 1980, returning a favour, as she put it.

She told mum exactly when she needed to go back and why, which, she said, seems weird.

"I know it's so strange and you probably think I'm crazy," she said, "but don't shoot the messenger. I'm just returning a favour to someone who helped me out many years ago."

"It doesn't sound weird at all," my mother had told her. "You don't know what this means to me!"

What was weird was that after Mum and Tina became reacquainted at the Leyland Retirement Home, it turned out they were cousins!

Tina and mum are best friends, which is great, if a bit weird for me.

Barbara passed away in 1983.

Tina opened her clothes shop, which she used as a platform to launch her own successful designs. She married a musician, travelled the world, came home, trained as a nurse, and found her dream job.

Of course, the reason mum was at the Retirement Home was Jimmy.

He had not been so easy to find. There was no Facebook or Twitter account for a James Randle, believe it or not.

Ironically, mum tracked him down through his brother, Charlie Randle, prisoner number 1291729. With some deep investigation work, mum got a home address from the prison visitors records.

It had been a beautiful moment when I was reading a book and mum was on the computer and she said, "I've found him!"

He'd enjoyed a full and charitable life since his conviction was quashed as he'd been determined to make the most of the opportunity he'd been given.

When the time had come, he'd chosen to move into the Leyland Retirement Home and waited for mum to call.

'Why didn't I look there first?' mum had said.

'I've been waiting forty years,' Jimmy said. 'I knew you'd find me eventually.'

They spoke on the phone every day for weeks during lockdown.

I tried not to listen in. It was lovers' talk, private and intimate.

Jimmy passed away from Covid in April 2020.

Towards the end of that first lock-down, I did some research too.

Most of my 'friends' from 1980 are still in Bedworth. I promised myself to look them up once we were free to do such things. It's still on the To Do list.

Boogie is now in his late sixties. He has a Facebook account and plays guitar and sings at an Open Mic in The Prince of Wales pub. I've seen him twice and he's quite good. I intend to introduce myself either next week or the week after.

Sarita is also on Facebook and judging by her posts, she is now the loving matriarch of a family of three children and eight grand-kids.

Johnny, Steeple and Pricey are all friends on Facebook, as is Mark (no Martin) Roberts, the quiet suedehead. They have families and 'lives' and they still hang out together after nearly fifty years of friendship. I am intensely jealous of that thing that they share.

Clair is living in California and is very private.

I haven't been able to find the wonderful Walter Jabsco, I wish him well, where ever he may be.

Banjacks and Twin-Tub own a building and demolition company, Bantwin Construction. In one of those small town coincidences, it was their firm that actually knocked down The Corner Pin in the 90s. I know what you're thinking. But, in this instance, it was an actual coincidence. I do now believe that there is such a thing.

Sharpie, who keyed the police car after Boogies Singles Party, is no longer with us. Violence marred his life. He served time in prison and it was there that he received injuries that he would never recover from. Drugs and alcohol were also ever-present, as were his friends who tried to help, but ultimately found they couldn't. He died alone. In the middle of the night, he fell in his bathroom and broke his neck.

Tomorrow we are having a girls' night out. Me, mum, Tina and Mia are going to a Caribbean restaurant in Coventry. Mum's treat. It's a step up from our weekly Costa coffee meets where we enjoy some philosophical chat and hearty laughs about our lives and loves. I look forward to it and if we don't get to meet up; it saddens me.

It's been a journey, and I've learned a lot, mostly about myself, but most importantly I've learned that a life shared with others is far richer than one that is not.

I still make a living buying and selling vintage stuff, (all in the here and now, of course). I'm getting into restoration too; I love that feeling of breathing life back into old stuff.

But that's only after I've reached out and touched the people who mean something to me. They come first and I make sure they understand they need to talk to me and let me know what's going on. If there's anything I can do for them, I need to know.

I'm also open to inviting others in. There's still room in my life for new friendships. I am fussy, but each day is a possibility to meet a friend for life.

And who knows?

One day we might look back and laugh and smile at all the years we've shared.

That's what this wonderful life is all about. And it's cute as ducks.

Very Special Thanks

I am exceptional thankful for the contribution of the following wonderful people

Jack, Mum and Dad, Lesley Wilson, Jason Beresford, Chris Twigger, Steve Suddens, Paul Harvey, Caroline J Clarke, Jenny Jones, Rob Summerfield, Nigel C, fish,

And I would like to thank you for reading and ask that if you enjoyed this book then if you could please submit a review rating and maybe some comments that would mean the world to me.

Thanks again and lets meet again soon

Paul

Printed in Great Britain
by Amazon